The Duration

The Duration

A Novel

Dave Fromm

TYRUS
BOOKS

Published by
TYRUS BOOKS
an imprint of F+W Media, Inc.
10151 Carver Road, Suite 200
Blue Ash, OH 45242. U.S.A.
www.tyrusbooks.com

Hardcover ISBN 10: 1-4405-9464-3
Hardcover ISBN 13: 978-1-4405-9464-9
Paperback ISBN 10: 1-4405-9463-5
Paperback ISBN 13: 978-1-4405-9463-2
eISBN 10: 1-4405-9465-1
eISBN 13: 978-1-4405-9465-6

Printed in the United States of America.

10 9 8 7 6 5 4 3 2 1

Library of Congress Cataloging-in-Publication Data

Fromm, Dave, author.
The duration / Dave Fromm.
Blue Ash, OH: Tyrus Books, [2016]
LCCN 2015043825 (print) | LCCN 2015046242 (ebook) | ISBN
9781440594649 (hc) | ISBN 1440594643 (hc) | ISBN
9781440594632 (pb) | ISBN 1440594635 (pb) | ISBN 9781440594656 (ebook) | ISBN
1440594651 (ebook)
BISAC: FICTION / Literary.
LCC PS3606.R633 D87 2016 (print) | LCC PS3606.R633 (ebook) |
DDC 813/.6--dc23
LC record available at *http://lccn.loc.gov/2015043825*

Cover design by Erin Alexander.
Cover images © Adrian Kollar/Olga Miltsova/123RF.

This book is available at quantity discounts for bulk purchases.
For information, please call 1-800-289-0963.

For Katie K.

"Can't be too picky in the deep."
Bob Schneider, "The Effect"

Author's Note

This is a work of fiction. While it uses real and perhaps recognizable places as settings, any similarities to actual people or events are entirely coincidental—*except*, that is, for the book's central secret, which is in fact based on an old Berkshire County mystery. Don't ask me to tell you what I think about it, though. It's a mystery, and you shouldn't believe anybody who claims to know the truth.

"You promised," Kelly said. "Two years."

We were sitting in that coffeehouse on the corner of Columbus and Clarendon. It was a freezing winter Sunday. Dressed in travel section attire—sweats and sneaks, bed-headed. I was stubbly. Kelly's long hair was pulled back from her forehead by a sort of wide headband, then pulled again, farther back, into a severe ponytail. Wrangle that shit, kiddo. Show it who's boss. The coffeehouse, an anti-Starbucks catering to the same South End crowd willing to spend $5 on a latte, was the sort of place I liked to mock while still frequenting. Their pumpkin muffins were obscene—each one a boulder of orange dough, big as your head, that left oil stains soaking through the to-go bag; sometimes they dropped a few green pumpkinseeds on the top to pretend it was a salad—and I'd sworn on several occasions, usually just after finishing one, to never eat another. Course, I was about to bust into one right then.

I frowned and broke a soft little wedge off the muffin boulder to buy time. Two years? I don't think I would have agreed to that. Two years was a blink. You'd have to suffer something a lot longer before you gave up on it.

But Kelly was resolute.

"Right up on that corner," she said, pointing out toward Dartmouth without looking. "You said we'd give it two years here and if it wasn't working we'd reconsider."

She was probably paraphrasing, but probably right all the same. Up there, where Dartmouth hit Columbus, where the kegs rolled into the service entrance at the back of Cleary's and they had live music every Thursday and you could buy a mammoth

9

cheeseburger at the takeaway place next door, I'd said a lot of things. Kelly wasn't the cheeseburger type, but we'd stumbled home together more than a few times, hand-in-hand, flush with the inebriants of one's upper twenties, one's first semi-domestic arrangement, plus, most likely, plenty of other inebriants, and I was probably thinking about putting the moves on her when we got back to the apartment, three narrow flights up, stumbling and crawling and laughing, hopefully, and maybe I'd even start the moves before we gained the landing, depending on what sort of attire she was sporting and how hard it was to find my keys, and anyway I could imagine at moments like that saying whatever it was I thought she wanted to hear. And I'd probably even meant it at the time.

They called me from the counter. Two lattes for Pete. Pete Johansson, Pete So Handsome, your mother's answered prayer. Best days behind me, but barely. I got the lattes and doused them with sugar, or doused mine at least, grateful for a reprieve.

I knew, vaguely, that she was unhappy. But, shit, we're all vaguely unhappy. That's just the human condition, right?

Something about not loving Boston. As if that were possible. What's not to love? She'd run her diagnostics at bedtime, softening the invective with toothpaste. These people. Six months out of the year, she'd say, everyone pops their parkas out like that *South Park* character who was always dying, and the other six months they walk around with big chips on pale, freckled shoulders. You can even see the chips under the parkas, she'd say. I loved watching her brush her teeth. The rich ones look like horses, she'd say, and the poor ones look like donuts. They have two interpersonal settings— resentment and overfamiliarity. They hate you until they love you and then they won't stop.

Something like that.

I came back to the table, sugar-fortified, sat down.

"I don't think I said two years," I said, pausing, watching her eyes flatten. I looked away quickly, before she could turn them to me. This line of attack had to be rethought. "And even if I did, look, promises are like sunk costs, right? That one, whether or not I made it, I made it two years ago. That's forever ago. We've invested here. We have equity now."

I was thinking of our jobs, our lease, the people we nodded to on the street who were little more than strangers we kept seeing over and over again, but who might, someday, if none of us ever moved on, become acquaintances. We need to operate from the present, the now. The market value of our accounts.

I was winging it, obviously, as I didn't truly understand economics. Or relationships, for that matter.

What was the market value of our accounts, anyway? I looked out the high front windows, onto the desolate and unlovely stretch of Columbus near the backside of the train station, a long block from Dartmouth. Brick nonprofits and parking garages, the wind curling up from the underground highway to spin leaves and trash and umbrellas into a vortex. Not glam. Our apartment was just a starter place, a rental, a foothold on the city. But we'd move on. Move on up, hopefully, like the Jeffersons did, to Newton or Back Bay or, maybe, who knew? Maybe Beacon Hill. Though those weren't really Jeffersons neighborhoods, this being stodgy Brahmin Boston after all. Whatever. We'd move around. Find new old coffeehouses, new Irish bars at which to cheer the Sox and boo the Yanks. Withstand new Januaries. Meet a whole new set of strangers.

But that sort of incremental stuff wasn't what Kelly was talking about. She was talking, again, about heading west. Like, way west. The West.

I reached for the muffin.

"If you don't stop eating that," she said, "and look at me . . ."

She left it blank and I tried to evaluate how much mileage I could get out of some sort of faux resistance to ultimatums, something defensible about, like, not negotiating with terrorists. I looked at her, but I kept eating the muffin. A man can be pushed only so far.

"What do you want?" I asked. "You want to just up and start over somewhere?"

That didn't seem rational to me. That seemed like, I don't know, something a certain kind of irrational person might propose with their certain kind of hysterical brain. You know what kind of person I mean? I mean, what about hard work? What about the nobility of suffering? Plus, it was winter, midwinter even, and it's never a good idea to undertake anything big, even big decisions, in winter. Tends to cut out nearly a third of the year, but still. Ask Napoleon.

I looked at Kelly. I thought she'd be crying, but she wasn't. I always thought she'd be crying when she wasn't.

She looked back at me. I was a big child in a small chair, swaddled in sweatshirt, crumbs on my cheeks. She glanced around the coffeehouse. An ominous glance, like something was coming.

Just then my cell phone lit up. A number I didn't recognize, which was good. Might be important.

"Who'd be calling on a Sunday morning?" I asked, in a tone that I hoped sounded both apologetic and frustrated, like all I really wanted to do was to sit there with Kelly and get to the bottom of our relationship.

She wasn't buying it.

I pushed out of the door onto Clarendon and put my hood up against the chill. The Escalade, my getaway truck, was parked down around a distant corner. Through the window I could see Kelly sitting at our table, back to the window, the foam on her latte pristine, the curve in her ponytail embittered. Then she got up, took her coffee, and came through the door, but instead of walking over to me, she turned the other way. I half raised my hands in a what-gives sort of way, but she put her sunglasses on and didn't look over. Somewhere it occurred to me that I was being a dick, that she might not shake it off.

Best not to dwell on it now, I guess.

"Johansson," I said into the phone, because it sounded badass, at least to me. I watched Kelly head down the block. There was a pause and I adjusted my hood to shield the wind. "Hello?"

Another pause, and then one word, an endearment.

"Guy."

You ever, maybe at your mom's house, come across a box of stuff from when you were a kid, and there's a little shirt or something inside, and you pick it up and see your name written in the collar? And it just kills you right away?

I came into the county from the east, picking up Route 20 just before it crossed the river and began to climb into the land of the Mahican. I rolled through the outer hill-towns of Russell and Chester and Huntington, one-horse towns, hamlets, through cuts in the ridges and along the icy banks of brooks. Cricks and creeks. Bogs and brooks. Dales and dells and glens and gullies. Too many sticks to shake a stick at. Five dead trees for every ten live ones, most denuded by winter, the pines and spruce left to shiver on the mountainsides like bristles on a boar. Two hours west of Boston, I drove past a plaster deer and a wooden Viking and a 7-foot beaver and an 8-foot bear. What people will do to amuse themselves in the sticks, I guess. Campgrounds. Shack bars. Tires in yards. The road a knotty umbilicus, bending in and out, up and down and around.

Route 20 was the best. You could come in on the Pike, which sagged like a belt on the belly of the Commonwealth, but you'd only save yourself twenty minutes and any sight worth seeing. The Pike was for tourists and long-haulers. It didn't do defiles or climbs or hairpins, just blasted its way through the ridge, through walls of ragged rock where icicles grew blue and busty in the south side shade while the sunny north side stayed bare. Kelly loved those icicles. She was from Los Angeles, where winter was a theory. "Look at that," she'd say, every time we passed through the ridge. "It's like the one side of the rock can't let go of the other." Easy, I'd say. It's just the way the sun hits.

It was two weeks since the call, early March, just about the finest time to be in New England if you didn't like color or pleasantries.

On this day, a nearly balmy Friday with temps approaching 40°F, fog hung on the crests and I wasn't in my best mood. That's why I was waxing poetic. In my best mood, I might stop in Chester, buy an antler or a jar of blackcurrant jam or some shit like that, just to feel like a man of the people, like I was representing. I might swing through the Gare Outlets and smell the leather at Coach, try on some waders at L.L. Bean. Be an engine of commerce. Pull the Escalade up to the curb outside the Batter's Box in Gare and nod through the windows to the reigning men's fast pitch softball champs. If I was in my best mood, Kelly would be with me, so we'd drive through town and I'd tell my usual stories about the basketball court that used to be next to the pizza place, how I'd balled there every summer evening from ages twelve to eighteen with Jimmer and Unsie and Chick because we couldn't get a good run in Gable, the four of us taking on all comers, all day, day into night, rising to the rock like wolves to the moon. And how whenever I drove by now and saw the dour daycare and haphazard plasticky playground which these days occupied what had once been the scene of some of the great contests of my youth I'd shed a single tear, like the Native American chief in those old Keep America Beautiful commercials. And Kelly would roll her eyes in her usual way, which, if I was in my best mood, I would interpret as condescension undergirded by a deep fondness—even a sense of near-spousal privilege—at bearing witness, again and again, to such florid nostalgia. We were engaged in the domestic equivalent of a John Cougar Mellencamp song. "Those same old stories," she'd be saying with that look. "I'll be hearing those same old stories over and over again for the rest of my life."

But Kelly was gone, as it happened, back to California, apparently not as interested in hearing those same old stories over and over again as I'd thought. Her departure, once decided, had been executed with ruthless efficiency—one carry-on, one box shipped from the FedEx down the block. One-way flight purchased with miles, a vague sense that she'd deal with the rest of her stuff later. Or not. Maybe she was making a clean break. Anyway, cab to Logan. I offered to drive her, but she said no, I'm good. Something furious and resolved about her on the sidewalk, waiting, a look like she was done with the Escalade, and whatever it symbolized. Wasn't clear to me, at that point, if she was totally serious. It probably should have been. I waited with her, my arms crossed, dressed for work, trying to affect both emotional availability and harried impatience: I am a busy man, but I am here for you when you want to work this out. I prepared to say something devastating, something stoic but vulnerable. To control the engagement. Stay, or some shit like that. Don't give up on us. But Kelly had her act together, and before I could say anything she'd kissed me hard on the cheek and gotten into the cab, and then she was gone, heading east toward the Ted Williams Tunnel, and I was stuck, freezing on the sidewalk, like damn. That was last Thursday, and I hadn't heard from her since.

So, not my best mood.

I passed the Dream Away, tucked up in a Becket hollow, and hit the cobbled streets of Gare. My mom liked to say there are only three families in the whole of Gare and that each rugged citizen is connected to one of them by some tendril of DNA. I curled through town and up past the lake and the brothel and the resorts at Blantyre and Cranwell. The brothel hadn't been a brothel when I was a kid, least as far as I knew, and Cranwell had been an abandoned prep school. Now they both offered massages, with significantly different price points. I passed the back side of Ventfort Hall, a massive brick chateau abandoned until 1994. We used to walk to middle school past Ventfort but stopped after somebody left a mannequin leaning against an upstairs window—I hope it was a mannequin—either way it scared the shit out of us at 8:15 A.M. Bypassed downtown Gable because why not, stayed on 20 toward the Knots, took in the glory of the Knotsford-Gable Road, the Luau Hale, the Price Chopper, the abandoned mini-golf.

Abandoned mini-golfs. Man, they're the worst. Almost the worst. Like just a notch above abandoned movie theaters on the depressive scale. Both of them can set you back for hours. You can be feeling pretty good about stuff, and then walk past an abandoned movie theater, its marquee empty or, worse, lettered with noncinema announcements, like "Senior Bingo" or "Rug Sale," both of which seemed sort of redundant, right? Like, of course it's senior bingo. You could just say "Bingo," and the seniors would show up. Or just "Rugs," because what else are you going to be doing with a bunch of rugs? But anyway, you see these sorts of things on an old movie marquee and you just know that somewhere back inside, back past the padlocked doors and the booth with the little half-oval ticket window and the lobby that once smelled like popcorn but now smells like seniors and rugs, there is a big amphitheater where people used to go and dream and watch Star Wars back-to-back-to-back, a three-peat, a trifecta my dad and I pulled off one great Saturday a long time ago, and now that dreamy space is herniated by this street-level infection of bad rugs and bad Nike knock-offs and bad coffee and bad real estate. Abandoned movie theaters suck. The Knots used to have three of them.

Chickie Benecik, he of the untimely phone call, wanted to meet at the corner of Council and Railroad Streets, the edge of what passed in the Knots for the wrong side of the tracks. The Knots was on the way up, relatively speaking, but it still had a ways to go, and parts of the city remained breeding grounds for disaffection and the things that came with it. Some of those parts were just down the hill from the entrance to the Knotsford Medical Center, which is where, I gathered, Chickie had recently been spending time.

I parked the Escalade and engaged the e-brake. Hah! With Kelly on the wing, it was all I was engaging these days. And better for it.

Chick and I had been toddlers on the same short street, only children, quickly inseparable, classmates at Cameron Elementary and altar boys at St. Barney's from nine until twelve, when that stuff with Bill Trivette came out. Unsie and Jimmer didn't come along until later, probably around 1995, when we started playing Catholic Youth Council ball. Our coach was a lunatic named George Harvey. He used to wear these cutoff sweatpants that must've been twenty years old. He had that big old gut and a big ass and he'd hike those bad boys up so tight that when he'd crouch to bark at us in the drills his nuts would press through the thin fabric of his sweats, right in our faces, like a tennis ball that hangs in your garage to tell you where to stop the car. It was hard for us to focus on what he was saying with his nutsack hung out like that, so we fucked up the drills, which infuriated him, and then we had to run sprints. All because he couldn't buy a pair of pants that fit. He was old school. One day after practice, Jimmer suggested we just find a way to snip that shit off, free George Harvey from the tether of his nutsack. Solution! He'd be less angry and we'd be less tired. We were still getting to know Jimmer at the time, and weren't sure if this idea was genius or sociopathic.

But yeah, George Harvey. He kept sticking me at power forward because I was already tall at the time, and I was like yeah I'm tall but I can handle the ball, I'm like Magic Johnson, put me at the point, but he wouldn't because his godson played point. You know Jim Flake? Yeah, he was okay but he wasn't going to get any quicker.

Chickie was our shooter. He had a stroke that was like half poetry and half automation, a grace note practiced ten thousand times. When he got older, in high school, if we could get him the ball in the right spot, I didn't even look for a rebound, I just ran back on defense as soon as he rose up. Chick used to let out a little whoop when he shot, until Coach Harvey made him stop, but he wasn't doing it to be a jerk. It seemed involuntary. Sometimes he whooped whether the ball went in or not. Unsie was our big man until he quit to ski and Jimmer eventually took over the point. Man, we rolled kids. They could not hang. We even rolled the Golacks, up at laconic Misconic. Colonic Misconic. One summer we were playing rec league there and as we're walking into the gym, the Golacks are outside just glaring at us. Ronnie, Robbie, and their little brother Tim-Rick, who was so nice they named him twice, except he wasn't nice at all, he was the meanest fucker we'd ever met. And they didn't like getting whipped. But we whipped them anyway, and then while we were still in the gym, they tried to push our car down an embankment.

I hadn't seen Chick in the eight years since my father's funeral. After high school, my decade had gone college, Dad's heart attack, law school, semi-engagement. Chick, I gathered, had done a couple of different junior colleges, drifting across the Southwest, then two stints with an international aid and education outfit called SmartSeeds. First one was in Guatemala, digging wells and building schools for Guatemalan kids. I got one postcard. Then the South Pacific, some island kingdom near the nuclear testing atolls where everyone glowed and the babies had twelve fingers. Just about as far away from Gable as it was possible to get. Somewhere in there he'd made it back to stand beside me at the wake. Then he was gone again. I hadn't really given him more than a passing thought in years. Just knew he was out there somewhere, doing his Chickie things. Everyone was doing their things. Figured we'd get together someday, reconnect, wouldn't really miss a beat.

Which seemed to be what was happening.

I stood on the corner and looked for him, trying to pick him out of the stragglers on Council Street. I wondered if I was sure I'd recognize him, but of course I would. By the end of high school, he'd developed this slouchy, limpy walk that looked like a strut. The sidewalk was sloped steeply down to the west, and KMC was just one distracted orderly away from sending a gurney rolling into the Housatonic. Up across Council, in the blocks off the rotary, sat St. Eustace, another hive of high school rivals, whose queen bee I'd dated briefly in 2000. She was a cute girl from the east side of the Knots, daughter of a judge, Shaunda Schorenstein or something like that. Shaunda Schoenstein. She'd taken me to her senior formal that year. I was just a junior from Gable, and we got a lot of dirty looks, which I think was what she was hoping for but sort of scared the shit out of me at the time because even though you'd think Catholic schools were full of sweethearts it's just the opposite, but I manned up and held her close and nodded at the dudes I knew from the courts, and later, in the downstairs girls bathroom, she pulled me into a stall and let me get to third with her, which I tried to do in a nice way, and, as I recall, she tried to help me do in a way that would make the experience meaningful for her too, until I think I came in my tuxedo pants. And that was that. High school. What do you want?

Chickie was already a half-hour late. I called the number I had in my cell, but it went straight to voicemail and that was full anyway. I walked to the entrance to KMC and approached the information desk, where the nurse receptionist looked at me suspiciously. Light brown skin, a robust waistline, a tattoo peeking out from the collar of her shirt. Big hoops hanging from her ears, wrong side of 28 and 215. Which made two of us, except for the hoops. She had long lacquered nails that looked unlikely to pass muster in an operating room. Her name tag said "Lemon."

"Hello, Lemon," I said. "I'm supposed to be meeting someone. I think he was a patient here."

She sort of rolled her face, as though skeptical of the very notion of meeting someone, and looked at her computer screen.

"What's the patient's name?"

"Chickie Benecik," I said. "Philip Benecik."

Nobody'd called him Philip in, like, the entirety of my existence. Even his mom called him Chickie.

Lemon kept looking at the screen.

"Your name?"

"Peter Johansson." I gave her a smoldering look, the one I'd used to reel in Kelly, the one I used to put on at the foul line when there were cute girls in the stands.

"Sorry," she said. "But you're not on our list. I can't give you any information about a patient. It's the law."

"So he was a patient?"

Lemon looked annoyed.

"What I mean is if he was a patient, and he's not a patient anymore, then you can tell me that, right? That's legal. Trust me. I'm actually a lawyer myself."

Feckless. But maybe charming in its fecklessness? I'd gotten by with it before.

Lemon seemed briefly willing to engage, the blinds of bureaucracy open an inch. Another nurse ambled by and gave me the evil eye, sort of impressively for someone wearing flower-print scrubs. Lemon glanced at her and harrumphed. Some history there.

"Come on, Lemon," I said. "Don't let her come between us."

Lemon rolled her eyes.

I laughed.

"I'm just messing," I said, chuckling, looking at my watch. Not a threat until it's too late. I could do this all day. It's where I excelled. "When life gives me a lemon, you know what I do? I say thanks. I'm not trying to squash it, either. It's perfect just the way it is."

Lemon returned to her computer screen, but she was smiling.

"This says he checked out two hours ago," she said, and then, "What did you say your name was?"

"Pete Johansson."

She reached down below her desk and came back with a manila envelope. Chickie's writing. Block letters. *Pete So Handsome.*

Her hoops swayed.

"This you?" she asked, raising her eyebrows sort of skeptically.

I took the envelope, held it up to the blinking hospital fluorescents, but the manila was thick and opaque. I considered not opening it. Sure, maybe there'd be something great inside, something that would make me feel less annoyed about having taken a vacation day to drive two and a half hours out of Boston just to be stood up in the entrance hall of KMC. But what were the odds? You gonna come through like that, envelope? Probably not. Once, looking to furnish our apartment via Craigslist in a style I liked to call "Victorian Indochine," I bought an old wooden cabinet for $20 from a guy who cleaned postmortem estate basements. It was a radio cabinet with a bad paint job, but the top lifted straight up like a treasure chest and I had visions of turning it into a bar. When I was putting it into the apartment, Kelly noticed that one side of it was hollow, and after a little inspection it became clear that there was a hidden panel on that side, a space beneath the main panel that wasn't there on the other side. I knocked on it. I could see, under the paint, the places where small stays had been hammered in to hold the wood in place. I got excited. Who knows what might be in there? A map? Of course it was a map. Or a will. Or a gun, the gun used to shoot a good man in a cold cone of streetlight. I got a lot of mileage out of that panel during the cocktail parties we threw in those early days. Sometimes I'd come at the thing with a screwdriver and the guests would almost shriek. But I left it sealed up each time. Kelly said maybe I should just keep it that way since, odds were, the fantasy was sure to trump the reality. Sort of a bedrock principle of our relationship, come to think of it. But then football season came, and one weekend I got a little drunk watching the Patriots short-yardage themselves into another loss and decided that the time had come, and the screwdriver was at hand, and the paint chipped all over the floor, and when I finally pried the board back, the space behind it was empty. Kelly got the little vacuum and shook her head.

I ripped the envelope open, sighed like I wasn't interested, and felt around inside. I came out with a glossy brochure for a local health spa called Head-Connect at Fleur-de-Lys, the kind of brochure that's folded into thirds and available at the front desk. That was it.

I looked at Lemon.

"Head-Connect at Fleur-de-Lys," I said.

Lemon just looked at me.

"You ever been there?"

She raised her eyebrows like I'd asked her to try a weird food or whether she'd ever been to Japan. A sort of protective revulsion, a do-not-want-what-I-haven't-got kind of thing.

"No, I have not," she said.

Head-Connect was a four-figure-a-night place down in Gable, a mystery spa whose guests roamed vast lawns and were chauffeured through the county in white vans. I'd never been inside. Well, that wasn't totally true.

I turned the brochure over. Looked into the envelope again. It was empty.

"Is this where he's staying?" I asked, more to myself than Lemon.

"Mr. Johansson, I can't give you any information about a patient," she said. "But the way he looked I doubt it."

I walked back to the Escalade, head on a swivel but no sign of Chick. I sat in the front seat and sipped the dregs of my rest-stop coffee. I had to take a piss, but couldn't bring myself to go back in and ask Lemon for the restroom. Our relationship, I felt, had run its course. Once, during a particularly rough period in college, I tried to hit on a young nursing student at the school infirmary after a panicked screening for syphilis. I was clean—jeez!—but the nursing student still wasn't interested, and I'd learned not to press my luck with nurses. Plus, I didn't trust hospital restrooms. The number of hand-washing posters, the industrial disinfectants, they all hinted at some bad shit lurking in the grout.

I tossed the envelope in the passenger seat and headed down to Gable, the glory of the Knotsford-Gable Road, the same garish landmarks in reverse. I took the spur off 20 and headed over toward the Church-on-the-Hill, in whose parking lot, in a long-ago January, I used to make out with a high school girl named Rochelle Scalise. It was one of the few places around town that the local cops didn't patrol, and we'd cut the engine and drop the seats back and yeah, sure, it was next to a graveyard and like 14°F out, but my thinking at the time was something along the lines of that'd just make Rochelle hold me closer. When you're young, you're strategic. On the matter of tactics, however, I could never figure out how to get my hand under her bra. In retrospect, maybe winter wasn't the season for it. There's something quintessentially adolescent, I guess, something almost noble, about trying to feel up a girl in a cemetery parking lot with a hand that is like *this close* to frostbite. I could still remember the beckoning warmth of

Rochelle's right breast as I stretched for it under the hem of her sweatshirt—the thing a small sun, a thermal reactor, a still-warm bagel. God bless her for letting me try too. She probably saved me a few fingers.

I pulled into the parking lot, just like old times, the same worn hedges, the same crumbling tablets. I guess not a lot changes in graveyards. I cut the engine and tried to figure out, having come all this way, what to do next. Option 1: turn off my cell phone, gas up, and be back in Boston in two hours, beating traffic if I left right then. Option 1 held some appeal.

Then there was Option 2. I picked up the envelope and shook its contents out onto the seat. The brochure came out and fluttered open like a bat. Something slipped from its folds and landed on the floor. I reached over and picked it up. It was a piece of medical scrip, folded three ways like the brochure itself. On it was a pencil sketch. The sketch was rough and not very good, but I probably could have figured out what it was if I studied it. So I didn't.

We'd sprung a fish from an abandoned mini-golf once. It was May 2002, after the annual Senior Appreciation Dinner. A quarter of our classmates skipped the dinner altogether, and another quarter left early. We'd stuck around for the presentation of the Senior Gift to Ms. J., the terrifying gnome who'd for years meted out discipline as our high school's vice principal. She was retiring that year, and our class had given her a fishing rod. No idea who had chosen the gift. It was hard to imagine knowing Ms. J. that well.

We were the good kids, relatively speaking.

Chickie was a sort of town ward—absent father, precocity, quirks. Forever showing up at your door with a ball just as you sat down to dinner, the kind of luck-struck kid who could, and did, pitch a no-hitter for Gable in a county pee-wee championship game when he was nine. After the Trivette stuff came out and his notoriety grew, Chickie started telling a story about how when he was a toddler, the daycare teachers took his class on a field trip to the bird sanctuary up on October Mountain and during a lunch break he'd taken a few wobbly steps down the trailhead they were picnicking at and into the path of a midsized brown bear. The teachers, not surprisingly, freaked out. One began yelling at the bear while the other tried to corral seven toddlers and shoo them back into the van. And the bear apparently got enraged and charged the one yelling teacher, knocking her down and bloodying her face pretty good, before returning to where Chickie stood and sort of nudging him deeper into the woods. And then they'd vanished for a half-hour. A pretty fucking frightful half-hour for those toddler teachers, I'd bet. Chick, according to Chick, was pretty calm about the whole thing, believing it to be theater, and folks surmised that the bear thought that he was a cub of sorts, a heartwarming attribution that did not stop the police from shooting it when they arrived. I suppose I don't need to add that most of this story was uncorroborated. Sometimes I'd ask him about it. I never got good answers. But it seemed like a story he wanted to tell, a story that wasn't another story, so we let him.

The rest of us didn't have near as much drama in our lives, real or imagined. We smoked our pot in the summer. We didn't sell drugs or come back from lunch break buzzing and Super Glue beer caps to the blackboard in Mr. Morris's social studies class. Unsie was an honors student and, our senior year, the best high school cross-country skier in the state. Jimmer had scored 1490 on the SATs without cracking so much as a practice test. He was heading somewhere big for college, somewhere with "Institute" in the name. MIT, RIT, RPI. Maybe it was Stanford. I was voted prom king, captain of the basketball team and most likely to succeed. It was a very small school.

On the night of the Senior Appreciation Dinner, Unsie had borrowed his parents' Suburban, the biggest car around. One or two girls had lost their bras in that car, but not much else, even though the way-back was large enough for a twin mattress—an accessory we often discussed obtaining but never did.

"We should get the fish," Chickie said, as we passed around a couple of purloined Zimas in the parking lot.

The fish in question was one of Chick's many obsessions, but this time, high school ending, twelve years of the straight-and-narrow behind us, nobody said no. Next thing I knew, we were in the truck.

The fish was a guppy, I guess. I don't know fish. Ten feet of cement poured over a mesh and wood frame, 4 feet high from her flat hollow belly to her stout dorsal. She was bright pink except for her fins and lips, which were a chipped blue, and her eyes, which were white and wide and lashed. She sat hidden near a copse of scrub pines along a commercial stretch of the Knotsford-Gable Road. A tube ran from her open mouth to a spot down on her tail, as one does, I guess, for all of us. She'd been a pretty easy third hole until the mini-golf went broke a few years earlier. All the other holes—the octopus, the submarine, the pirate ship, et cetera—were gone, taken off to who knows where, and nothing else remained of the course except a rusted chain-link fence around a plot of weeds.

Who knew why the fish was still there? Maybe she had resisted.

The glory of the Knotsford-Gable Road coursed on—a Dairy Queen was operating out of the mini-golf's former rental office, and the fish sat forgotten about 50 yards away from it, surrounded by spring vegetation. As you drove past, all you could see was her dorsal fin peeking out above the weeds, and then only if you knew where to look.

Unsie cut the lights of the Suburban and pulled as far as he could down an old driveway that bent around the back of the trees, until we got to a chain across the drive. We got out.

It had rained earlier that night, and the glow from a nearby McDonald's glittered across the damp field. Chickie lowered the tailgate, and we crept through the underbrush, past the shadow of the Dairy Queen, over to the fish.

We hadn't really thought much about what to do next—we hadn't anticipated getting this far. But now it seemed obvious, sort of. Free the fish.

The fish watched us mutely. We were all still wearing our slacks and button-down shirts from dinner, a style we might one day call business casual if we ever got jobs. Chickie and I got on the sides and Jimmer bent over the tail. Unsie stayed at the car. We designated him the getaway driver, but I had little doubt that if the cops came, Unsie wouldn't hesitate to leave us where we stood. He wasn't stupid. Wind rippled through the brush, and the fish sort of seemed glad for the company. We counted to three and strained.

The fish did not budge. It was heavy as shit. We tried again, until Jimmer said he felt something pop in his abdomen.

We reconvened at the Suburban and spoke in whispers.

"So, uh," Jimmer said, hand on his pelvis.

I shrugged, a little relieved. Chick limped off a ways and kicked at some tall grass. It was getting late. My curfew was 12:30, a notional concept in a town like ours. There was rarely anything going on, and if there was we'd probably missed it already. Unsie started talking about St. Lawrence, a school at the North Pole, where he'd been offered a scholarship. I still hadn't chosen a college—my top four choices had rejected me—and I left the conversation and crept back toward the fish. Chickie had migrated there, and I joined him next to it.

We didn't speak.

I could remember playing mini-golf at the course with my dad after Little League practice. We were always happy to see the fish, a straight shot and early enough in the course that we weren't yet bored. But I'd put away mini-golf when I got to high school and hadn't been there in years. And apparently I wasn't alone. Once she'd had a whole oceanography around her. Now she was an orphan, swimming in the weeds.

Chick bent down on the fish's left flank and patted the pocked cement.

"Maybe we can roll her," he said.

He looked at me and grinned, like all this time we'd just been thinking about a better way to do it.

My slacks were damp and stained at the knees, and my tie was rolled up in a pocket. The ground sank when I kneeled down.

I slid my hands under the fish's belly, got a purchase on her hollow interior. Chick knelt next to me, our shoulders touching.

"Ready?" he asked.

I didn't say anything, so he counted to three and we went for it.

Nothing happened for a second, but then the fish slowly tilted, 20 degrees, then 45, and then it rolled from one side to the other, traveling about 4 feet and ending up lying on the side we'd been pressing against. Nearly a full rotation. We fell forward into the uncovered divot and I clipped my chin on the fish's blue pectoral. Unsie and Jimmer were still shooting the shit back at the truck. Chick scuttled forward on his knees.

"Come on," he said, not a command or a request, because at that point my participation was assumed.

Another roll. Hey, that was 8 feet. I looked up. The open tailgate was still about 20 yards away.

Fuck, I thought. We're going to get it there.

Chick put his hands on the top of the fish. He was grinning from ear to ear. "The Egyptians built the pyramids," he said. "And they weren't even wearing shoes."

I cruised down from the Church-on-the-Hill into Gable village. Olde Gable, settled in 1750 and don't you forget it, now full of boutiques and farm-to-table restaurants. The town was built on a sort of midsection of hill—north was a climb; south a descent. There were few flat roads—everything rolled somewhere or bent somewhere else. In the summer evenings of our youth, before we devoted our time to girls and hoop and stealing fish, Chick and I used to take our bikes up to the Church-on-the-Hill driveway at the apex of the village, look out over the nighttime town, and then turn our wheels south. We'd drop our heads and speed down the hill, past the dark library and locked town hall, right down West Street, left to Prospect Hill Road or into the marshes around Stonover Farm, through clouds of fireflies blinking in the night; you'd be at Lake Mackinac almost before you had to touch the pedals. Hill-to-Bowl, we called it, a solid 4-mile drop. Of course, then we had to get back.

Gable was the sort of place that, when I finally left for college and told people where I was from, would usually get a response like, "How lucky you are!" Which is true, in the grand scheme of things. Gable's a walk-to-school, public park, historic home sort of place. A "25-Best" list sort of place. We had a select board, a local diner, Little League. High property values and low crime rates. We had two lakes to swim in—Laurel Lake and Normanton Bowl. Hills and fields and clapboard churches and a typhoon of foliage in autumn.

But growing up Rockwell wasn't uncomplicated. Gable was the historic seat of Berkshire County, the thin Massachusetts municipality that stretched from the Vermont border to Connecticut. Out here in the woods, across the state from our putative capital, it was easy to feel a little isolated from the rest of the Commonwealth. The rough citizens of all those grim and gritty boroughs of Bostonia had an identity. They were Massholes, and proud of it. They went to the Cape and Maine in the summers, kept their attention on themselves and their tenuous place in the national urbanism. We were their forgotten cousins, their woodland folk. Stick-children, as it were, separated by 30 miles between us and the next eastward exit. In the summer months, Manhattan drove up with its money, a sort of foreign aid that tethered us to the Empire State. In the winters, our storm forecasts came from Albany.

Of course, it had ever been thus. We were our own country, a protectorate, a bucolic Sudetenland. For two hundred years, the artists and oil barons and steel magnates of New York had come to gambol across the Berkshires, drawn first by a copper vein and held by the rolling hills. The Gilded Age of summer palaces began in 1845 and lasted until the federal income tax took effect in 1913. The Great War followed, and then the Depression. When the millionaires left, they abandoned their cottages to the hills. Aspinwall, Springlawn, Shadowbrook. Elm Court. Two dozen more at least. Some burned down, fell apart. Others became prep schools or convents or conference centers. Some became one thing, failed, became something else. All of them were haunted.

When the Boston Symphony Orchestra started coming out to Tanglewood in the late '30s and money started to flow again, the cottages began reappearing, rising from the woods like Avalon. In Gable alone, Blantyre and Wheatleigh became hotels. Shadowbrook, which had burned down, was rebuilt in austerity and became a monastery, then a prison, and then a yoga retreat. Cranwell put down a golf course. The same thing happened in Normanton, in Great Barr, up and down the Hudson River. The estate in the woods behind my house, called Fleur-de-Lys, stayed empty and shattered off of Bramble Street—Fanny Bramble, mother of our ghosts—until the mid-90s, when an outfit called Head-Connect decided to expand its lucrative holistic health racket from the dry heat of Nevada to the cold comfort of the Berkshires.

I parked on Church and walked over past the Knights of Columbus hall. The K of C sponsored our Little League team in 1992, the year we won it all, and then hosted the trophy ceremony in that hall. Now it was a bistro where you could buy an heirloom-tomato flatbread and a faro salad for about $19, but I could still see Coach Cimini handing us our shiny little batters right where the espresso machine now sat.

Screw it, though, you know? They made a good flatbread. Nostalgia's fine but you can't eat it.

I kept walking to the corner of Church and Housatonic. With Head-Connect and some of the other luxury spas operating year round, Gable had money in the winter, and Unsie, who had made the Olympic cross-country ski team as an alternate in Torino, had bought the old Kirkwood pharmacy and turned it into an outdoor sporting goods store called Asgard. Skis and snowshoes and $9,000 road bikes for the finance enthusiast, sold by fit locals in a shop whose pale planks and straight lines evoked a probably inaccurate version of Scandinavia.

I walked in and found him toward the back, taking inventory on a shipment of rock-climbing shoes.

"Homeboy," I said.

He looked up. Put out a palm for a tap and a half hug. Kept it short. Real life wasn't touching him so far—he was still long and lean, elbows and knees. He smelled piney. I have this picture in my head of what the word "hale" means, and that picture is Unsie.

"So Handsome," he said back. "How's Boston?"

I shrugged. "Fine. You know."

Unsie nodded. "The big city."

"I guess," I said. My sense of Boston was that at any given moment it was pretty convinced that it was in a three-way tie for the biggest city in the country. But the law firms paid well, so I shouldn't complain. "Hub of the universe. That's what they say."

Unsie didn't reply, didn't seem to think a reply was called for. After a second, he nodded to himself and looked up.

"Have you seen him?"

I shook my head. "He asked me to meet him up in the Knots today, by KMC. He never showed."

I looked around the store. Early March, but still three couples wearing North Face and sunglasses inside. "You?"

Unsie looked at me and raised his eyebrows.

"Yeah. Not great. Fun, sort of, but not great."

"What's he doing here? Last I heard, he was in the Pacific. Saipan or Tortuga or some shit."

He shrugged.

"Don't know. I think that ended, not sure if he had a next thing lined up. Sort of floated back, that was my impression."

"Where's he staying?"

"KMC emergency room once or twice, I think. When he's not there, he's at the Horse Head."

"The Horse Head?"

The Horse Head was a motel up along the Knotsford-Gable Road. I'd driven past it twice today already.

"Yeah, that's what I said. He asked me for a tent. Too cold for that, still. I mean, we have some good tents, but you have to know how to use them. I told him he could stay with Sara and me, but he said he was okay."

Unsie turned back to his shoeboxes.

"Sara was relieved," he said, sort of reluctantly. "He looked a little rough. Accident-prone. And she's pregnant."

Conditioning being what it is, it took me a second to realize that this was happy news.

"Hey," I said. "Hey!"

Unsie turned a little red. His neck, mostly. His cheeks were sort of always red.

"Yeah," he said, shrugging.

I clapped him on the shoulder.

"My boy," I said. "Yours?"

He flipped me the finger and continued to sort boxes. I paused a decent interval.

"Why was he at the E.R.?"

Unsie shook his head. "Not sure," he said. "But it's Chick."

I nodded. Chick once got concussed in his driveway because he decided he could do a backflip.

"Dude is leaving me clues," I said, digging in my pocket for the piece of medical scrip.

Unsie unfolded the scrip, looked at it. It was of a curved, pointy thing. Might be a sword. Might be something else.

"This supposed to be you?" he asked.

"Fuck off."

Unsie laughed to himself, looked at it for a second longer. Shrugged. Gave it back to me.

"I've seen bigger."

I waited him and his stupid jokes out, until eventually he had to re-engage.

"I haven't seen him in a week," he said, finally.

A customer beckoned from a rack of ski poles and Unsie clomped away, his feet both heavy and light on the floors like a marionette.

We strained against the fish's side and it rolled again. It was a little off-line.

"Psst," Chick whispered.

Uns and Jimmer looked over at us, realizing what we were doing. They didn't look thrilled, but they trudged over and got down on their knees next to me. Jimmer positioned himself at the fish's tail, turning it like a rudder. We rolled and rolled again, and within twenty minutes, we were at the back of the truck.

"Put the tail up there and then we all lift the front?" Chick asked breathlessly. He was sweating. Into it.

None of us nodded, except Chick at his own idea. We knew the drill. Chick and I pivoted the tail up, and Jimmer backed the tailgate under it. The truck dipped under the strain. Jimmer climbed into the back and held the tail steady. Chick and I bent down on either side of the massive head. We looked at each other and lifted.

Slowly the fish rose off the wet ground. Unsie, surrendering, got between us and applied his substantial lower-body strength, while Jimmer pulled from inside the truck, which didn't help at all. But we got the head up over our belts and leaned in with our bellies. "I can't hold it," Unsie said, but he did, and then we got leverage and slid the fish right into the back of the truck.

Or almost, at least. The Suburban's way-back was thinly carpeted, and the fish slid tail-first up over the collapsed second row of seats. But then the dorsal fin hit the lip of the roof, and she stopped moving. The fish's round pink face sat on the tailgate, hanging out over the edge. We tried to tilt her, roll her, and then we tried to pull her back. She wouldn't budge.

"Maybe if we just bash the head in a little," Jimmer said, measuring with his hands from somewhere inside the truck, and in our adrenaline-flushed state, it sounded reasonable. If we could clear five more inches, the whole fish would fit in the trunk.

I shrugged. Unsie was in the driver's seat. He was ready to bolt.

I found a thick log on the ground and swung it at the dorsal fin. The log struck with a muffled thump and flew into pieces—damp wood against cement. The fish was unscathed.

"Don't," Chick said as I searched for a rock.

Then he laughed.

"I mean, you know. But don't."

We paused and considered our situation. It was late on a spring night, the sort of night our local cops lived for, and there was a giant stolen fish sticking out of Unsie's mom's Suburban.

"Isn't there a blanket in here?" Jimmer said.

Unsie passed one back, and we draped it across the fish's head. It was a small blanket and didn't even reach the gills. Now it just looked like a fish with a fever.

"Let's take it to school, drop it outside the office," Chick said.

There was a certain logic to that, since we'd just given Ms. J. a fishing rod. Still, it seemed dangerously close to vandalism. The previous year, some seniors had put toothpaste and shaving cream on the middle school windows on the evening of Senior Skip, and they'd been banned from graduation.

My parents would kill me if I got banned from graduation.

Chick looked at us. I could feel my heart beating beneath my wet shirt. The clock was ticking. In Gable, this time of night, about 40 percent of the cars on the road were cop cars. We knew some of the cops—one of them had been the assistant soccer coach a few years ago. They loved catching local kids, seeing as how they'd each been local kids themselves. Last Halloween, when people were out egging, Gary Lenehan had chased our high school's current track star 4 miles on foot. Caught him too.

"In?" Chick asked, and one by one we each nodded.

Jimmer got into the passenger seat. Unsie started the engine. I sat in the back with Chick and held onto the fish's tail. It would be bad, I thought, if the fish fell out of the car. Four seniors, out on a springtime lark, drop a giant cement fish on top of some poor young family. That would be next year's public service announcement.

"Take side streets," Chick said, as Unsie veered onto Route 7 and headed south a quarter mile until he could pull off. We were all quiet. In the back, I held the tail both tightly and loosely. I didn't want the fish to slide out, but if it did, I didn't want to go with it.

Midafternoon and the sun was a pale penny sinking toward the western hills. It was cold outside Asgard. I couldn't bear to hike back up to the Horse Head just yet. And fuck Chick, anyway, for standing me up. For a little while, at least. Fuck him while I got myself a flatbread.

We still owned a house on Scrimshaw, I guess my mom owned it, but she was living in a condo up in Burlington with my dad's ashes. I drove up our dead-end street, drawn by the magical magnetism of . . . what? Boredom, probably. Or muscle memory. Whatever. I could see the renters' kids in the front yard. Two boys and a girl, each under nine from the looks of it, passing around a purplish ball in need of air. Didn't those kids know there was probably still a hand-pump in the garage and a bent needle in the top left drawer of the kitchen? Silly kids. Even without the extra air, I could punt that ball right over the garage, I bet, send them off to hunt for it among the hydrangeas. But I'd never do that, of course. It was bad enough to be lurking there as it was. I was going to spook the neighbors, and then I'd probably recognize one of them, or not, whichever was worse.

It was nice to have kids in the neighborhood again, frolicking like when we were young. Made me happy. Not really. Neighborhoods have life cycles, right? I wondered if they climbed the sugar maple in the back, where the treehouse had been, or if they'd found the coffee tin full of Hulk action figures and the Kris Kross mixtape I buried in the side lawn in 1992. I wondered if they followed the trail that went all the way through the woods out back, a couple of miles to the Magic Meadow, to the rear flank of the Fleur-de-Lys property. Our places. The doorjambs were full of our pencil marks, the briars were full of our blood. Chick's dad had left when Chick was tiny and his mom had moved to Florida, to a golf course near a lake. Their house, a small ranch that used to be across the street from mine, was gone, subsumed by a barn-like home built by a barn-like man whose late-model SUV sat next to a boat and a lacrosse net in the driveway.

The barn-like man stood on his porch, staring at me.

It was five o'clock. I'd wanted a reason to get a beer for a while, and now I had one.

✤

Our high school was 3 miles from the abandoned mini-golf. The fish swayed and pivoted but stayed in the truck. We passed two cars going the opposite way, each of which we were sure was a cruiser, and when we got to the parking lot, it was lit up like a football field.

"Ready?" asked Unsie.

There was no cover in the lot, and we'd have to get in and out fast.

Unsie pulled in and raced to the school's main entrance. The truck jumped up over the curb by the doorways, and we scrambled out and pulled on the fish with all our might. It wouldn't budge. We were fully exposed.

Unsie was pushing from the back, whispering "Shit, shit, shit!" Jimmer had a crazy look on his face. Chick and I were pulling and twisting as the truck's exhaust heated up my pant leg. Then the dorsal fin cracked, and the fish tumbled out onto the walkway. There was no time to do anything aesthetic. Chick and I dove into the open back of the truck, and Unsie peeled out onto the road. Behind us, the fish stared balefully into the parking lot.

"Oh shit!" Chickie yelled, smiling ear to ear.

I couldn't believe it had worked. Jimmer started to giggle, and it was left to me and Unsie to be the serious ones.

"We can't say a word," Unsie said eventually. "Nobody can say a word."

We each nodded. Unsie drove to the all-night carwash, and we got out and hosed the grass and mud out of the trunk. It seemed prudent. Could they dust for mud? It was past midnight, and my shirt was smeared with pink. Events were irreversible.

"Look," Unsie said, pointing at the ground. A big toad, the biggest ever, had washed out of the trunk and sat on the carwash floor, staring at us. He'd been inside the fish. Like Jonah. He croaked his thanks and hopped off.

We dropped Jimmer off at his corner, then Unsie drove me and Chick to the bottom of Scrimshaw. We had to pass the high school. The fish swam in the glow of the parking lot lights. Our humanities teacher liked to remind us that Melville wrote *Moby-Dick* while sitting at his cottage right up the road, imagining the great whale breaching beneath the white winter curves of the distant mountains. We looked quickly over at the fish—ahoy, Tashtego! Thar she blows!—and then quickly away.

✦

I sat on a stool at the Heirloom and tried to catch Ginny Archey's eye. She was bartending. We'd dated for the length of a party once, near the end of junior year. Her dad owned the bar, a proud testament to tradition and Keno in a rapidly gentrifying downtown, and she'd been working there since she was fourteen.

"Hey," she said when she saw me, with a smile that turned quickly into a scowl. She slid a bowl of peanuts toward me. "Still allergic?"

"Only to you, peanut," I said. I wasn't allergic to either of them.

She laughed, said "I'm just kidding, Petey," and ambled down the bar toward me. Her belly was round and heavy. First Sara, now Ginny. Everybody was pregnant but me.

"Well, look at you," I said. "If you'd looked like that back in 2001, we might have had something."

She blushed. "You wish, pal."

"I do wish," I said, and meant it.

"Hah," she said. "No you don't."

I leaned across the bar to kiss her cheek and made a point of looking around the room at the collection of flannel and early drinkers.

"Just tell me whose it is," I said. "I'll make him make an honest woman out of you."

She kissed me back and extended her left hand.

"Pull my finger," she said, showing off a dainty rock on a silver band. "If I wasn't swollen like a whale, I'd let you try it on."

I'd done some preliminary rock shopping over the course of the past year, and hers looked to be about a half-carat, and if the ring was platinum it wasn't a bad little buy.

"Who are you marrying?" I asked, trying to sound like I was trying to sound incredulous. Had to be careful with pregnant women, or so I've been told.

"You don't want to know," she said, looking at me pointedly.

I thought about that for a second. Who was she marrying? Me? Nope. Chick? Too soon, though I wouldn't put it past him. Then it hit me. She was marrying Tim-Rick Golack.

"You've got to be kidding me," I said, this time trying to sound like I was trying to sound like I was joking.

"I'm not kidding you," she said, "and don't make me regret that kiss. What are you drinking?"

I ordered a beer and let both it and the conversation sit for a minute. Ginny moved with cetacean grace inside the bar, no bumping, no wobble, her belly like the central star of the system. I remembered that I'd heard, in the way you hear things on social media, that she'd been dating Tim-Rick Golack, who had emerged in recent years as a local businessman and, according to Unsie, a regular at Sunday Mass. But a ring and a baby I did not know. There were some chicken-egg questions that I didn't ask.

I sipped my beer, which tasted watery and vaguely funky, like the taps needed to be changed. A novice Heirloomer might have sent it back, but they'd just find out that all the beers tasted like that. It was almost a source of pride.

In the corner, some girl was setting up a karaoke booth.

"I saw your boy," Ginny said, having rotated back over to me. She was still smiling but her eyes were subdued.

"Has he been coming in here much?"

She shook her head. "No, just the once. You know, the stuff with T-R."

I nodded. I knew the stuff with T-R.

"It's so stupid," she said. "That was high school. Time to grow up."

I looked at my beer and raised my eyebrows. "Tell me something I don't know."

Ginny put a hand on her belly.

"Petey, tell him he can come in. Or better yet, you bring him in with you. There'll be no trouble."

I sipped my beer and shrugged.

"I can't find him," I said. "Dude called me out from Boston and stood me up."

Ginny put both her hands on the bar and leaned forward so that her belly canted toward the floor.

"I hear he's spending a lot of time in Sink City," she said. "Back and forth."

She sighed heavily. I gave my beer more attention.

"That's what I hear."

"That's what you hear, huh," I said. "In your condition?"

She gestured with one hand around the bar. "I'm in no condition to be in my condition. But I hear a lot."

I finished my beer, stood up, nodded to no one in particular. Ginny swept the bar with a wet cloth.

I pulled $5 from my wallet. She tried to wave it away, so I stuffed it into the tip jar next to the cash register.

"When are you due?" I asked.

"Easterish," she said, rapping her knuckles on the bar. "When things warm up a bit."

"Well, there you go," I said. "Something to look forward to."

It was dark when I left the Heirloom. The streetlights were coming on, bright lozenges wrapped in gauze. Gable wasn't much for neon, but I could see farther down on Church Street an orange smear glowing through the windows of the tapas restaurant, formerly a hardware store. The Foodtown was closed, but the lights in The Bookstore— "Serving the community since last Tuesday"—burned on.

What did I know?

I knew the thing with T-R. The thing with T-R was a series of fights during our senior year of high school, two during basketball games and one shortly after graduation, each progressively bloodier and more serious than the last.

It was a weird thing. Chick was neither a lover nor a fighter, his notoriety creating a sort of buffer around him. His friends were loyal. His enemies, if he had any, kept quiet. He did some dumb things to property, but never had problems with anyone.

Except Tim-Rick Golack. Those two were like oil and water. Hoop-wise, Misconic was our main rival, a tough city school from the west side of the Knots, and Tim-Rick was one of those overmatched hustlers that people called either scrappy or thuggish, depending on their biases. The first fight had been mainly pushing, some language, as we pulled away in the fourth quarter. The second fight had ended both Chick's and my basketball careers, which were probably ending anyway but might have carried on at some midlevel college for a bit, and the third one had left Tim-Rick with a scar from his ear to his chin and Chick with a suspended sentence of a year in jail, pled down to simple battery from assault with a deadly weapon. With the third, they'd just crossed paths at the Berkshire Mall on the wrong day, Tim-Rick with his brothers and Chick with a hard plastic frost scraper in his back pocket. Why he was walking around with a hard plastic frost scraper I don't know—it was July—but mall security had to call the state police and a hazmat team to deal with the blood.

As for Sink City, I knew that too. It was a reference to the faded factories and coarse canals of a town forty-five minutes to the east, the Venice of Western Massachusetts, where they used to fit porcelain to pipes and, more recently, where one went to bargain-hunt for anything harder than weed.

❦

The Horse Head Motel advertised free Wi-Fi and a hot tub but both were suspect, and the tired dude at the front desk gave me a key to Chickie's room even though I wasn't Chickie. I didn't even say I was Chickie. I just said "Benecik, and I don't have a key." Dude had never seen me before, but he had an Italian sub and an issue of *American Sportsman* behind him, and he just did not give a fuck.

I'd never known anyone to stay at the Horse Head, which was distinguishable from the Comfort Inn and the Pine Ranch next door only by the big red horse head next to its empty pool. You could walk to the Price Chopper and to an all-night gas station, and those were just about the only advantages I could see to staying there. The key had a plastic diamond attached to it that said "15." I walked across the parking lot and knocked.

Nobody answered.

I knocked again. It felt like the beginning of an episode of *Law & Order*, normal things happening and then a body.

I put the key in and turned it. The door opened.

"Chick?" I said through the gap.

No answer.

I pushed the door open wider. The room was tiny. There were two twin beds, one rumpled and one still made, dusty sheets at right angles. Papers were spread out across the made one.

I checked the bathroom. A toothbrush. A towel over the shower bar, slightly damp. Trash in the bin. A plastic grocery bag full of underwear hanging on the interior doorknob.

Back in the main room, I moved some papers aside on the made bed and sat down. There was a backpack, one of those serious ones, leaning in the corner, all zippers and ties and mesh. A pair of snowshoes, probably several hundred dollars at Asgard, but I doubted that Chickie had paid that much. It was nearing nine and I was beat. The outside temperature was already into the low 30s and descending. I wasn't driving back to Boston, that's for sure. Two hours on the cold road and then a night in a cold apartment, thanks but no thanks.

The papers on the made bed seemed to be a mix of maps and brochures and copies of microfiche. I scanned them quickly with determined disinterest. Whatever it was Chickie was getting into, it was not my problem. I was a workingman now, an adult with my own life to lead, my own crosses to bear. The sentiment felt about 70 percent true.

I flipped on the remote and checked the TV. The Horse Head's cable was a joke, and if you weren't going to watch grainy porn or hockey, there wasn't much to watch. I considered ordering the porn and sticking Chick with the bill for wasting so much of my time, but couldn't bring myself to do it after such a stupid day.

The morning after we emancipated the fish, I slept late. Seniors weren't required to check in until 9:30, when the buses left for graduation rehearsal. I drove to school, wondering if the fish would already be gone—indeed, if it had ever really been there at all—and parked near the back of the lot. Even from there I could see a crowd around the entry. I began to sweat. Walking across the lot, I passed Denton, our grizzled custodian. He seemed grouchy.

"What's going on?" I asked.

"You should know," he said angrily, and for a split second I almost shat my pants.

"Seniors," he said. "Somebody thinks they're real funny."

I kept walking and tried to catch my breath.

That was one big-ass fish. A bunch of my classmates surrounded it.

"Had to be eight or nine guys," someone said.

"The Lesters have a trailer," another said, invoking the previous year's ne'er-do-wells. "Coulda been them."

We got onto the buses to head to rehearsal and I slid into a row next to Jimmer. When we were all seated, Ms. J. appeared at our bus's open door and stepped up into the well. She was a wide woman, with a white helmet of hair.

The bus fell silent. Halfway back, I focused on my sneakers.

"I just want to say," she said, gesturing with her hand. "To whoever put that fish there . . . "

Ms. J. paused. For a moment, she looked like she might cry. I could feel my nuts retract into my stomach.

"To whoever put that fish there, thank you. I love it. I'll be taking it with me when I leave."

Then she smiled, for the first time in our collective memories, and stepped back off the bus. The seats filled with whispers. Jimmer stared at me. I couldn't look at him. Two rows in front of us, the back of Unsie's head quivered. Through the window, I saw Chickie. He was over by the fish, wasn't even on the bus yet.

In the morning, I opened my eyes and he was in the bed across the room, pale and thin, asleep. Mouth open a crack, chin turned toward the ceiling. In repose he looked as young as the last time I saw him, shortly after high school. I watched him until I felt confident that his chest was moving and then closed my eyes again.

An hour later, I woke back up. I'd been having a dream about canoes, like the kind the natives would make from saplings and birch bark. First guy who made one of those must have been a genius. This time Chick was sitting across from me, on the edge of the other twin. He was wearing a full suit of long underwear, the fabric pocked like soundproofing. He had a beard I hadn't noticed before—had it been there before?—and looked a little brittle, but his eyes were smiling.

"Guy," he said, in this fucking saccharine way that combined "it's great to see you" with "don't be mad." But sometimes it's still sweet even when you know it's saccharine, you know?

I rolled over toward the wall, still clothed, still on top of the sheets.

"Be that way," he fake-huffed. Then he bounded over and jumped on me, holding on the way a koala holds a bamboo spear, his arms around my chest, his legs thrown over mine. What you call spooning when you're trying to get a girl to trust you.

"Shhh," he said. "Let it happen."

I felt his beard on the back of my neck.

"Dude," I said, my mouth full of cobwebs. "Get the fuck off me."

I should have been mad, but instead I felt like I imagine a soldier feels when he's reunited with his unit after leave. Kind of sad, but also kind of relieved. It was the feeling I always got with Chick. Got it again, even after our long estrangement.

He rolled onto his back and lay beside me. I could almost hear him smiling.

"Guy," he said again, both the beginning and the end of a sentence. Then: "What are you doing here?"

I lifted my head. Wan sunlight filtered in through the high window. I snorted.

"Don't even," I said. "Asshole."

"You're the asshole, asshole," he said. "Breaking into someone's room and sleeping here. Who do you think you are? Goldilocks?"

He threw his arm back around me.

"It's a good thing you're so handsome."

I shrugged free again.

"Off," I said.

Chickie put his head on my cheek. His breath smelled burnt, sleepy. Then he stood up, over me. I opened one eye and braced myself. This was the kind of situation where, back in the day, you'd get an elbow-drop to the ribs just because. A friendship equal parts tender and macho, landing in the middle most of the time. It probably sounds weird. I don't know what to tell you.

I levered his leg away from the wall and sent him off balance. He leapt across the short gulf to the other bed. I could hear the springs buckle. The sunbeams registered the turbulence.

"You got my message?"

"Fuck I got your message," I said, rolling onto my back and rubbing my eyes. "What do you think I'm doing here?"

He was lying down now, on his side, looking at me as if we were at a sleepover.

"Horse Head. I thought you came, you know, for the Horse Head."

I closed my eyes. So it was going to be like this.

"Where were you yesterday?"

I could hear him bouncing, but at least the question shut him up for a second.

"I waited up there for an hour."

I looked over at him. He was smiling, but his face was red. He wouldn't look back.

"Haven't seen you in forever. Random calls. I drove my ass all the way out here because you asked me to. And you leave me hanging."

Nothing.

I picked up the envelope he'd left for me.

"And what is this, anyway? Fleur-de-Lys and a picture of a dick."

Chickie looked up. Almost like he'd forgotten about the envelope. His face brightened.

"It's not a dick," Chick said. "It's a horn."

He crouched between the beds and inclined his right hand up and away from the bridge of his nose.

"A horn. Get it?"

A horn. I should have known that. Maybe I did.

"I get it," I said.

In the spring of our seventh grade, our history teacher, Ms. Bitz, got caught in the weight room after hours, pinned under the captain of the wrestling squad. The sub, Ms. Flemmy, who was about a hundred and eight years old, came in looking to buy herself a week or two of adjustment time and immediately gave our class a project.

"For the next week, each of you is to write a report about a famous historical figure who is buried in town," she said. "Fifteen pages."

Jimmer had suggested we write about Ms. Bitz herself, since she was now both famous and buried, at least reputation-wise, but that seemed sort of cruel. Plus she was pretty hot, and who knew when and under what circumstances we might meet again. Maybe there was wrestling in our futures as well.

Anyway, there was no shortage of candidates. What with the village's history, the cottages and such, we'd been milking our ghosts for a hundred years already. Local lore was the go-to for every teacher from home ec to humanities. It was inescapable. Our high school mascot, the Gable Millionaire, was a rich dude in a top hat and tails running around the bleachers at home games, fake-smoking a cigar and handing out Monopoly money. He was our patron and sovereign and albatross all at once, the tycoon who'd carved up the woods so he had somewhere to go on the weekends. And none of us were even rich. We were all service-industry kids, ice-cream scoopers, lawn mowers. We walked your dog and delivered your paper. Our great-grandfathers kept Carnegie pools clean. Chandeliers swaying overhead and naked ladies in the gardens. Write about a famous figure buried around here? Shit, we would dig them up just to bury them again.

As it happened, on the very day that Ms. Flemmy gave us the assignment, Chick and I were already a couple of hours into a report on Guy Van Nest, whose estate, Fleur-de-Lys, sat about 200 yards off of Bramble, past a chain-link fence and a marble gatehouse in disrepair. The property was hidden behind a brocade of pines and cedars and, from the road, if it was winter and the leaves were down, you might just catch sight of a ruined corner of the Italianate main building, maybe a column or two, maybe the edge of what was once a fountain. Nobody had been in there regularly for fifty years, roughly since the Sisters of Mercy bought it at auction in the 1940s and then didn't have the money to restore it. A fire in the '70s gutted the second floor and was locally attributed to a nun-sponsored insurance gambit.

From the back of my house, it was a couple miles walk through the woods to get onto the Fleur-de-Lys property. We used to hike over there all the time, hunt for turtles in the old pools, look through the broken windows of the main house. Run around for hours, trails to more trails to statues and gazebos splintered by time. Cowboys and Indians. Capture the flag when we had numbers. The estate was a labyrinth, and the main mansion its center. All the windows were damaged, and the rooms inside looked dank and gangrenous. It was a mess. We snuck out to it every chance we got.

Chick and I'd been there just the week before, in fact, trying to force open a window above the porch, when we were surprised by Officer Grevantz, the newest member of Gable's police force. Slick son of a bitch was on an ATV, an appropriation for which the police department had lobbied just the past summer, and when folks asked what do you need an ATV for anyway, our jowly Chief Winston could probably have said "to bust kids trying to sneak into Fleur-de-Lys," but didn't.

The ATV was loud as shit, but the window was nearly open, and we just weren't paying attention. Grevantz jumped off that thing like he was roping a steer, light shining off his sunglasses, gum snapping between his teeth. He pointed at the two of us.

"I know you two," he shouted, I guess to forestall any thoughts we might have of escape. He was wearing a cross between a smile and a snarl. "Benecik and Johansson. I know your parents. Get your asses down here."

Grevantz was only about twenty-six years old at the time, in his second year on the job. Man, you just knew this was the best thing he'd done all week and that he could hardly wait to get back to the station. I think he was hoping we'd run for it.

The thought did cross my mind. Chick gave me a look—part panicked, part thrilled. I shook him off. The ground was wet, we were wearing boots, and the motherfucker was on an ATV. Plus, he had a gun, not that he'd use it.

Anyway, it was irrelevant. He knew us. Even if we shook him, he'd just be waiting at our houses.

We climbed down. Grevantz called for a cruiser. A little unnecessary, I thought, until I noticed how cool his walkie-talkie was, and how staccato and totalitarian he got to sound speaking into it.

Chief Winston was a big man with a wide head and an avuncular quality that I associated with gardeners and the '80s Celts coach K.C. Jones, who I admired despite his having ruined my Magic-Johnson-loving childhood. Chief Winston was in-laws with George Harvey, our CYC coach, and had a daughter our age named Ava who went to private school in Connecticut. We knew her from the summers, from Tanglewood where we parked cars and she wandered with her private school friends through the mazes, girls with names like Karina and Ellis, girls who ignored us until they needed someone to smuggle in a fifth of blackberry schnapps and make out with and then throw up on. But nobody messed with Ava, probably because she was the daughter of the local police chief and maybe also because she didn't make herself available, as if she felt a little torn between her school world and her home world and didn't want to throw up all over the latter, at least not yet. And as long as she kept bringing hot chicks in to slum with us, that was fine.

Maybe because we'd never tried to lay a hand on Ava, or maybe because he knew about the stuff with Bill Trivette, Chief Winston went easy on us. Grevantz had marched us to the rusted gates of Fleur-de-Lys and stuffed us into the back of a cruiser driven by another of our local cops—there were only six—named Mulvaney, who had been on the job forever and didn't say anything to us except "watch your heads." Then Grevantz had led the cruiser back into town on the ATV, like he was at the head of a big parade, a hunter towing in the bucks he'd brought down. People on Main Street stared at the cruiser. Chickie stared back. Sometimes he waved.

In his office, Chief Winston fixed us with a glare he'd probably been practicing for years. An old yellow dog lay curled at the foot of his desk.

"Where'd you stash it?" he asked, squinting first at Chick and then at me.

We looked at each other.

"Stash what?" I asked.

"We didn't stash anything," Chick said.

"So you have it on you?" Chief Winston said.

"What?"

"Don't get smart with me, son."

"What?"

The chief let me shake for a minute, then started chuckling. Man, these fuckers were bored. I recognize that now. At the time, I almost started to cry.

Then he picked up his phone and dialed a number.

"Yeah," he said, after a pause. "They're here. I'm sending them your way. If they aren't there in the next"—he looked at his watch—"five minutes, let me know. I'll send out the dog."

Chief Winston hung up the phone and snapped his fingers. The dog at his feet raised its head. The chief looked at us.

"You're wanted," he said, "at the library."

The town library was three-quarters of a mile away. Chick and I sprinted across the street, through the back parking lot of the Curtis, over the fence at Lilac Park, almost got hit by a car crossing Housatonic, and arrived at the doors just as the head librarian, a wizened octogenarian named Florence Banish, bent her bun to check her watch.

"You are the miscreants?" she asked, holding the door handle with fine fingers, her bones sheathed in parchment. With her other hand, she pressed her glasses back over the crook of her nose.

We were keeled over, wheezing, our hands on our knees.

I looked up and nodded.

"Chief Winston says you are here to write a book report on Fleur-de-Lys. An apologia of a sort. It is to be thirty pages long and is due by the end of the month. Fortunately for you," she said, "I am the definitive resource."

She turned in the door and headed inside.

"Follow me."

Guy Van Nest was the only child of Forsyth and Helene Van Nest, a late baby, a gift to the tycoon's second wife when he was in his fifties and she was already pushing thirty-five. In photos from the late 1800s, Guy appears as a small boy in short pants, pale—but that might be the tint—and surrounded by knees. Forsyth had made his fortune in the West, sliding needles into mineral veins, fueling the factory fires of the Cuyahoga, the construction of highways across the Atlantic Coast, the general choke and rattle of the late Industrial Revolution. Perhaps in response, he built Fleur-de-Lys deep within the Berkshire hills, surrounded by trees and fields, an Eden, a solace, a place where he could pretend to be a naturalist. Fresh air and clean water. He shipped Helene and baby Guy up here and rarely visited, and when he died, not soon enough, he left the entire estate, all 36 acres and 900 statues and forty rooms, to the child, who was eight at the time.

Life was a series of nannies and clowns and croquet parties for Guy and his lonely mother, who cared less for the sleepy hill towns and their inhabitants than her husband seemed to want of her. Guy made few friends among the local children, many of whose parents worked for him, and his summers were spent in carriage rides from one cottage party to another, social events where the bonhomie was largely ceremonial. After Forsyth died, Helene was less and less in residence, taking the train back into the city at every opportunity and more often than not leaving Guy behind, on his massive estate, with his handlers and his jugglers and his short pants. As he hit his teens, things got a little crazy: wilder parties, construction projects commenced and halted, visitors of all shapes and sizes. Skinny-dipping. Naked lawn bowling. He developed something of a reputation.

Then, in his early twenties, Guy went big. He'd hosted a traveling circus at Fleur-de-Lys, putting them up for the entire summer, the performers in the main house and the animals in stables and tents he'd commissioned. In the evenings, servants regaled the uptown taverns with stories of bearded women and dwarves and sword-swallowers, and some days you could catch an occasional glimpse of great gray beasts wandering aimlessly across the property's back fields. When that summer ended, rumor had it, Guy had kept a rhino.

We learned all this from Florence Banish, who had a whole folder of Fleur-de-Lys material in a fireproof cabinet in one of the library's archival spaces. At that point, Head-Connect hadn't yet purchased the property, although some of the local realtors whispered of overtures from Lake Tahoe. Chick and I sat at a circular table and spread the contents of the folder out in front of us. Grainy pictures, newspaper clippings, yellowing photocopies of deeds. Florence Banish watched hawk-like as we sifted through them, her voice a cross between a croak and a flute: no bending, no drinks, careful with the artifacts. Of course no drinks. Jeez, couldn't she see we had no drinks?

By our third day of research at the library, I was bored and had started to try and work out how big we could make our margins. Chickie, on the other hand, was engaged.

"Shit," he said, sliding a frail slip of newsprint my way.

It was a clipping from the *Berkshire Record*, an old weekly newspaper now subsumed by the *Franchise*, an inside page dated April 1927. The paper was brittle and the color of Florence Banish's hands. It was an obituary. Guy Van Nest, erstwhile owner and sole occupant of Fleur-de-Lys, died of pneumonia at the young age of thirty-eight and was buried on Long Island.

"Shit," I said. I got it right away.

Florence Banish hissed at me.

"Shoot. Sugar. If he's not buried here, we can't use him for Ms. Flemmy."

We were combining our probationary report for Chief Winston with our history paper, of course, but the latter depended on the subject being buried in town. Now Guy Van Nest didn't qualify. We could still use the material for Chief Winston, but the one for Ms. Flemmy was due in a week and that's the one for which we were suddenly without a subject. Chick groaned. Then he began shuffling through the papers again.

"Maybe he had a kid?"

I checked the obituary. Van Nest was divorced, no kids.

"No luck."

We itemized the papers. Records from a bankruptcy, deeds of transfer. World War I going on somewhere, the stock market heading south. We settled on a grainy black-and-white from late August 1914, according to the thin scratches along its margin. The steps to the Italianate main house, a spread of people in front, a white tent top off to the left. Thin and mustachioed Guy Van Nest at the center of the spread, on the pea-stoned entry, dressed for dinner and flanked by women with parasols, then farther out by dark and hairy and dramatic creatures, acrobats in jumpsuits belted at the waist, a pair of midgets, a body builder, a 7-footer. A bearded figure of indeterminate gender with his or her arm around a clown, and past them, housemaids and gardeners and livery on the upper steps. Everyone staring at Guy, who had a smile on his face, a lion at his feet, and an elephant looming behind him, its trunk draped around his shoulders like a shawl.

"What about the rhino?" said Chickie.

I looked up.

"What rhino?"

"The one he kept at Fleur-de-Lys after the circus left. What happened to that?"

I shrugged.

"Heck if I know," I said, out of deference to Florence Banish. "How do we know if there even was a rhino at Fleur-de-Lys?"

"There was a rhino at Fleur-de-Lys," Florence Banish said. "There still is."

We looked at her. She was standing in the door of our little project room, leaning a frail hip against the frame and looking dreamily out a side window. If she'd had a thin cigarette, she could have been in a movie. After a second, she gathered herself, took a look out to the main reading room, and then crossed slowly to us. She moved some papers around and centered the circus photo before us. She stared at it for a moment, then bent a bony finger toward one of the housemaids, second step, third from the edge.

"That's my mother," she said.

Chick and I walked from his room at the Horse Head. He was limping a little bit, holding his left side.

"What'd you do?" I asked.

He shrugged. "Don't know. Probably nothing. Just getting old. The knee aches when it's cold out."

He was twenty-eight, six months younger than me.

I clicked the unlock, and the truck blinked. Chick had blown his ACL out in the second fight with Tim-Rick Golack, somewhere near our foul line, at the bottom of a pile of kids. It had never healed right. They had to call the game with six minutes left in the fourth quarter. Tim-Rick had been in a different pile of kids near the baseline, his head in the crook of my arm, but the game was in our home gym and he took the blame for the injury, both from the fans and, the next day, in the paper. Which is what made his resurrection as a local businessman such a surprise.

"Nice ride," Chick said, looking at the Escalade. "Not as nice as Jimmer's, but not bad."

Jimmer was somewhere in Silicon Valley, doing something with numbers.

I'd had the Escalade for two years, got it shortly after law school, a gift to myself from those bottomless first paychecks. It was a stupid ride to own in Boston, where everyone either took cabs or the T, and where 15 feet of available curb was hard to find. And driving it I always felt like I was heading to an AND1 Mixtape game. But I liked it. It looked good parked next to all those little BMWs in the South End, like a killer whale in a school of clownfish. It announced my presence in the city, a kid from the sticks no longer. I came to play. I came to scale the walls. Plus, it helped me to feel wanted, because someone was always moving a couch.

My ride was the only ride in the parking lot.

"Where's your car?" I said.

Chick opened the passenger door.

"Don't have one."

"How'd you get here, then?"

He looked at me.

"Where? Here, Gable?"

"Like, here." I motioned to the Horse Head. It was a long walk from anywhere. "Last night, how did you get here?"

"Oh," he said. "Buddy dropped me off."

"Buddy? Buddy dropped you off?"

We didn't know anyone named Buddy. And anyway what buddy did Chick have who was dropping him off at the Horse Head?

"A buddy. Elvis LaBeau, from Misconic. You remember Elvis LaBeau."

I did not remember Elvis LaBeau. I got in the truck. Chick climbed in the passenger seat and looked around. He put his hands on the dash and pretended to be taking it all in.

"Boston is treating you well, I see," he said.

So transparent. My head was starting to hurt.

"Dude, hold up. Back up."

Chickie looked at me, then lowered his eyes.

"I need a little chronology," I said.

"Fine," he said, staring at his socks. "Can we do it over breakfast?"

✣

We drove into town and stopped at Gina's, one of the few places where you could still order an omelet with the yolks. The waitress, a woman in her early twenties whose hair looked wet but was in fact dry, brought coffee.

I decided to start with a banality.

"How, uh, how's life in education?"

Chickie was shaking salt into his coffee, he'd always done that, and started grinning at his memories, though whether it was genuine or strategic I wasn't sure.

"Less educational than advertised."

"You did it twice, right?"

He nodded.

"You do it twice, you get extra credit."

The coffee was thin and the mug was diner-ceramic, clunky, all rounded edges. I took a sip and put it down. I cleared a space before me on the table and put my hands there, palms down.

"Can you, like, give me some straight answers?"

Chickie took a deep breath and squared up in his booth. People used to call me So Handsome, but, growing up, Chick was the one of us who made the heads turn. My look, which didn't do much until I started to grow into it around junior year, was sort of Harlequin Romance cover, strong jaw, oversized face. When I could grow stubble, it was all over. Chicks throwing their panties onstage, that kind of thing. Not really. But anyway that took years. Chick's look, which he had from, like, fourth grade on, was straight out of a S.E. Hinton novel, Ponyboy all the way. He didn't take a whole lot of interest in the girls, but they'd taken a whole lot of interest in him. Everybody did.

He looked that way now, despite the beard. Skin a little rougher, vaguely feral, but still. He looked like someone you wanted to protect.

"So, what's going on?" I said. "Why are you back here?"

There were a lot of places in the world with slates cleaner than this one.

He shrugged, took a deep breath. Looked out the window at the parking lot.

"SmartSeeds was good, gave me something to do. Sort of like the Peace Corps for screw-ups. Man, the island where I was, the second time? It is far. Like, far far. No buildings, really. Just, like, shanties and hammocks and bike paths. I kinda wanted to stay there forever."

He paused, looked at the table.

"But you know how it is with colonialism. Never lasts. Plus, they stopped paying me. I had to leave. Flew to San Francisco, so I saw Jimmer for a couple of nights. He's like Future-Man now. After that, I was in Florida for a while. My mom's there."

He looked at me.

I nodded.

"She's the same. Anxious. Medicating with gin. I was working at some grade school, a teacher's aide like. SmartSeeds has a pretty good network for when you come home, but they wanted me to finish my degree and go to grad school, and I'm just not into it."

He stopped and sipped his coffee.

"What are you into?" I asked.

Chick looked back out the window.

"Not grad school. And not Florida. Holy shit, man. Alligators and snakes everywhere. There's not a body of water in that state I'd feel safe in. Not even the tub."

He smiled, trying to tunnel his way back to comedy.

I stayed on him.

"And?"

His smile faded.

"And, I don't know. Met a teacher at the school, she asked where I was from. I said here, and she knew it from when she was a kid. She used to go to Camp Whippoorwill, started talking about what a wonderful place it was, the usual shit, and I was like, lady, you don't even know."

He shook his head.

"But then, like, here I am, right? Got myself to the other side of the world and all it ever felt like was a test. I can't see starting over. Not in the Pacific, sure as shit not in Florida. Ponce de León said the Fountain of Youth was in Florida. Dude was fucking high. So I got on a train."

Our wet waitress came back and sloshed more coffee into our cups. We ordered. She scribbled on a pad and then looked at Chickie. He was holding up his coffee mug.

"This coffee tastes like salt," he said.

She squinted at him. Her nails were long and shiny. She rapped them on the Formica.

"Did you say 'shit'?"

"Salt," Chick said, nodding. He started smiling at her and then at me. He handed her the mug.

"Go ahead," he said. "Try it."

She looked at the mug warily.

"It's okay. I'll just get you a new one."

"No, no, no," Chick said quickly, taking the mug back. "I love salt."

He brought the mug to his lips and took a big sip, but he was already laughing and the coffee sprayed out across the table.

The waitress started to smile. She couldn't figure this dude out.

"Do I know you?" she asked, an easy switch from sullen to coquettish.

Chickie smiled back at her and extended his hand.

"You do now," he said.

❦

"So what's your plan?" I asked after we'd finished eating. We were walking up toward Asgard, to see if we could catch Unsie before the weekend got too busy. "You can't stay at the Horse Head. Especially without a car."

The wind bit. Friday's fog was behind us, and temps were back in the 20s. Low for this time of year, but not by much. I ducked my chin into my collar. Chick didn't seem to notice. The morning was bright but faint, with a cloudbank on the southern horizon. People said if you don't like the weather in the Berkshires, wait five minutes.

"My plan?" Chick asked, looking sideways at me. He shrugged.

"Are you, like, thinking about staying here permanently then?"

He shrugged again, all shrugs these days. He started to say something. Stopped.

Asgard was closed. A sign on the door said it opened at ten on Saturdays. We still had half an hour, so we kept walking, past the Heirloom, also closed, up toward the library.

"I saw Ginny Archey in there," I said, hooking a thumb back toward the bar. "She said to bring you by."

Chick made a small move with one corner of his mouth and said nothing. We kept walking until we got to the library and ducked out of the wind.

"So," I said. "Permanently?"

"Dude," Chick said, quietly. "Can't we just enjoy each other's company?"

He still wasn't looking at me, but "Dude" was the functional opposite of "Guy."

"Well, all right, dude," I said, throwing it back at him. "Maybe I should just be heading out then?"

Chick huffed like a teenager for a second, then put his hands out and closed his eyes.

"No, you're right. I'm sorry. It's just . . . I don't know. I don't have a plan. So, like, I sort of wish you'd stop asking."

He suddenly looked exhausted. His hands dropped and his head seemed too heavy for his neck.

I looked around the library foyer, trying to figure out what to say next, trying to muster the emotional wherewithal for this sort of triage. Part of me, a rational part, a smart part, wanted to just light out of there, go back to Boston, get some mass-produced coffee and either sit on a couch and watch the Celts or go out in the Back Bay and hit on an accountant. But of course I couldn't do that, because that day when Bill Trivette caught us goofing around in the bell tower, he sent me home and kept Chickie behind.

There was a rack of brochures by the door and a bulletin board on the foyer's back wall. I focused on the board to have something to do. There were a surprising number of events coming up. Story time. Knitting circle. Gable Reads Together. Good stuff. Community stuff. I drew strength from it. To consolidate that strength, I tore a tab off the fringe of the knitting circle flier. It was the first one to go.

"Okay," I said, feeling stronger already. "How can I help?"

Chick peeked at me from the underside of his own head.

"Well," he said, then paused. "No. Forget it."

I looked at him. Crossed my arms.

He waited a respectful amount of time, then raised his head. "I guess I do have one plan. The rhino. At Fleur-de-Lys, remember?"

I did. There was only one.

Chick reached over to the rack of brochures and pulled out a glossy pamphlet for Head-Connect, the same one he'd left for me at KMC.

"The horn," he said, tapping the pamphlet in his hand. "It's there."

True to her word, Florence Banish, whose mother had been a chambermaid and, briefly, a midwife at Fleur-de-Lys in the early 1900s, was in fact the definitive resource on Van Nest palace intrigue. Among the many rumors circling lonely Guy Van Nest in those fitful first years of his post-adolescence, the one about his sexuality seemed to bother him most. His house staff reported that his most frequent summer visitors were young men, like himself, from the counties around Manhattan, and that he was more interested in lawn tennis than debauchery. That, to Florence Banish, was a thin reed on which to hang a conclusion. I didn't have a strong opinion about it. But I mean, shit, the poor kid grew up with everyone calling him "young Master Guy," with a dad who wasn't around, and then dead, and with a mom who would have rather been somewhere else. I'd be desperate for a little lawn tennis with my friends too. But apparently, Guy took the rumors to heart.

The rhino, a white double-horned brute originally from the savannahs of Zimbabwe, had roamed the rolling acres of Fleur-de-Lys all summer long with its circus cohort, eating the grains and grass and marigolds, rolling in creek beds, sleeping with its siblings in a roomy stable after Guy had the horses sent off. During performances for the Van Nest entourage, the ringmaster, a thin Hungarian named Asko Hoge, coaxed the great beast into charging at a brace of hay bales stacked in a pyramid, sometimes, for extra effect, setting the top bale on fire first. The young rhino's larger lower horn, nearly 3 feet of curved keratin, would dip and sway, and the beast would emit a deep bellow, and then it would be off, its speed always a surprise to the spectators, five thousand pounds of muscle crashing into the hay, which would tumble and flare and bounce, and the crowd would cheer, and the rhino, spooked, would rush off to hide in the stables, later to be coaxed out by the zebras and rewarded with a bucket of warm apples and a scrub bath. The lions would roar and the twin elephants would perform a cloying trunk-to-tail dance, but for Guy, the rhino, with its mighty horn, was where it was at. He briefly entertained the idea of putting a saddle on it.

The rhino was also ill, or cursed, or otherwise problematic, which is probably why Asko Hoge agreed to leave it at Fleur-de-Lys when Guy Van Nest offered him a ridiculous amount of money for it at the summer's end. Guy, of course, didn't know or care that the rhino was ill or cursed or otherwise problematic. Rather, Guy, whose own childhood had impressed upon him the importance of having children before you were too old to be bored of them, had decided that he wanted an heir, that an heir would put certain pesky rumors to rest, and that the great white rhino somewhere outside his back veranda would provide him with both the spark and the symbol of virility he would need to woo and then impregnate one of his female visitors, about whom he was otherwise ambivalent.

And so it was that the rhino stayed behind when the circus left for Albany on Labor Day 1914. As local extravagances went, it wasn't even that over the top. Florence Banish's mother told her of rare birds at Naumkeag, swans in the ponds and flamingoes in the swamp. Idlewylde had an incendiary carousel. And there were rumors that at Elm Court the house staff was bioengineered to be mute. Guy fenced in 13 acres of rolling fields and woodlands toward the back of his property and, late at night, would come and stand at the edge of the stables, listening to the beast grunt and dream. And something must have worked too, because soon there was a wedding both lavish and perfunctory, and a young woman from a Scarsdale trading family took up residence in the east bedroom of the main house. Florence Banish's mother was promoted to midwife. For a time that autumn, Fleur-de-Lys had a hum to it that transcended the hollow frivolity and general end-of-the-world-ness of society America on the cusp of a distant war. Guy himself, then just twenty-five years old, was seen to be walking taller, a more serious figure, his hair oiled and slick, his gaze quicker.

"I have a memory of him coming up the drive in his fancy car," said Florence Banish, who had been four in 1914. "Just a whirl of finery, everyone moving."

Alas, the pregnancy did not take, and the girl from Scarsdale went back to Scarsdale, and winter pushed fall aside earlier than usual at Fleur-de-Lys. The white rhino stopped visiting the back meadows and stayed closer to its stables, snorting and chirping and pawing at the same parcels of muddy lawn. The dogs, no longer afraid, nipped at its tail. Guy left for the city for nearly all of November, and in his absence the stable-hands, who in their defense were horsemen and cow-milkers by training and somewhat terrified of exotic animals, gave the rhino a wide berth. The warm apples and scrub baths ended.

By the time Guy returned, around Thanksgiving, the rhino was despondent. It rubbed itself raw against the walls of its stall, stabbed its huge horn into the trunks of elms, ate little. It keened in grunts throughout the night. Guy tried to contact Asko Hoge, but of course the Hungarian was long gone, miles past Albany, never to return. Forsyth would have seen that one coming.

Guy took to his chambers.

One December morning, as the house staff of Fleur-de-Lys readied the breakfast and the grounds crew swept the first snow of the year off the pea-stoned walkways, a great crash echoed from the ground-floor ballroom. Florence Banish's mother had been one of the first to reach the room, and to have seen the great white rhino twirling and stomping at its center, a wooden window frame impaled on its horn, blood on its muzzle, a jagged hole where just the day before French doors had led to the back patio, and to the lawn, and then down to the stables.

Florence Banish's mother was herself relatively unflappable, and had in fact once coolly stuck a gardening fork into the meaty palm of an opportunistic handyman—rather less handy after that—but when the beast turned and looked at her, its eyes cloudy and mad, she screamed and took off running back down the hallway toward the front of the house. She didn't need to look back to know that the rhino was charging after her, nor did she need to warn the other household staff, who were already hiding themselves in closets. When Florence Banish's mother reached the landing of the curling stairway that led to the second floor bedrooms, she took them two at a time and, about halfway up, caught her toe on her skirt and went down hard, splitting her lip on the marble steps. Nine stairs below, the rhino came into the main foyer and snorted. Florence Banish's mother looked at it. It didn't seem to see her, focusing on ground-level nuisances like a marble bust of Cleopatra and an urn purportedly from the Greek island of Naxos, both quickly destroyed. The rhino whirled about the foyer, bludgeoning the walls. Portraits fell, windows shattered, and it occurred to Florence Banish's mother that there would shortly be nothing left for the rhino to smash except her. But then Florence Banish's mother heard a click and looked up to see Guy Van Nest at the top of the stairs, his hair askew, his pajamas wrinkled, and a rifle in his hands.

The rhino apparently heard the click as well. It lifted its head to the stairway. Its great flat snout dipped and sniffed, and then it pawed at the Italian tiles on the foyer floor. It assumed a stance recognizable by a hundred hay bales, and by Florence Banish's mother, as trouble.

At the top of the stairs, Guy Van Nest leveled his rifle and fired.

Guy Van Nest was not a rifleman, and the rifle he held was, as both a weapon and a metaphor, woefully unsuitable for the task at hand, and to nobody's surprise the shot shrugged off the rhino's massive shoulder, barely leaving a mark. The sound of the blast, however, echoed off of the marble walls of the foyer, a booming thunderclap, both sharp and rolling. It appeared to spook the rhino, which executed a hop-like pivot on its back feet and blasted through the mansion's front door, left partially open by a fleeing butler. The rhino widened that opening considerably, snapping one of the door panels clear off its hinges and sending the other careening into the building's outer wall like a sail in a storm. Guy Van Nest, rifle still in hand, hustled down the stairs, barely acknowledging Florence Banish's bleeding mother, and raced to the door. Past him, Florence Banish's mother could see the rhino, well down the drive, moving at a fast trot toward Bramble Street. For a minute, it appeared as if the animal might gain the road, perhaps pick up some momentum on Bramble and trot himself right down to Normanton. But then, as Florence Banish's mother watched, the rhino turned its head and charged off, across a side lawn, its tracks in the snow as straight as a rope. In seconds, it vanished into the rolling woodland.

Two hours later, after the front door had been braced and boarded, after Guy Van Nest had dressed and shaved and gathered several of the men who worked in the stables, after Florence Banish's mother had cleaned her lip and applied a packet of ice wrapped in cheesecloth to it, and after young Florence Banish herself had kissed her mother's cold damp hands, three large booms sounded in the forest. A bit later, Guy Van Nest and the stablemen came marching out of the rolling woodland, their own footprints obliterating those of the rhino. Guy Van Nest had a closed face and carried something wrapped in a towel. Two of the stablemen held grim larger-bore rifles of the sort that came in useful when one of the plow-horses splintered a fetlock. A third held a hacksaw. They'd dropped those in the toolshed and come back out with shovels.

Guy Van Nest did not mention the rhino again.

Some in the house staff concluded that Guy was humiliated by the whole episode, from the animal's impulsive procurement, to its apparent inadequacy as a talisman, to the disastrous finale. A young master's grand attempt to set himself up as a man of vitality, only to fall on his face. He'd picked his big fight and lost.

Others, including Florence Banish's mother, suspected that there were deeper emotions at work, having to do with the vagaries of the womb and the intergenerational transmission of trauma. Whatever it was, the effect on Guy was profound. Time passed, silences were procured, and the property was restored, but Guy's absences from Fleur-de-Lys became more frequent and the parties less so. On the nights he was there, he no longer dressed for dinner and spent long evenings in his upstairs salon. He took to medicinals. The staff, which was always whispering, now whispered about money. Was it running out? Was there enough for them all?

Eventually, the answers to those questions became clear, and the property was abandoned by 1920. Guy Van Nest retreated to a considerably smaller estate on Long Island, and was not seen in the Berkshires again.

As for the rhino, those stable-hands who had accompanied Guy into the rolling woodlands were usually too drunk to be reliable, especially after they lost their jobs, but one or two spoke of following the rhino's tracks, and, where the tracks were faint, of following a break in the undergrowth the size of a train tunnel, until they'd found the beast. They spoke of a fast march across hard earth, and then a short shale drop that opened onto the soft swamp below. They spoke of half a ton of animal at the bottom, upturned and fearful, already part buried, its eyes foggy and its chest rattling. They spoke of oaths and recriminations and curses, and, finally, of shots fired by the master of the house.

We knew all this because we'd put it into our reports for Ms. Flemmy and Chief Winston, which wound up being probably just about the best goddamn reports you've ever read, probably. Got an A from the former and a paternal pat on the shoulders from the latter. We dropped in big block quotes from Florence Banish, pages at a time, the prose both flowery and square. The master of the house. The leveled muskets. Only thing missing was someone getting the vapors.

"It was never seen again," Florence Banish said, in the quote we ended on. "The beast of the wood, a secret locked away forever."

Far as I was concerned, that was the end of it. Good story, but once we turned in the reports I was ready to leave it behind.

Chick wasn't, though.

These were the months after the Trivette stuff came out, and we'd been upping our time in isolation. The trails, the practice courts. We hiked Monument, found the West Normanton quarry. Chick started talking about his time with the bears. It was just easier to be out of town, I guess. Nobody giving us the look. Nobody changing the dynamics. Eventually, the next scandal would drop and we could return. So we shot threes and poked through the ruins of our environment, trying to find something else to process. A new identity, a cause. And then Ms. Bitz and good old Florence Banish came through.

Once the weather warmed up and school ended, Chick took our report and began directing forays into the woods off of Bramble, expecting to stumble right onto the body of the rhino. Jimmer and Unsie came twice and then bailed. I stuck it out initially. First few times, nothing—looking for a shale cliff and a big lump of earth in those woods was like looking for a rotting tree. They were everywhere. The fourth time, a site felt promising and we lugged a couple of shovels through the woods from my dad's shed, but all we hit was the rusted frame of a VW Bug.

After that, I lost interest pretty quick. Shaunda Schoenstein was working concessions down at Tanglewood, and I was too busy trying to charm my way into her apron to want to waste more time in the woods. Plus, there was poison ivy back there, and no matter how many times you tell a girl it's not contagious, she never believes you.

Chick stuck with it. He had a little map that he'd worked on with Florence Banish, and he was checking off quadrants. We found the Bug here, he'd say, marking a spot with an *x*. We radiate out from that.

"This is dumb, Chick," I said one day, as I was urinating against a maple tree and eying a nearby vine suspiciously. Its leaves were shiny and triplicate and a little close for comfort. "We are never going to find it."

Chick was shuffling around, looking at his map. "It's okay," he said. "You can go."

I put my junk away carefully, without touching it, by lifting the waistband of my sweats out and back. Go into the woods, brush up against a plant, put a hand down your pants—just to scratch your balls, for example—and presto, poison ivy on your dick. Happened to Mark Pacheco. More than once, I think. He was a weird kid.

"Come on," I said.

Chick looked at me and shrugged. "What?"

"Come with me."

He shook his head.

"Can't," he said, smiling. "I've been called."

"Yeah, well, I'm calling you back. Shaunda and them are in the maze. Let's go."

Chick looked up into the trees. The sun was bending away to the west and sending shadows down onto the forest floor.

"Fine," he said, folding up his map. "But we're coming back. It's out here. We can't just leave it."

"Shit," I said. "If it's out here, it's not going anywhere."

But it was, in fact.

Head-Connect purchased the property in the fall of 1997 and set about bulldozing the grounds into someone's idea of Sherwood Forest. They smoothed the hills and put down fresh cedar chip trails, color-coding the trees along the way. They unrooted the rot and dug out the poison ivy and the broken fountains and the VW and replaced them with reading nooks and meditation moments. They put really well-made footbridges over the creeks. You can always tell when developers are serious by the quality of their footbridges.

If they found a big skeleton in there, we never heard about it. Of course, from the cockpit of a backhoe it might be hard to notice one among all the dead roots and boulders and such. Anyway, after they were finished, the woods were pristine and unrecognizable, and any reference points we might have hoped to use were gone. Chickie and I watched from Bramble as Fleur-de-Lys disappeared into a cocoon of all-weather siding and then re-emerged from fifty years of overgrowth as a bright ship of marble and glass. They built new wings for a gym complex and a test kitchen. Horses returned to half of the stables, while the other half became an aquatics center. The servants' quarters were expanded and fitted with hot tubs. Gardens were seeded with astilbe and bee balm. Everything was sustainable, whatever that meant. The whole thing took about eighteen months, but pretty soon after that, strangers with unlined faces and southwestern roots started buying up the midlevel real estate on the outskirts of town, and limousines and livery cabs started pulling in from Bradley and Wassaic, ferrying stars with bad habits, overweight team-building executives, the one-percent looking for either an edge or a break.

The Gilded Age had returned.

Later that first summer, Chickie got arrested again, and released again, for trespassing in the woods around Fleur-de-Lys. At first the Head-Connect folks thought he was paparazzi and were sort of disappointed to learn he wasn't. He was persistent, though, and eventually they put him on a special list of nuisances, like crabgrass and fire ants. They hung his picture in the contractor's shack. The third time, Chief Winston and Chick's mother negotiated an agreement to rein him in, and in exchange, the Head-Connect folks didn't press charges. After that, he got really quiet whenever the subject came up.

"What do you mean, it's there?" I asked.

We were still in the entryway of the library. Chickie looked around warily, like he was checking for eavesdroppers. I caught myself doing it too.

"Well," he said. "I get back, what, a month ago?"

It was less than that, far as I knew.

"Don't know what I expected, but it's all weird now. It's not fun anymore. You're gone. Uns is always busy. We're not kids like we used to be. But then, then, there's this other part, it's almost a ghost part, comes and goes, but it's this part that feels like I never left. Been here the whole time. One day I wind up at the library, looking for old Banish, even though I know she's gone. And instead I start chatting with this new librarian—you know how it is when you get them talking—telling her about how Banish had turned us on to the rhino and all that. Just for someone to talk to."

He was more animated than he'd been since early morning, jumping on my bed.

"And she says, 'You know Ms. Banish passed away in 2002, right?' And I'm like, shit yeah, we were at her funeral. Except I didn't say 'shit,' of course. And she felt so sorry for me, or something—these librarians stick together—that she takes me back to the office and opens a drawer and says, 'This was her special file.'"

He slung the backpack off his shoulder and dug a manila folder out of it.

"Guess what was in it?"

He pulled a small square of photo stock out of it, grainy and blurred at the edges. I squinted at it. It looked like a picture of a furnace.

"What is it?" I asked.

"It's a safe," Chickie said.

I looked again, more closely. He was right. There was the heavy door, partially open. There were the rectangular bars along the bottom, stacked like chocolates. Papers and small boxes took up the middle shelves.

"A secret locked away forever," Chick said, bending a finger over the picture and tapping on the topmost shelf. It was hard to see what was there. I brushed his finger aside and squinted, but all I saw was something that looked like a bat in a sack.

"She knew the whole time," said Chick. "That's the horn."

We left the library an hour later with a plan. Or plans.

Chickie's plan was insane. It involved infiltrating Head-Connect via a sort of hillbilly parkour, sneaking into the basement of the main building—where Chickie was sure the old Van Nest safe remained—*cracking* the safe, removing the now 100-year-old rhino horn from its shroud, spiriting it back out of Head-Connect, and committing it to the woods in some druidic fashion. If we couldn't locate the rest of the rhino, at least we could make it whole. A rhino's soul is in its horn. It's what it's got. Something like that.

My plan was, to my way of thinking, more realistic. It involved figuring out who we knew at Head-Connect—we had to know someone—and asking them if there was a rhino horn sitting around, or if they'd ever heard of one. Was there an abandoned safe on the property? It seemed unlikely. Even in his despondency, Guy Van Nest wouldn't have just left his valuables behind, right? No safe meant no horn—if indeed there ever was one—and no horn, then, you know, no need for any insanity.

My plan might have lacked the drama and excitement of Chick's, but it was just about the limit of what I was willing to do. I'd borrowed upward of $75,000 to finance a law degree and, as tangled a history as we had, I wasn't prepared to surrender it in the pursuit of Chick's lunatic errand. There were legal and ethical issues to consider. As it stood I was due back in Boston for work by 8:30 Monday morning.

"So, let's talk to Unsie about this," I said as we walked away from the library.

Chick, so focused and impassioned a few minutes earlier, was now fidgety.

"Uh, yeah," he said, checking his watch. It wasn't yet noon. "Can we do it later?"

I shrugged. We were two blocks from Asgard.

"Let's do it later," Chick said. "I actually have a thing in a few minutes."

"What thing?" I asked.

Chick shrugged. "Just stuff. Errands."

I looked at him.

"What's going on, man?"

Chick gave me his big smile.

"Don't worry about it, dude. Listen, we are going to find that thing, and it's going to be great." He looked me in the eye. "Thank you for helping me. It means a lot."

"You're full of shit," I said.

A purple Trans Am idled at the corner of Church and Main, because in Gable it could always be 1983. Chick spotted it.

"That's my ride."

I scanned the Trans Am. A driver and the waitress from breakfast in the front. A guy in the back.

We were outside the Heirloom. If Chick was going to pull this shit, I was going to extract a price, the past for the future.

"Fine," I said, hooking a thumb toward the door. "Meet me here at six sharp,"

Chick looked up at the establishment, and his eyes narrowed.

"Meet me here or come find me in Boston," I said.

The big smile came back.

"Heirloom it is. Six o'clock."

I nodded skeptically.

"See you then," I said.

Chick gave me an enthusiastic double thumbs-up and jogged off toward the waiting Trans Am. I watched him go.

"What the fuck, dude?" I said to Unsie, when I found him in the back of Asgard, folding performance T-shirts into shiny squares. "Drugs, right?"

Unsie kept folding.

"I think so. I mean, it's not my area of expertise, but sure seems like it."

"Ginny Archey says he's been going back and forth to Sink City."

"I guess. Seems to me that there's probably plenty of local options, no need to make the drive. Things are bad out here. But, again, it's not my thing."

I picked up a shirt and folded it. His square looked better than mine. He took the shirt and shook it out, then folded it again.

We'd smoked a little in high school, except Unsie, who was too focused on lung capacity and had already begun researching ways to up the red blood cell count in his plasma. Jimmer and Chick smoked the most, the former using his high to deconstruct the moral arc of certain video games, the latter sinking into a poetic stupor. Never anything harder than weed, though, almost never. There were plenty of kids we knew pushing pharmaceuticals, and once in law school I tried to convince Kelly that we should enhance a Hootie & the Blowfish concert with Ecstasy, but it didn't work. I knew nothing about real drugs.

"What are we going to do?" I said.

Unsie looked at me.

"Hah," he said.

"Come on, man."

Unsie stopped folding the performance shirts.

"You come on," he said. "What do you want me to do?"

I looked around the store. Eight or nine people were milling around, trying on fleece vests and alpaca socks.

"Can you give him a job?" I asked.

Unsie looked up and spoke firmly, as if he'd thought it all out already.

"The kid is on drugs. I'm not going to give him a job. If he was not on drugs, I would consider it."

He gestured to the quiet store.

"But look around. How long you think a job like this would hold Chick's attention? How many shirts you think he could fold before he tied one around his forehead? Some days even I want to take a blowtorch to the place."

He sighed.

"Look, Pete, I know you feel like you owe him."

He stopped. I sensed an opening, thin as it may be.

"Kid saved your life," I said. "You owe him too."

Unsie rolled his eyes.

"Please."

"If I can get him to give up the drugs, you give him a job. If he screws up, fire him."

Unsie shook his head, but more in exasperation than in resolve.

"You're just going to get him to give up the drugs, huh?" he said. "What drugs is he on?"

I didn't know.

"You should probably start there, don't you think?"

I nodded.

"So that's where we'll start. Let's find out what we're dealing with."

The "we" was on purpose, again.

"Hah," Unsie said again.

I decided to shift gears, circle back later and act like we'd agreed.

"Hey, do we know anyone who works over at Head-Connect?"

Unsie finished the shirts and walked over to an inventory console.

"Yeah, sure. Why?"

I shook my head.

"You don't want to know."

He looked at me and raised his eyebrows.

"So," I asked. "Who?"

He tilted his head. I like people who have little unconscious tics that manifest when they're thinking. It's like you can see into their minds. I really like people who make little clicky noises with their tongues when they think. Like they're micro-processing or something. I trust them, trust that they're thinking. I've been working on emulating those gestures. They seem like useful gestures, deployable in a number of situations.

"Well, some friends of friends work there. Sales, outdoor rec. I think Ava Winston is in there somewhere. They contract out their snowshoeing and Nordic to us in the winter."

"What does it mean to contract out a Nordic?"

Unsie looked up and made a sad face.

"It means we lead the cross-country ski tours through the property. Out to the Magic Meadow, through the woods. Bunch of bankers and entertainment types, can't ski worth a shit. But they pay well."

He clucked his tongue.

"Longest ninety minutes of your life, though."

"That's probably not true," I said. "So, so far we know you and Ava Winston."

I thought for a second.

"You ever get in there?"

Unsie looked at me.

"Ava?"

"Head-Connect. You ever hang out inside?"

He shook his head.

"Not if I can help it."

Unsie didn't like the idea of fitness retreats, preferring the idea of fitness lifestyles. He was disdainful of anything that smacked of a shortcut.

"What's Ava Winston do?"

Unsie returned to the console.

"Don't know. I never see her. But she was in the paper a few years ago when they promoted her. Local interest story, something like that."

"Her dad still around?"

"Yeah, in the existential sense. He retired a few years ago. Moved west."

"Shoot," I said.

I looked around the showroom. A rack of skis. A fleet of kayaks.

"You ever see a rhino horn down there?"

Unsie looked up at me.

"Are you on drugs too?"

When we were sixteen, Unsie broke his leg playing spring soccer after sneaking out with us on a day that he was supposed to be grounded. His punishment was six weeks in a foot-to-hip cast and a cat that bit his exposed toes. One hot June day we sprung him from his house and drove him out to the quarry in West Normanton, where Shaunda Schoenstein and the other rising seniors on St. Eustace's girls' field hockey team had installed themselves as sirens. Shaunda had a plastic baggie full of pot and a two-piece bikini whose top she would untie when she was sunning on her stomach, and as we swung Unsie and his leg across the narrow creek that separated the access road from the winding path to the quarry, we discussed various ruses that we might use to get her to sit up suddenly. Jimmer said that if she, or frankly if any of the other girls there, put themselves in a compromising position, we should feign a drowning. They would probably feel compelled to dive in, breasts unfettered, to save us.

The quarry was a mile back in the woods off of Route 183, a rectangle of limestone, shades of green and bottomless. One long edge was crowded with trees, but the other sloped gently down into the water. On the eastern short side was a sort of altar of rock, 12 feet up at its highest point, with sloping sides and a perfect flat top for lounging. On the western edge was the sacrificial cliff, a promontory 65 feet high, with leap spots at 30, 40, and 60 feet. I'd done the 60-foot jump once, in my sneakers, after a half-hour of mind games. Chickie did it every time we went, even though he couldn't swim very well.

We pushed through the undergrowth, a determined expedition, Unsie on his crutches and the rest of us in swimsuits. Eventually we emerged at the base of the quarry. Shaunda and a bunch of the other St. Eustace girls were crowding the altar. A couple of disgruntled junior males scuffed along the edges. Girls like that always had body men. Someone had to buy the Slush Puppies.

Shaunda waved at me. Alas, she was wearing a T-shirt.

The four of us waved back.

"Hello, ladies," Jimmer said, but it came out sounding skeevy and he frowned.

We crossed the vestibule and emerged at the water's edge. Nods were exchanged and we began unfurling our towels, marking off our plot of quarry. We weren't there just for the girls. Of course, Unsie couldn't go in on account of the cast, and Chick didn't swim on his own. But the girls didn't know that.

"Shirts off?" asked Jimmer.

I nodded.

"Let's do it."

I grabbed the hem of my T-shirt and began to lift. Jimmer pulled his over his head.

I stopped lifting mine. Chick and Unsie didn't move. Jimmer's chest was a pale concavity, too much time in front of the PlayStation. It blanched in the sunlight, made him look like Casper.

"Fuckers," Jimmer said.

Messing with Jimmer about girls was one of the best things we did.

He took a running leap and piked into the water. The St. Eustace girls eyed him like gators.

Jimmer emerged and went back under, vanishing like a frog, his head coming out thirty seconds later across the quarry. He flashed us the finger.

"He's the fucker," Unsie said. He frowned at Jimmer, then looked at the girls and ducked his head.

Unsie was also not great with girls, but for opposite reasons. Where Jimmer was determined, to the point of awkwardness, to crack the code of gender relations, Unsie was acutely self-conscious. Unsie could run for miles, even farther if a girl was chasing him. Whatever. They'd grow out of it.

Unsie swung himself off toward the western promontory.

I flicked my eyes toward Shaunda.

"I'm gonna go . . . " I trailed off.

Chick raised his eyebrows.

I nodded.

"Wish me luck."

Chick stepped to me.

"I'll do more than that, you big bear," he said, and threw his arms around me.

I pushed him off.

"But I love you, man," he said, loud enough for the gallery.

I gave him the finger and took a second to compose myself, check my hair, the tuck of my T-shirt. All good. I turned and tried to be casual in my walk toward the altar.

The body men were waiting. I knew a couple of them from the soccer fields. I nodded. They closed ranks, acted like I was there to talk to them. Not much danger of anyone starting shit, as that wasn't really their role and anyway I had my boys with me, but they weren't entirely welcoming. Then Shaunda called to me from the top of the block, and I was like what do you want me to do? I slid past them and climbed up.

"Hey," I said, when I got up to the flat.

She was lying on her back on a towel, propped up on elbows, pink toes pointed toward the water. Her T-shirt was one of those gray scholastic practice shirts that said "Work Hard" on the front, no doubt pilfered from some poor lacrosse slob now in the rearview mirror. She'd knotted it at her golden midriff.

She took her sunglasses off and looked at me.

"Hey," she said back.

I sat down next to her on the rock.

"Your friend," she said, gesturing to Jimmer down in the water. "He's a little pale."

"Uh, yeah," I said. "I guess so."

"And the other one," she said, turning her head slightly toward the far promontory, where Chick and Unsie had vanished into the ledges. "What happened to him?"

"Which one?" I asked, and meant it, but it was also sort of good, I thought, to act like we were all complicated guys.

"The one with the cast," she said.

"Broke his leg."

She looked at me, trying to figure out something. I gave her my best Clooney smile. She burst into giggles.

I was rocking this shit.

"Want a hit?" she asked, lifting a small pipe from a crevice in the rocks at her side.

I shook her off. "Maybe in a minute."

The day was sticky hot and the sun blasted off the white rocks like a concussion. Below, Jimmer had swum to our end and was making small talk with one of the body men, trying to entice a nearby center-half with a nice rack into the water.

"You gonna go in?" I asked Shaunda.

She shook her head.

"Nnnnn. This isn't a wet T-shirt contest."

She looked at me, daring me to react. I kept my eyes on the quarry.

"So," I said.

She started laughing again.

A voice came from below. One of the midfielders.

"Shaun!"

She wrinkled her nose.

"What!"

A ponytail bobbed below the altar, a short girl who couldn't make the climb.

"It's three. We gotta go."

Shaunda sighed. The ponytail receded. She turned back to me.

"My friends call you 'Pete So Handsome.'"

I blushed as strategically as I could.

"Everyone calls me that."

Shaunda sat up and wrapped her arms around her knees.

"Why?" she asked, grinning.

Just then we heard a splash echo across the quarry, and a gasp rise up from the gallery below.

"Oh shit," said one of the body men. "He slipped."

I looked out at the water. Beneath the 30-foot ledge, a pile of bubbles was effervescing through the green water and making a jagged circle on the top. Then a hand came out, splashing around.

I stood up. Shaunda put her hand to her eyes like a visor.

Damn, fellas, I thought. Appreciate the effort, but she's not even wearing a two-piece.

Then I saw Chickie standing atop the sacrificial cliff. Checked on Jimmer, still below, now staring out toward the far end. Who'd that leave?

I saw Unsie's face in the water. Even 50 yards away, I could see he was scared.

Above him, in a flash, Chick pushing off the quarry wall, a random spot between 60 and 35, torqueing in the air, and hitting the water with a slap.

"Oh, shit," said Shaunda. From that height, anything but a foot-first entry could break bones. And Unsie's bones were already broke.

I flew off the altar, 12 feet up, knifing into the water and coming up near Jimmer, the two of us hauling ass across the surface.

It still took forever. Or felt like forever. Swimming, we couldn't hear much, just sort of a localized commotion along the quarry walls. We just swam and swam, grabbing a breath every fourth stroke or so.

When we got to them, they were underwater, Chick holding Unsie around the chest and kicking as hard as he could. Bubbles leaked from under Unsie's cast and broke for the surface. Beneath them, the water was gradations of shadow. We grabbed Unsie and pushed for the side. When we got there, the juniors reached out and pulled us onto a low ledge. Unsie's cast was dead weight, but he was a skier and had good lungs and rolled onto his side to cough and spit.

"Hey," someone yelled. We looked back at the water and realized that Chick was still struggling, still below. I dove for him, 10 feet down, got a hand on an arm and pulled. Female legs splashed along the edge and female hands reached out for us. We pulled Chickie to shore by the collar of his shirt.

His eyes were closed.

"Oh my God," said a midfielder. "Oh my God!"

We levered him onto the ledge. He was splayed like Jesus. Shaunda scrambled out of the water and knelt at his head. She'd gotten wet after all and even with the drama of the moment I made a quick mental note of the swells on her shirtfront. Like, I didn't feel anything about them, but I noted them anyway. Felt like the least I could do. They were notable.

Shaunda put her hands below Chickie's chin and lifted it slightly so that his lips parted. Then she pressed her mouth to his and blew.

Chick's chest rose, but the rest of him was still.

Shaunda put her ear to his lips, feeling for breath. She brushed his wet hair from his face, then blew into him again. I grabbed his foot, shook it, just to do something. Unsie watched.

"Chick!" said Jimmer.

Then he coughed. Water dribbled out of his mouth and he turned his head. A second passed. Shaunda burst into tears and wrapped her arms around Chick's neck, bending to him and crushing him to her chest. Chick continued to cough, but his eyes opened. The field hockey team cheered. The junior boys high-fived.

I scrambled up behind them and threw my arms out, sandwiching Shaunda between Chick and me. I put my hand on the back of Chick's head and kissed Shaunda on the ear. She was flat out sobbing now.

"Holy shit, Shaunda," I said. "You did it!"

She sort of shifted from holding Chick to being held by me, and buried her head in my shoulders. Soon, her teammates began attending to her. The junior boys huffed a little and returned to their towels. Chick bent on the ledge as Jimmer rubbed his shoulders.

"Damn, man!" said Unsie, reaching over from the side. His cast was bleeding plaster onto the rocks. Chick looked around and grinned at us.

"Everyone okay?" he asked.

What we were dealing with quickly became apparent when Unsie and I got to the Heirloom at six. The place felt on edge, the way a pick-up game feels on edge when some new guy shows up with his elbows. Ginny Archey gave me the eye when I walked in and gestured toward a booth at the back. As I crossed, I could see Chick on one side, slouching on the bench, and Tim-Rick on the other, upright and alert.

"What's the word?" I said as we closed, nodding to Tim-Rick the way you might greet a strange dog.

Chick looked over hazily. A half-empty beer was on the table in front of him. A full beer was in front of Tim-Rick.

Tim-Rick slid out of the booth and stepped to me.

"He's high as a kite. I don't know what's going on, but," he said, leaving it hanging there.

"Hey," Chick slurred, his face clammy. "What's that prick saying about me?"

Tim-Rick's face darkened and he half turned toward Chick.

"I'm kidding," Chick said. "It's love. I love that prick."

He picked up his beer as if to drink it but just held it in front of him for a second. Then he let it drop to the table, a tiny bit hard, and slouched against the far wall of the booth. Unsie slid in next to him and pushed the beer away.

"I'll take care of it," I said to Tim-Rick.

He looked skeptical.

"Look, he comes in here, Ginny asks me to sit with him because he's clearly fucked up," he said. "But, I mean, come on."

I nodded.

"I'll take care of it."

Tim-Rick seemed to be debating, weighing objectivity against the prerogatives of the past. Then he headed back toward the bar. Halfway, he turned around.

"That's one sad son of a bitch," he said, louder than he needed to. Patrons fell silent.

Chick roused from his catatonia and tried to push out of the booth, but Unsie held him in place with a steel thigh.

I turned toward Tim-Rick, caught between bad options.

"T-R!" Ginny hissed from the register.

He looked a second longer at us, then turned to Ginny and spread out his arms, palms up, before huffing out the front door.

Ginny turned back toward the register and put one hand to her cheek. Chatter resumed.

I slid in across from Chick. Even spaced out, he appeared sheepish.

"Prick," he said.

We'd been stoned plenty of times, but this wasn't stoned, at least not the way I remembered. Back then, there was a humor to it. There was none of that now. Chick looked pale, unhealthy, his eyes both fidgety and lidded.

"What are you on?" I said.

Chick looked down and reached for his beer. I slid it out of his reach.

"I'm serious," I said. "What are you on right now?"

I don't really know why it mattered to me, since I wasn't a pharmacist. I think I just wanted confirmation. I wanted him to acknowledge that he was betraying something.

Chick looked back up at me and leaned his head into the corner where the booth hit the wall. He raised one hand to his lips and locked them with a phantom key. Then he smiled and closed his eyes. In seconds, his breathing was slow and steady.

Unsie adjusted in his seat and looked across at me.

"Well," he said. "Not quite old times."

I picked up Tim-Rick's untouched beer. A hefeweizen. Figures, that pansy. But I drank it anyway.

Ginny Archey maneuvered her swollen belly over to the booth like a magic bumblebee, bar stools seeming to move out of her way on their own.

"Bottoms up," she said, a smile on her face but not in her eyes. "You've got to get him out of here."

Unsie and I carried Chick out to the Escalade and deposited him in the passenger seat.

"Don't overdo it," Uns said, patted me on the shoulder, and headed off on a fast walk down Housatonic. I wasn't sure what he meant.

Chick was snoring by the time I started the truck. I drove him through town, past the library, rounding away from the police station. We headed toward the long rise up to the Church-on-the-Hill. At the bottom, I heard evening bells, like vespers, but not from the hill. They were from the tower of St. Barney's, just on my right, silent and dark on a weekend night.

When the shit with Bill Trivette went down, people didn't know what to do. He was some sort of youth leader, young and engaging and relatively new, on loan from an archdiocese out East. He hung out with the altar boys and the Scouts, organized picnics and just-say-no-to-drugs stuff. One Sunday after Mass, Chick and I were up in the bell tower, killing time before basketball practice, passing copies of *Sports Illustrated* and *Victoria's Secret* back and forth. We weren't supposed to be there. Bill Trivette caught us, took our magazines, told us to go home or he'd tell our parents. Then, at the last second, he called Chickie back. I waited outside for a half-hour.

Chick's mom was a regular at the 8 A.M. service, and she didn't want to believe that anything bad had happened. Chick was dramatic, everybody knew that. Bill Trivette swore it was some sort of misunderstanding, but my mom pushed it with Chief Winston and threatened to go to the *Franchise* if something wasn't done.

Bill Trivette left soon after that. We never heard where, just that St. Barney's had sent him away. Events receded. Trivette's departure became another local mystery, its gaps filled with whispers. For his part, Chick just stopped going to church. Me too, come to think of it. That's when we took to the woods. But of course people treated him differently. At least for a while. The tenor changed when he walked into a room. Something had happened, something bad, maybe, though nobody knew details. It just became part of the fabric, like a fire scar on a tree trunk, a cross on the side of a highway, a memory of a thing that became the thing itself. There was plenty of stuff like that in childhood.

Chick snored on, and I turned the Escalade onto a side street, unwilling yet to face the garishness of the Knotsford-Gable Road. I drove down Old Normanton Road, past Elm Court, looped back around Tanglewood and the big summer houses on the hills. I wound the truck up toward Richmond, sliding below Saranac and the Apple Tree Inn, above the cow pasture where one summer night Unsie had been getting his first hand-job (allegedly!) from a mildly intoxicated junior named Yolanda Sepulveda and they'd stumbled into an electrified fence. Then above the other pasture where, that same summer, a feeble local kid named Billy Glib got a flat tire on his Mustang, and we were so drunk we jacked up the wrong side of the car. Billy Glib's Mustang was a stick shift with only four gears, but he didn't drink and it was the only regular ride in our high school class. He used to say, "Nowhere you can't get around here in fourth gear."

I pulled the Escalade into an overlook at the top of Richmond Road, empty on a frigid March night, and got out of the truck. From the overlook, you could look down onto Normanton Bowl. The big lake was limned with moonlight and I watched the clouds roll past the dim distant swell of hills. Lights blinked in the surrounding hillsides, homes and barns and bars, furtive headlights.

The hopes and sins of our forebears. My breath floated up into the speckled galaxy. In summer, the woods would be humming with insects, but right then there was no sound, just a sea of stars, an ambient glow, all the dark curves of the majestic nighttime county.

In the parking lot of the Horse Head, the only other car was a purple Trans Am. I pulled up next to it. It was empty, but the lights in Chick's room were on.

I left him asleep in the truck and crossed to the door. It was open a crack. A quick scan of the lot suggested that we were the only guests staying at the Horse Head, which, I guess, was hardly surprising since it was March, and the Horse Head.

I pushed open the door.

Inside, the overhead light was unflattering. A short, scruffy guy in jeans and a hoodie was sitting at the desk, and a longer, balding guy with a potbelly was lying on Chick's bed. The longer guy was wearing a Danny Ainge replica Celts jersey under a tracksuit. Fucking Ainge. They were watching the Bruins on NESN.

"What's up, gentlemen?" I asked.

The smaller guy looked up quickly, his eyes darting around for exits and weapons. The longer guy was more languid. Sloth-like. He looked familiar.

"Oh, hey," said the scruffy character. "Uhh, Chick with you?"

He stood up, stuffed his hands in his pockets.

I shook my head no.

"Haven't seen him. I thought he was with you guys."

I looked at the smaller one.

"You LaBeau?"

He looked at me nervously, then nodded.

I nodded back and turned toward the other one, who was still lying on Chick's bed.

"Feet off, please," I said, pointing to his boots.

Dude said, "Oh hell yeah, sorry," and swung himself up to a sitting position. A fat Beantown Buddha. Then I recognized him.

"You're Robbie Golack," I said.

Dude nodded.

"I know you?"

I shook my head.

"Naah. But I just had a beer with your brother."

He tilted his head, not so much thinking as trying to remember.

"Well, you must mean Tim-Rick, because ain't no beer where Ronnie's at."

The scruffy guy gave a courtesy laugh.

"Yeah," I said. Whatever. "Tim-Rick. Down at the Heirloom."

Robbie looked almost wistful.

"Yeah? I haven't seen that kid in forever. How's he doing?"

I shrugged.

"You all must be excited about the baby. Gonna be an uncle, huh?"

Robbie looked up, semi-sharp, a butter knife of attention.

"No shit?"

He looked bewildered and, for the briefest of moments, hurt.

"Little fucker never calls anymore. When I see him, I'm gonna kick his ass."

Well, that should fix it.

LaBeau checked his pager even though it hadn't buzzed. Dude had a pager.

"Yo, we gotta go," he said.

Robbie shook his head.

"I ain't leaving until that motherfucker shows up with the money."

LaBeau blew air out of his cheeks.

"Shut the fuck up," said Robbie Golack.

"You guys got something for him?" I asked.

LaBeau didn't say anything but Robbie Golack did because he was dumb as a stump.

"Shit yeah, we got something for him," he said, looking me over. Seemed like he was doing it more for my benefit than his own, like he wanted me to know I was dealing with a seriously bad dude. "And he already owes us from this afternoon."

"How much does he owe you?"

Robbie shrugged.

"Fuck."

He gestured to LaBeau without the decency to look at him.

"All in? Two fifty," said LaBeau.

"Goddamn," I said. "For what?"

This was one Golack could handle.

"For this," he said, taking a small plastic pill jar out of his tracksuit pocket and rattling it. "Yahtzee."

He put the jar back in his pocket.

"And for lunch."

"Easy, Rob," said LaBeau.

I thought for a minute.

"Okay," I said. "You guys going anywhere?"

"Fuck no," said Robbie Golack, swinging back onto the bed. "And I'm gonna put my boots up until that piece of shit comes back."

LaBeau sank down into the desk chair but kept his hands on the sides, as if, should an opportunity present itself, he might get right back up. Any opportunity at all. Elvis LaBeau did not want to be there, which made two of us.

"Give me five minutes," I said.

Golack shrugged. "Give you all night, fuck I care."

I cut through the parking lot, stealing a glance at the Escalade's interior. It was dark and still. I jogged across the Knotsford-Gable Road to the gas station, where there was an ATM. I took out $300 and slushed a large cherry Slurpee into a cup. I stuck a straw in it but left the lid on the counter. The attendant, a pockmarked woman in her early thirties, barely looked up.

On the way back, I could see LaBeau in the parking lot, peering into the passenger side of my truck.

I walked up.

"Who's that?" he asked.

"Don't worry about it."

He looked at me, and then whistled back toward the room.

"Hey, Robbie!"

"Give me the stuff for Chick," I said.

LaBeau just fidgeted. Cars went by, and they were making him nervous.

Robbie Golack appeared at the door of the room, looked around, and did a fat-man jog across the parking lot, all shoulders and tiny, shuffling steps.

"Give me the stuff for Chickie," I said, when he got to us. He was about my height, but slouchy and balding already.

LaBeau pointed to the truck.

"Chick's in there."

"He's passed out," I said. "From lunch."

Robbie Golack looked at me, then peered into the passenger seat.

"Look, here's three hundred dollars," I said, taking the money from my pocket. "Give me the stuff. I'll make sure Chickie gets it."

I made a point of looking around the parking lot, like we might be under surveillance. Prodding them toward a decision.

LaBeau focused on the money. Robbie Golack kept peering into the truck.

"Rob," said LaBeau.

Golack kept looking, but reached into his pocket for the vial. He gestured toward LaBeau.

"Fuck it. Give him the money."

I handed LaBeau the wad. He counted it, the new bills both slick and sticky.

"Three hundred," he said.

Robbie Golack gave me the vial. I stuffed it into my pants pocket.

"He nodded out, huh?" he asked.

I shrugged. "Stuff must be good," I said.

It seemed like a thing to say in a situation like this. Vaguely complimentary.

Robbie looked at me.

"Well, next time we ain't waiting around. You tell him to get his shit together or I'm going to kick his ass."

It had been a long day. I felt like I'd made good choices for most of it.

"Cool," I said. "But let's do it this way instead."

I took a sip from the Slurpee and handed it to LaBeau.

"Hold this," I said. "Don't spill."

He looked at me for a second, then took the Slurpee in his right hand.

"Two hands," I said. "Please."

Robbie Golack smiled.

"Hold up," he said. "Why he gotta hold that shi—"

When LaBeau put his left hand on the bottom of the cup, I coldcocked Robbie Golack—bam!—caught him right where his jaw line would've been if he wasn't such a saggy turtle-headed fuck.

I hadn't punched anybody in a long time. But it's sort of like riding a bike. You don't really forget how to do it, and when you finally get a chance, you remember how much fun it is.

The punch made a noise like a ball hitting a glove. Robbie Golack made a noise like "Guunh" and went down hard on the tail of the Trans Am. Something flew out of his mouth—a tooth, spit, part of his tongue, I didn't really care. I could see it in the neon from the Horse Head. While he was down, I kicked him once in his midsection, not super hard but hard enough to lay him low for a minute.

I turned to LaBeau. It seemed like he might initially have felt obligated to jump in, albeit reluctantly, if he hadn't been trying not to spill a Slurpee, but now that it was just the two of us he sort of froze. I was a pretty big guy.

"Here's the deal," I said to him, getting right up close. "I see you anywhere near Chick again, two things are going to happen. First, I'm gonna kick your ass. Like bad. Second, I'm gonna turn you all in to the cops."

LaBeau still had two hands on the Slurpee.

"You got it?"

He nodded.

"Keep the money. But no more rides, no more nothing. I see you again, you're fucked. I know where you live. I know your parents."

That last bit was a nod to Officer Grevantz, who'd employed it so successfully on me as a kid. I reached into my pocket and LaBeau flinched. So I left my hand there.

"You have thirty seconds to get out of here."

I took the Slurpee from him.

"Put that underachieving son of a bitch in the car," I said.

Robbie Golack was struggling to his knees back by the fender.

"Mother-" he said, reaching for his pockets.

In my experience, people who are drunk or on drugs, or who have just been decked, or who are wearing tracksuits, tend to have a real overestimation of their motor skills. Robbie Golack was probably all three of those, and he was still fumbling around for his pockets when I decked him again. LaBeau grabbed him and pulled him around to the passenger-side door. I opened it and LaBeau stuffed him in. Golack started to stick his head out to say something—something like "You're fucking . . . " something, who the fuck cares?—and I slammed the door into him, the window smacking him in his nose. For a fat guy he had a skinny-ass nose. But it wouldn't be skinny tomorrow.

I took my phone out of my pocket and held it up so LaBeau could see it.

"Fifteen seconds," I said, taking a big pull of Slurpee. I pointed to Robbie Golack. "You tell him what's up."

LaBeau nodded.

"Fuck, man," he said.

"That's right," I said, tapping myself on the chest. "Fuckman."

LaBeau hustled over to the driver side and slid in. The Slurpee was giving me a brain-freeze. I stood on Golack's side and kicked the door for good measure. Just a glancing kick. It was a nice car.

LaBeau backed up and I could see Robbie Golack yelling something, at him or at me, whatever. I put my phone to my ear and LaBeau peeled out of the parking lot. He hit the Knotsford-Gable Road heading north, running the light by the Grub-n-Grog and vanishing around a bend.

My knuckles were red and swelling a little. I pressed them against the Slurpee. I felt good. I felt like an MMA guy. Then I felt bad, almost instantly. Almost thirty years old, a member of the bar, beating up some sad-ass mule in a motel parking lot in order to help my druggie pal. Not mature. It was the sort of behavior that one might have hoped to leave behind by now.

I took the vial out of my pocket and looked at the label. It said "Oxycodone: 40 mg."

The dude behind the Horse Head's front desk was reading an issue of *Bowhunter*.

"Yo," I said, dropping my Slurpee onto the counter with a mild thud. "Benecik. Fifteen. We need to change rooms."

When Chick opened his eyes, it was 8 A.M. I'd been awake for an hour, my stuff already in a duffle bag in the truck.

"What's up?" I said.

He looked around. Different room. His stuff was in a pile by the bed.

"What's going on?" he said.

"You had some visitors last night."

Chick slowly patted himself, as if checking for bruises.

"I took care of it."

I held out my purple knuckles. What a badass.

With my other hand, I took the vial out of my pocket.

"They left this," I said.

His eyes focused slowly. Then he dropped his head back on the pillow.

"Shit."

I put the vial on the desk.

"You remember anything? You remember seeing Tim-Rick Golack last night?"

Chick stared at the ceiling and didn't answer. After a minute, he got up gingerly and went to the bathroom. I could hear him rubbing water onto his face. When he came back out, he ambled toward the vial. I picked it up, put it in my pocket.

"When did it start?" I asked.

He looked at me, sat down on the bed, put his head in his hands.

"This shit. When did it start with the Oxy?"

They called it "hillbilly heroin" in the *Franchise*. A blight on all these rural towns.

"I don't know." He rubbed his temples. "End of high school, I guess. After my knee. Doc gave me some pills for the pain. They helped. A lot."

"Ten years?" I asked.

He shrugged.

"Off and on," he said. "Probably more on. Varying in intensity. SmartSeeds was good, it helped. Thought I was solid. Wasn't. Slipped up out in the Pacific, they sent me home. Florida didn't help at all. Dudes hand shit out like M&M's down there. I get back here, scene of the crime, turns out I know half the orderlies and two of the orthopedic docs at KMC. They pegged me the minute I walked through the door."

I shook my head, bewildered.

"Guy. How come you never told me?"

He wouldn't look up.

"I thought you knew. Everyone else, when you have a bum knee and a reputation for being a weirdo, they overlook stuff."

That broke my heart a little.

"Can you stop?"

He didn't look up, sort of shrugged.

"Trying. There's always tomorrow."

I looked across the room. This is where it was at, a motel room and drugs. But at least he said he was trying.

"Look," I said. "I can't be a part of this if it doesn't change."

Chick looked up, confused.

"What do you mean?"

"You gotta get your shit together."

I handed him a slip of paper, the address of a local substance abuse clinic on it. I'd Googled it during the night.

"Here's a place. Have you heard of it?"

Chick looked at the slip, saw what it was, and crumpled it.

"Can I have my stuff, please?" he said.

I took the vial out of my pocket and tossed it to him. It was empty.

"I flushed it," I said.

Chick's face darkened. I could see him trying to contain himself.

"That was pretty stupid. It was a lot of money."

"No shit," I said. "My money."

He looked at me.

"I paid for it. And don't bother calling them back. They're not taking your calls."

He sat still for a minute, then flicked the vial across the room and through the bathroom door, where it hit harmlessly against the shower curtain. He lay back down on the bed.

"You don't really think that this is how it works, do you?"

I sort of did. I think I was wrong.

He covered his eyes. Seemed like he was having a little internal debate. When he took his hands away, he was smiling.

"Okay. Fine. What do you want me to do?"

"I'm glad you asked," I said.

I had it all figured out.

"Go to that place. They've got a bed for you. Call Unsie and ask for a job. Apologize to Ginny Archey. I can't babysit you. I have to go. But stay clean for a week, just this week, and I'll come back."

He didn't move.

I played my trump.

"We can look for the horn. Just one week. I'll come back and we can look for the horn."

Chick rubbed his face, still smiling, his eyes focused somewhere in the middle distance.

"You don't understand," he said, shaking his head. "I appreciate it. But you don't understand."

I stood up.

"You don't understand," I said. "I'm out. I cannot stay. If you want my help, leave your phone on and answer it when I call. Put me on your list at that place and tell them to talk to me. Do that and I'm here for you. If not, you're on your own."

I went to the door and paused. Like I was really going to walk away.

"You coming?" I asked.

Chick looked at his knees. He stretched one leg out and reached for it in a weird pantomime of loosening up. Took a deep breath, then another. Finally, he stood up.

"Where else do I have to be?" he said.

I drove Chick out to the clinic, a drab, one-story institution surrounded by the Becket woods. The sign at the entrance to a long drive read "The Birches—Your Wellness Source," like "wellness" was something you could buy, aisle six at the CVS. There were no fences, but Chick didn't have a car, and the isolation seemed beneficial. Was it the right place for him? I had no idea. Was one week there going to do him more harm than good? Possibly. Here's what I knew—it was within my budget and the only drug rehab place around that wasn't in the Knots. I helped Chick fill out the paperwork and sent him off to intake. Right before he went in, we shared a little manly hug. It scared the shit out of me.

I spent my junior year of college in Spain, learning enough Spanish to try and convince Spanish girls to sleep with me. I did not have much success, but when I came home I figured I should just run the labs and make sure that I wasn't carrying any unwanted visitors from the more progressive stretches of the Costa Brava.

I'd never been to a walk-in health clinic before, so I tore out the "Cl" page from the Yellow Pages and headed off to Great Barr. There were a few clinics listed. At the first place, a Planned Parenthood outlet off Main Street, the receptionist recognized me. She'd been in the Garden Club with my mother. I acted like I'd walked through the wrong door and left immediately. Then I went around to another place, steeled myself for the humiliation, walked up to the receptionist—an attractive young woman whom I might have hit on, were I not seeking a test for sexually transmitted diseases—and explained my predicament. She wrinkled her nose and said, "This is a mental health clinic."

This is a roundabout way to say that I didn't know much about clinics and that I felt capable of dropping my drug-addled friend off at the wrong sort. But the Birches was an actual drug treatment clinic, if not a terribly in-demand one. It had featured prominently in the Scared Straight presentations our high school had put on years ago, and I'd vetted it just that morning on Yelp, where it got mostly good reviews from the drug addicts who had been sequestered there.

I went back into town and filled Unsie in on what was going on. Told him about Robbie Golack and the oxycodone and where Chick was. Extracted from him a reluctant promise to visit Chick on Wednesday. Said I'd be calling. Heard the bells at St. Barney's herald the start of eleven o'clock Mass.

Then I hit the Pike and didn't breathe until Boston.

I wasn't a huge fan of my job, but that week I loved it. I loved my colleagues, I loved my city, I loved riding on the urine-scented subway with people I didn't recognize. With Kelly gone, my apartment was quiet and boring, and I could do pushups and try on suits and walk around in my boxers holding a beer and nobody was like "How's that 'Most Likely to Succeed' stuff working out?" Not that Kelly ever said that. It was more something I said to myself.

Kelly and I had one of those photo wall-collages that happy couples make, vacations and hugs and beaches and such, and when she left she took about half of the photos, the ones with us and other people, the ones where we looked happy, and the pattern that remained was like an archipelago of melancholy. So I took the rest of the photos down, boxed them up carefully, shelved them in one of the now-empty closets, and covered the holes with a long horizontal poster of spread-armed Michael Jordan, circa 1991, saying "No bird soars too high if he soars with his own wings." I spread my own wings, could have touched both sides of the kitchen if I wasn't holding a beer.

And the city! Boston could be great when you didn't expect it to care about you. Maybe that's true of most cities, but it's truer of Boston. Boston! Badass, unfriendly, steel and cement and glass. Beefy cops and bent Brahmins, students and Jamaicans and Irish, the pale tribes of the Hub, gaunt but sturdy, brittle but unfrail, their traumas weaponized like bionics. Every day I left my apartment at 7 A.M., walked to work through the fragrant frost, stayed at my desk until nearly midnight, and walked back home again in the dark, when the steakhouses along Faneuil Hall made the air smell like meat. My supervisors at Huey Huckle—my firm—were impressed. Most of the work was mindless—discovery responses, motions to compel, document review—but I plowed through it with the endurance of a gunner. I invented witnesses to depose and prepped the outlines. I wrote several really nasty letters. I researched opposing counsel, opened new matters. Midweek I even won a dismissal in a stupid premises liability suit in which a woman had sued my client, a big box retailer whose name I'm ethically prohibited from telling you but it rhymes with Ball-Mart, after she rammed one of those Mart Carts into the in-store Pizza Hut counter and sustained a pepperoni-sized burn on her right breast just above the nipple. Unfortunately for her, toxicology said she'd been drunk at the time.

And every day, at 6 P.M., I called the Birches and checked on Chick. On Monday, he was shaky, resentful. On Tuesday and Wednesday, he sounded better, weak but resigned. Unsie went on Wednesday and said Chick seemed together.

On Thursday, he was gone.

On Friday, my office phone rang at noon. I'd been there all night. The partners thought I was a lifer.

"Johansson," I said.

It was Unsie.

"He's in jail," he said. "I'm inclined to leave him there."

For the young Bollywood star Vishy Shetty, it had been a rough year. She'd first come to prominence in late 2008, in a film called *Tiger Tiger*, in which she played a rookie zoologist racing against time to save the big cats of Rajasthan from an urban development project spearheaded by the rakish industrialist Anil Dutta. Shetty had brown eyes that were as big as milk saucers and curves both hidden and accentuated by a completely impractical *ghagra choli*. Dutta never stood a chance.

A string of movies followed, fluff pieces that padded her bank account(s) and kept her in the public eye but didn't advance her into superstardom, and she was beginning to feel a little desperate. Her last picture, a song-and-dance number about the Indian Ocean tsunami released in the spring of 2011, had been poorly received, and she had sought refuge on the set of an English reality series called *All Eyez*, which tracked the interactions of a rather toxic mix of young celebrities forced to spend a trimester as students at one of Oxford's less prestigious colleges. The reality show route had proved lucrative for other rising Indian B-listers, much of whose viewing public retained a sort of Stockholm syndrome curiosity for all things British, but the set itself had turned out to be less of a refuge than Vishy Shetty had hoped. At the end of week four, she was shown having a vaguely racist row with one of the other cast members after her purse was lost on an Oxford double-decker—hint: one of the producers took it—and later that season, she'd been caught by the night-vision cameras, set up about the back patio of the Woodstock Road flat where the cast was imprisoned, making out with the same cast member. The season descended into fights, flirtation, pints and biscuits and chips, and a brutal website called *All Thighz* sprang up that purported to track the weight gain of the female cast members—hint: one of the producers created it. Things really went south, however, when Vishy Shetty attempted to send a rather unchaste selfie via Twitter to a magnificent West Ham striker named Alo Djibouti. Ms. Shetty had apparently intended to send the photo, in which she was poorly lit but nonetheless stood in marked contrast to the insinuations of weight gain made online, as a direct message but, somehow (hint: you already know) it wound up being transmitted to all of her 675,000 Twitter followers.

Alo Djibouti, who was himself already engaged to a proper English rose named Saffron Leeds, strenuously denied soliciting the photo, and at first claimed to not even know who was in it. However, subsequent digital investigation by media outlets suggested a closer relationship than either party initially let on. Saffron Leeds appeared on the plush couches of a Sussex television studio to publicly dump Djibouti, after which West Ham lost its next three matches. The British tabloids, while sparing Djibouti, leapt on the young Bollywood temptress, with the *Telegraph* running a full-page denunciation (complete with the incriminating photo, of course) and the headline "A Vishy Shetty Thing to Do." The *Sun* went with "Delhi Belly: Not Enough Saffron for Djibouti." Enraged West Ham fans began picketing the Woodstock flat and, citing security concerns, the producers pulled Ms. Shetty from season two of *All Eyez*. (Hint: There's a comeback in the works.) For the time being, she had to get out of England, but was being financially cautioned by her handlers against returning home in disgrace.

Where could she go that didn't care about Premier League soccer and naked tweets and the subcontinent? Where could she go that presented a plausible recuperative cover story while not implicating drugs or alcohol or other serious vices, which might resonate with the masses of South Indian youngsters for whom the West remained a land of manners and manors and puritan refinement?

Which is how Vishy Shetty came to be spending a month at Head-Connect in snowy, blasé New England, as opposed to snippy, jaded olde England, in the late winter of 2012. Which, in turn, is why security around the spa's perimeter, which was normally (relatively) lax, eyes out for deer and thrill-seekers, was on (relatively) high alert the night that Chick tried to sneak in.

I found a lot of this out after the fact, of course, after I left Boston, breathless badass Boston, late on that blustery Friday night, and wound my way back into the Berkshires. I went to the Gable police station, where Chick was not, and then met up with Unsie at the Heirloom and got the story of Chick's ill-fated attempt to breach the walls of Fleur-de-Lys with a hook-and-ladder type thing he'd found in a toolshed at the Birches. Apparently, he'd slipped and landed on topiary, right next to where Vishy Shetty had been furtively smoking her last pre-intake cigarette. She screamed, and the jig was up.

"What the fuck?" I asked.

Unsie blew through his cheeks.

"On the plus side, he was sober."

I considered that. It seemed promising, actually.

"Have you seen him?"

Unsie nodded.

"Chief Grevantz knew that we were pals and came by this morning."

"Grevantz is the police chief?" I asked.

Unsie nodded again.

"Is that weird?"

He shrugged.

"I don't know. Is it?"

My turn to shrug.

"Seems weird to me. Seems like he shouldn't still be here."

Unsie looked at his beer.

"Why not? He put in his time, worked his way up. Made a future for himself. There's a way to do it."

I felt like I'd insulted him somehow, and we fell silent for a minute. Then he picked it up again.

"Not a bad guy, actually. Good skier, good with the local media, such as it is. Coaches T-ball. Supports the town, supports the store, et cetera. That's about all it takes for me."

I thought for a minute about how to use that information, if indeed it was usable.

"So where is Chickie now?" I asked.

Unsie shrugged, and then pulled out his cell phone.

Unsie had his best, and his most important, customers on speed dial. Chief Grevantz was one of the latter. Head-Connect was one of the former. After a couple of calls, he'd located Chickie at the lockup next to Berkshire Superior Court, half an hour to the north in Knotsford. His arraignment was set for Monday morning at eight.

"No visitation on the weekends," Unsie said.

I was sort of relieved. But then my own phone buzzed. It was the lockup. Which meant it was Chickie.

I stepped outside, onto the Heirloom's wheelchair ramp, to take it.

"Guy," I said.

"Guy!" he said back, chipper and upbeat. He sounded great, actually.

"What the fuck, guy?"

"You heard?" Slightly more downbeat, but not by much.

"Uns."

"This is my phone call! I'm calling you with my phone call."

"I'm flattered, guy. How are you?"

"I think I broke my back," he said. "But not too bad. But listen! I can't talk long."

"Why not?"

"Regulations. I don't know. Guy, I saw it. I saw it!"

He was practically yelling into the phone. Whatever he saw, the rest of the lockup was going to hear about.

"You know this line is recorded, right?" I said.

He made a noise like *pssssh*.

"I don't give a shit. I saw the safe. On the way out, they led me through the lobby. It's right there, in a room off of the middle. Like a display or something."

"They led you through the lobby?"

"Yeah, they thought I was a guest at first, probably because I said I was a guest, but then when I couldn't give them a room number, they thought I was paparazzi or a hooligan or some shit. Called the cops. Guess what?"

He was humming.

"What?"

"Grevantz is the police chief now! He remembered me. That didn't help. And guess what else? Ava Winston, from Tanglewood? She works there too! In, like, guest services. I think she was trying to help me out, but the main guys weren't having it."

"Wow," I said.

"Yeah, wow! And the safe. Right there! I knew it!"

My fingers were freezing and it felt like my lips were turning blue. I stomped my feet.

"Dude, do you have a lawyer?"

"Don't need a lawyer."

"What do you mean? You got a hearing on Monday."

"It's just an arraignment," he said, sounding like a guy who knew more about it than he should. "Court will appoint a lawyer for that."

I'd gone to law school and had spent the past three years as a litigator at a pretty decent little firm, but I had almost no idea what actually happened inside a criminal courtroom. People would sometimes ask me for help with their DUIs and speeding tickets and I'd feel like a dentist looking at a guy's foot.

"Okay," I said. "So what now?"

"We gotta get it!" he nearly shouted. "Get in there. Get into the safe. Take the horn. You know what they call a rhino without a horn? A hippo!"

This was stupid. I looked around the sidewalk. It was so cold that when I exhaled, the breath seemed resentful. So cold you could almost see the black air shimmering like oil. Anyway, what was wrong with hippos?

"How do you know it's in there?" I asked.

"Come on," he said. "Of course it's in there."

Well, it either was or it wasn't, I guess.

"Dude, I'm fucking freezing out here. What is the point of getting it? What then?"

"Well, first, let's strategize. How are we going to get it?" he asked.

"Fuck if I know!" I said. The fricatives helped my lips. "Wait, I do know. We are not going to get it. I'm not going to get it. But let's say that you can somehow magically get inside the safe, and the horn is there, and you take out the horn, all without getting arrested. What would the point of that be?"

I looked up. The volume I was conducting this scheme in was good for my circulation, but maybe not for logistics.

"So," continuing in a whisper. "What would the point be? What then?"

There was a pause. A long pause, like he was doing it for effect.

"Then," he said. "It's obvious."

"It's not obvious to me."

"Well if it's not obvious to you, I'm not going to tell you," he said. "Drug free, by the way. Five days and counting."

"Right, right," I started to say. "And that's great. But, I mean, what the—"

The phone went dead.

Asshole.

"Ain't gonna work," a voice said behind me.

I turned around. It was Tim-Rick Golack. He was standing on the sidewalk.

"No shit, Sherlock," I said. Paused. I didn't disagree with the conclusion, but I also wasn't sure how much he'd heard. "What's not gonna work?"

He stepped up onto the ramp.

"They run the place pretty tight," he said. "Most of their clientele are both rich and image-conscious. I can't even get past the guard booth."

I nodded.

"Thanks for the info."

We were silent.

"I heard you saw my brother the other day," he said.

I shifted my weight slightly, holding it on my back foot, ready to launch an overhand right.

"Are we going to have a problem about that?" I asked. Seemed like a dumb question. It was his brother.

Tim-Rick looked down and shook his head.

"Nope," he said. "Not about that. My brother's a drug addict. Like your boy. But unlike you, I walked away. I haven't talked to him in years, and I plan to keep it that way."

I shrugged, but held my position.

"What is it with you and him, anyway?"

Tim-Rick looked at me.

"Who? Robbie?"

"Chickie," I said. "What was all that bullshit about?"

Tim-Rick looked uncomfortable. He was quiet for a long time.

"I don't even know. Just, something about the guy. It's like he thinks he should get all the breaks."

I frowned.

"I can pretty much guarantee he doesn't think that."

Tim-Rick shrugged.

"Well, he gets them anyway."

I snorted.

"You have any idea about the breaks he's gotten?"

Tim-Rick scrunched up his face a little, preparing to be un-PC, maybe.

"Oh, right. One perv gets a little handsy in the choir and now this kid is the golden child? Please. Bad shit happens to everyone."

That was true enough. But, come on. Some kids get dumped. Chick got more than that.

"Careful," I said. "He's my best friend."

"I know he is," Tim-Rick said. "And I'm glad he's yours and not mine. I didn't mess up his knee or do anything else to him. I don't owe him anything. I don't owe anyone and nobody owes me. This life, man. Get with it."

There was shit here I didn't have the bandwidth for. I decided to try and steer the conversation back to transitional pleasantries. If we were clear on his brother, I was gonna mosey.

"Well, good for fucking you," I said. "Whatever. Nobody's looking for handouts anyway. But, hey, I guess I should warn you, I think I let the cat out of the bag a little when I saw your brother."

"About what?" Tim-Rick Golack asked.

"About Ginny," I said. "I hear you're going to be a father."

Tim-Rick blanched.

"You told my brother?" he asked, slightly panicked. "Jesus Christ."

Then he took a deep breath and spat into the snow. He raised a finger and pointed it at me.

"Stay out of that," he said.

He turned to go back inside, but then reversed himself and headed off down the street.

"Yo," I started to say. "I'm sorry!"

But he was gone.

Goddamn, this shit was exhausting. First Chick and now this dude. I was legitimately happy for him. Or for Ginny at least. I didn't know it was classified info. Ginny wasn't fooling anyone.

I gave it a second, then went back in and cut a path through the Friday night crowd to our booth. It was closing in on 9 P.M., and the bar was packed and sweaty. It felt desperate. Unsie looked impatient.

I slid in across from him and coddled my beer.

"So he still wants to break into Head-Connect," I said, putting my phone on the table. "He says he saw the safe in the lobby, and he thinks the rhino horn is inside it."

Unsie nodded.

"There is a safe in the lobby," he said. "But there's nothing inside it."

"You've seen it?"

He looked at me.

"I've seen a safe in the lobby. An old one. That's where we meet for the Nordic tours. The thing is decorative. It's not the Royal Bank of Scotland or something."

I banked with the Royal Bank of Scotland, and they sucked.

"For a guy who hates going inside, you sound pretty sure. Tim-Rick Golack just told me that he couldn't get past security at the front gate," I said.

"Is Tim-Rick Golack an Olympic skier? Because I am," Unsie said, veering as close to ego as he got. "Does Tim-Rick own a business that lets Head-Connect claim to locally source their cross-country and snowshoe excursions? Because I do."

I acted impressed. It was impressive, but I was still acting.

"Wow," I said. "So can you get us in?"

Unsie put his hands flat on the table and took a deep breath. "No."

I looked at him.

"Why?"

He glanced around the booth.

"Come on, Pete."

"What?"

"They are my biggest client. They trust me. I have friends who work there. I also live in this town all year round, with my wife and, soon, my kid. I have a reputation. You are not seriously asking me to jeopardize those things to help Chick—who, sure, is a very important friend, an old friend, but who is also out of his fucking mind—look for something that is (a) not there in the first place and, (b) if it was there, would be of no real use to him in solving whatever problems he has to solve?"

He looked me in the eye.

"You aren't asking me to do that, are you?"

He gave me a hard stare, and I let him because he'd earned it. That was a compelling goddamn speech.

"Yeah," I said finally. I didn't want him to be right, but he was. "I'm asking you to do that."

Uns looked sad.

"I know you are," he said. "And I am saying no, reluctantly but firmly. There's a limit, you know?"

I waited a second, but he wasn't reconsidering.

"You're right."

I sipped my beer and thought about it.

"I just want to help the guy."

Unsie nodded. "Sure. But why?"

Why? Because that's what friends did.

"Figure out why," Unsie said. "Then you'll know how."

All right, fucko. Let's not push it too far.

My beer tasted bitter.

"I wish Jimmer was here," I said. "Jimmer would help me."

I wanted to make Unsie feel as bad as I did.

"Only say my name," said a voice from near the side door. "And I shall appear."

I looked over.

It was Jimmer.

Jimmer was older and slicker, a slight weight at the jowls, but the rest of him seemed more svelte than in youth. He was wearing a shiny belt and gray slacks. Maybe it was the clothes that were streamlining him. His skin looked moisturized. His teeth were bright and straight. His hair was wet without being wet, but expensively so, not like the waitress at Gina's. He came over to our booth and I slid out to hug him. I'd never been happier to see someone in my life. It was like seeing Chick again in the opposite bed, except sober and uncomplicated. I couldn't stop staring. I think I thought if I stopped staring, he'd up and vanish.

"Jimmer!" I said.

"I'm like fucking Dumbledore," he said, raising a finger. "But, uh, it's James these days."

I looked at him. Couldn't stop smiling. I kissed him on the cheek and he relented.

"To everyone else but you guys, I guess" he said, sliding into the booth next to Unsie. Unsie threw an arm around his shoulder and that was it.

"What are you doing here?" I asked. "Like, what? What are you doing here?"

Jimmer scanned the table for a menu and, seeing none, shrugged. He pulled out a very shiny phone and glanced at it with practiced nonchalance. It glowed subtly like a glowworm.

"Bat signal," he said, tilting his head toward Unsie. "And I was able to set up some business in Boston to make it work."

"Business in Boston?" I said. "I live in Boston. Do you want to stay with me?"

I felt like a fanboy.

"Uh, yeah, man. Sure. Of course."

"Cool," I said. "What's your business, anyway?"

Jimmer was still looking around at the people in the bar. He seemed fascinated in the way one might be watching an early music video, or visiting a museum display on primitive societies.

"Eh, VC stuff. Not very interesting."

"VC like venture capital?"

Jimmer nodded. "I help a few startups out. With money."

"Wait," I said. "Are you an angel investor? Goddamn, man! That's awesome."

Jimmer sort of shook his head without actually denying anything. It seemed more embarrassed than corrective.

I didn't really know much about angel investors except that they sounded cool and usually had shitloads of money.

"Do you have like shitloads of money now?" I asked, before I could rein myself in.

Unsie laughed and Jimmer looked even more embarrassed. I might have felt more embarrassed too if I hadn't seen Jimmer vomit onto a Northampton girl's lap in the summer before our junior year, thus ending the evening for all of us. Or if I hadn't been there that night when, after a fairly minor rejection by a hot sophomore named Jemma Bergdorf, Jimmer lay down in the middle of Walker Street and waited to get hit by a car. It was more a symbolic gesture than anything else, because it was late and Walker Street was long and well-lit and lightly traveled, a gesture sort of like walking into the sea at low tide while carrying one of those noodles, but I'd been there for it and had sat on the double yellow line by his head, and we'd talked it through until he stopped feeling so bad.

Jimmer sort of nodded his head back and forth for a second, and then leaned in.

"Okay, so, right, you've heard of Sment?"

I nodded, then shook my head no.

"We digitize odors so that they can be transmitted electronically. That's my company."

It took a second to process.

"You digitize odors? I didn't know you could do that."

"Right, like the smell of your mom's hair, or your grandfather's cologne, or gingerbread, or oatmeal cookies, or whatever. You click the link, download the scent, it fills the room. Endless applications."

My mind was blown.

"How do you do that?"

"Well," Jimmer said. "You know how music is made up of sound waves? Well, odors are made up of smell waves. We figured out how to digitize those."

I looked at Unsie. He was smiling.

"Bullshit," I said.

"Yeah," Jimmer said. "It's more complicated than that, but the algorithms would bore you."

"Huh," I said. "And people will pay you for it?"

"Well, Yahoo! did," Jimmer said.

We sat silently for a second.

"So," I said. "How much do you know?"

Jimmer gave an exaggerated shrug.

"Something about our boy busting into Head-Connect, some drugs, arrests, sounds like a clusterfuck."

I nodded.

"He's on a vision quest."

"That's Ginny Archey," Jimmer said, looking over at the bar, like he'd spotted a manatee.

I nodded.

"And this guy's gonna be a dad," he said, clapping Unsie on the shoulder.

"Indeed," I said. "All grown up."

Jimmer looked at me.

"How about you," he said. "You okay? Still seeing Kylie?"

I made a face.

"No more Kylie, I don't think. Or Kelly either. But I'm good. Other than not knowing where I'm going to sleep tonight, I'm good."

Jimmer raised his palms up, as if I'd missed the obvious.

"Well, I can fix part of that," he said. "You're staying with me, of course."

I finished what was left of my beer.

"Sounds great," I said. "Where are we staying?"

Jimmer looked at me. Then he raised his arm to signal the waitress. When she got to us, he raised three fingers.

"Tequila," he said. "For my compadres."

Then he looked at me, with as hard a look as I imagine he could muster.

"Where do you think we're staying?" he said.

❖

I followed Jimmer's rented Range Rover slowly down Bramble and past the turnoff to my old house. The dashboard temp gauge on the Escalade read 15, and the woodland around Fleur-de-Lys seemed absolutely still. It was a long 2 miles downhill from the philistine comforts of the town center to the marble gates of Head-Connect, nothing in between but a few houses and some overgrown meadows. Head-Connect was famous for its restrictions on what you could bring in—it was sort of like a dietary airplane—and sometimes in high school, we'd see desperate spa guests trudging like refugees along the side of the road, heads down in shame, heading up to O'Brien's Market for nicotine and Oreos.

At the gatehouse, Jimmer went first, pulling up to the long plank across the drive and lowering his window. A guard leaned out of the gatehouse and waved a flashlight over the car like a wand. In my headlights, I could see Jimmer reaching for documents in an attaché case on the passenger seat. The guard had Jimmer press his palm onto a sensor. A second guard came out and walked around the car with what looked like a golf club. The process took about ten minutes. Then Jimmer was past and rolling slowly up the long drive.

I pulled ahead. The entry guard flagged me down. He was leaning out of a little cottage-like structure, a dwarf-house, but I could see the glow of monitors inside.

"Hello, sir," he said. I didn't recognize him. "Can I just take a quick look at your identification?"

I reached for my wallet.

"I'm with him," I said, gesturing to the taillights meandering ahead of me as the other guard, a younger guy no doubt lower on the totem pole, did whatever he did with the golf club.

The security guard gave the interior of the Escalade a quick once-over with his flashlight.

"Oh, I know, sir," he said. "It's just protocol."

The guard took my license and pecked on a keyboard, my data filling some sort of form. He held out the pad for me to press. When I took my hand away, an outline of it glowed on the screen.

"Thank you, Mr. Johansson," he said. "Valet is just up the drive."

I nodded to him, as if this was just one of many luxury spa entry exams I would endure this week, as if this was my life. He smiled back, a professional smile of both warmth and distance.

Up the drive, the pea-stones crunching under my wheels. Speed bumps. Walking paths and resting benches. Private villas appearing beyond an iced-over pond. A row of pines to the right, beyond which fifteen Jesuits lay buried. Relics from the mansion's brief Sisters of Mercy interregnum, once in the ground there forever. To the left, 50 yards of snow-dusted lawn and then the woods, thick and quiet. I tried to imagine a rhino trudging down this drive, battered and raw, having had enough. I looked, as I'd done in my youth, for a break in the woods, an entry-point that might have appealed to the mad, cloudy eyes of an ungulate, but, as always, none revealed itself.

After a hundred yards, the mansion came fully into view, glowing like a cruise ship on a white sea. Where before there'd been saplings and broken rock, now planters and smaller courtyards formed a moat around the ground floor, beyond which French doors opened out from the marble. On the second floor, tall half-moon windows, eight a side, looked out onto the lawns. They'd been broken and boarded up for years. Despite the season, despite the hour, they blazed like a portal to some galvanized era, lavish and imperturbable. As I approached, I could see trails wending their way from the main house out onto the property, lit every 50 yards or so by torches, half of them looping back and the other half vanishing into the distant tree line.

I bent my truck around to the left and into the graceful roundabout that led to the guest entrance and reception. The Head-Connect facilities occupied a series of one-story outbuildings, clean lines and glass wings radiating from and encircling the main mansion. This was all recent construction, tastefully done, the colors muted and local and blending with both sight lines and surroundings. No nuns had seen these buildings, no carriage-men or acrobats or midwives. They were new to me, even. I couldn't tell how big the place was, where it stopped. It felt like origami.

At the top of the rotary, six valets waited in pine green jackets, youngish, fit, but standing with a poise that marked them as professionals. Who were these guys? Private schoolers? Full-time valets? Actors from the Shakespeare troupe up the road? I couldn't place them. Felt like the twilight zone.

Jimmer was already out of his Range Rover, and the Rover was already gone, and a porter had already swept the sleek shoulder bag from his arm by the time I pulled up. As I looked right, to the entrance, my door opened on the left, and another valet stepped gracefully away from the truck.

"Welcome, sir," he said.

I put the truck into park and got out.

"Bags?"

"Nah," I said, fishing in my wallet for small bills. "I'm good."

I pulled out a couple of ones and offered them up. The valet raised his palm.

"Thank you, sir, but not necessary," he said. "All gratuities are included in your package."

I nodded like I'd known that. My package includes gratuities. Not the first time I've heard that. Hey!

The valet extended his arm toward the entrance.

"Right through those doors there," he said. "Enjoy your stay."

I crossed to Jimmer, who was moving a thin stylus across a small flat screen. He looked up only long enough to confirm I was there, then walked in through the sliding doors to the Head-Connect lobby. I followed.

Inside, the lobby was bathed in flattering light. The floor was marble, edged with sound-swallowing rugs. A glass table in the middle of the room held a huge vase of snow-white calla lilies. Water fountains and warm wood. Modern, vaguely Native American art adorned the walls. Doors opened onto meeting rooms. Low tables held swaths of lifestyle magazines and glossy brochures. The banquettes coddled you. The mirrors made you look taller and less indecisive.

I scanned the lobby for a safe.

There was no safe.

Relief.

Jimmer was at the front desk, where a stunning young woman of indeterminate ethnicity was handing him a sleeve of keys and a dossier. I saw her gesture toward the concierge desk, off to the right, and signal for a porter to relocate Jimmer's minimal luggage to its proper place within the establishment.

Ava Winston stood at the concierge desk, looking at a computer monitor. She had her hair pulled into an upscale ponytail, a perfect golden spout pouring off the back of her head. I'd forgotten it was blond. In my memories she always wore baseball hats.

We approached, Jimmer more assertively than I. I think I was waiting for an invitation. When we crossed the 3-yard threshold, Ava Winston looked up. They must drill on that threshold, I thought, the perfect distance, remaining engaged and inconspicuous right up until the moment before a guest initiated contact, then fully present and ready to help. As if the guest was carrying a fob.

"Mr. O'Neill," she said, her voice warm and smooth. "Welcome to Head-Connect at Fleur-de-Lys."

She came out from behind the concierge desk and stood the perfect distance from Jimmer. She was in a charcoal skirt and jacket. Her hands were clasped behind her back. Her calves looked aerodynamic.

"We are so happy to have you join us."

Jimmer nodded, acknowledging their gratitude. He looked around the lobby as Ava Winston continued to talk.

"We have a tour tomorrow morning after Welcoming that we recommend for first-time visitors," she said. "Or I am happy to show you around now."

Jimmer made a point of checking his watch, a thin, lovely thing that managed to look ostentatious in its restraint.

"Actually, I've got a couple of calls to make," he said, handing me a room key. "Perhaps you can give my associate here a tour?"

He turned to me and winked.

"Of course," said Ava Winston, looking at me quickly and then back at Jimmer. He was pretty clearly the main attraction here. It must have been some algorithm.

"You're in . . . " She checked her console quickly. "Birch. That's a suite here in our main building. One of our bellmen will show you to it."

Jimmer was already back on his tablet, ambling off toward an ascending hallway by the main desk as a shadow figure appeared to escort him.

"Thank you," he said without looking back, unpresent, gone.

Ava Winston watched him go, a mix of professional attention and mild affront on her face. Then she turned to me. She looked at me for a second with a courtesy smile on her face, and then let it widen, almost grudgingly, into a toothier one.

"I know you," she said. "Don't I?"

"No you don't," I said. I was Obi-Wan and she was the storm trooper.

"You're Pete Johansson."

"Nope."

She turned back toward where Jimmer had gone and spoke in a low voice.

"Oh my God, and that's Jimmer," she said. "James O'Neill."

She looked for a second like she might snort-laugh, but pulled out of it.

"James O'Neill. He only booked the room yesterday, we didn't have time to double background."

She turned back to me.

"You little fuckers," she hissed, and punched me on the arm, and then immediately caught her breath and looked around the lobby to see if anyone had heard the profanity, if anybody was watching. Nobody was.

Ava grinned broadly.

"Sment," I said. "Have you heard of it?"

"Sment the digital fragrance system?"

I nodded.

"Sment. He is Sment."

She looked after him again.

"Huh."

She turned to me.

"Well, that explains the deposit."

"Sment," I said, taking a deep, appreciative breath through my nose. "I'm using it right now, actually. A little something I call 'Trouble in Marrakesh.'"

Ava Winston looked me up and down, the smile creeping back onto her face. She sniffed the air and frowned.

"I would have thought yours was factory-installed," she said. She took my arm and led me down a long hallway out of the lobby. "Let's go."

⚜

"It's great to see you," Ava said, stopping me when we'd rounded a corner and were no longer visible to the reception staff.

"You too," I said. Awkward pause, then hug.

Ava broke it and looked around quickly.

"How's your dad?" I said.

"He's good."

Her cheeks flushed slightly.

"Sorry. I'm not used to coming across real people here. He's good! Oh man, he won't believe this. Ah, he retired a couple of years ago. Happy in his retirement. Still has a house here but spends a lot of time in Nevada."

"Nevada?"

"One of the perks of working for the company. Family discounts. He's just about the healthiest sixty-eight-year-old on the planet. Or, at least, that's my goal for him."

I nodded. "Got it. And you're here, doing this."

"Yeah," she said. "Right, come check it out."

We kept walking down the hallway. On the wall there were charcoal drawings and chakras, shit that seemed to be trying very hard to be covertly motivational. Must have been working, because I felt like some yoga. Never did yoga before. Kelly used to do yoga. It looked like a lot of work.

"Guest rooms are this way," Ava said, gesturing down a side passage. "Yours is down there to the left. The main spa building is straight ahead."

I looked around. I hadn't seen another guest since we arrived.

"You guys do good business in the winters?" I asked.

Ava Winston nodded.

"We're fully booked. We were able to fit you in only because of a cancellation."

"Where is everyone?" I asked.

"Around. You'll see. It's easy to fill your time."

She paused.

"So, like, are you Sment too?"

I shook my head.

"Nah, I'm just along for the ride," I said.

"Nice ride," she said, a little self-congratulatorily. "What are you up to?"

"I'm a lawyer," I said.

"In Boston, right?"

I nodded.

"I see Unsie sometimes," she said. "He's my link to the outside world."

We'd reached smoked-glass doors at the end of the hall.

"Wait," she said, stopping short. She looked at me closely. "This is about Chickie Benecik, isn't it?"

I tried to look surprised.

"Pete, tell me it's not about Chickie Benecik."

"I don't know what you're talking about," I said, and as I said it I could hear that I had no future in the courtroom.

She could hear it too.

"Listen, I don't know what that stuff was about the other night—last night, Jesus. It was last night. But I swear to God, you better not screw around with me here. Sment or no Sment, I will run you guys out of here on a rail."

I put my hands up.

"Ava, when have I ever screwed around with you?"

That came out sounding more suggestive than I'd meant it to. Ava narrowed her eyes.

"I'm sorry, I didn't mean it like that," I said. "I swear to you this isn't about Chickie."

It was easier the second time.

She straightened her skirt.

"Promise?"

"Promise. Jimmer's in town, I'm just tagging along."

She took a deep breath and pushed her shoulders back. After a minute, she resumed the tour.

"Fine. Good."

She looked around, as if she'd forgotten where we were. Smoked-glass doors, right.

"This is the main spa entrance. Steam rooms, pool, massage, treatments, you name it. We can wrap you in anything from seaweed to fettuccine. That's a joke. No carbs."

I looked at her and grinned. She grinned back, grudgingly. Then she shook out her arms and took another deep breath.

"Sorry, that's part of the script. If you want to do any classes or outdoor activities, you can arrange those through me or use the on-demand system on your room monitor. Or just show up, they'll fit you in."

"Classes?"

"Mindfulness, Pilates, landscape architecture, whatever you're into, really. Colorwork."

"Colorwork?"

"Crayons," she said. "Very therapeutic."

I pretended to evaluate that.

"You guys have a knitting circle?" I asked.

Ava made a face.

"You'd be surprised. The dining room is across the way in the main building. That's where we do our Welcoming."

"Welcoming, right. What's that?"

"It's an initial personalized evaluation that we ask our guests to do when they arrive. Sort of like a physical, but with some nondenominational spirituality and environmental elements taken into account. It helps us customize your Head-Connect experience."

"That sounds awesome," I said.

I must have looked skeptical.

"It's really easy," she said, looking me over, taking in the billow of my shirttails, the bovine thickness of my neck. "Nonjudgmental."

What was she suggesting? I'm a big-boned man locked into a sedentary lifestyle. And I can still almost dunk a basketball.

I widened my mouth in mock surprise. She blushed again.

"No, no, no," she said, palms up. "That's not what I meant."

I gave her my smoldering look.

"Sure."

"Ha," she said, in not-a-laugh, and patted me on the arm. "Now, seriously, you'll want to be over there tomorrow morning at eight. It's all in your folder."

The glass doors slid open silently, and a trim woman in white sweats walked briskly past us. Ava slipped back into business mode.

"Okay, well, I'll leave you to it, then," she said. "Have, uhh, have fun."

I nodded.

"Sounds good. Hey, do you guys have a safe?"

She paused.

"For valuables? Each room has a safe in the closet. You program the lock yourself."

"Cool," I said. "No, like a big safe?"

Ava looked confused, and her wariness returned. "Do you need something safeguarded? We can hold it behind the front desk. Security guaranteed."

"Nah. It's okay."

She started to go, paused.

"You sure? Not a problem."

I shook my head.

"Okay," she said.

I could see her trying to suggest a solution for a problem she couldn't identify, the helpfulness drilled into her.

"The only big safe we have that is accessible to guests is our Vice Safe, and that doesn't have a lock."

"What's a Vice Safe?" I asked.

But now she was already moving back up the thick carpet, away from me, fast and silent.

"You'll find out at Welcoming," she said.

I padded around the hallway for a second. What was a Vice Safe? I'd find out at Welcoming. When I stepped near the smoked-glass doors, they slid open silently. The spa entrance was shallow and quiet and taupe. White towels, each one rolled into a perfect cylinder, were stacked in baskets next to the door. Smaller baskets held flawless green apples. There were water bottles everywhere, both chilled and room temp. A counter stood in the middle of the room with a small bell on top. Behind it was a slate wall with daily services written in different colors of chalk, like ice-cream flavors. Tropical sugar scrubs. Sevruga caviar facials. Something with cranberry essence. Off to one side was a list of "Today's Steams": eucalyptus, rosewater, espresso. What the hell was espresso steam? Would that be good for you? I thought about going back to the lobby to ask Ava. Once, in LA with Kelly, we'd gone to some hipster beer bar, and there was a big slate behind the bar with all of the place's guest taps listed on it. Next to the list, someone had drawn a picture of a gnome, like your run-of-the-mill garden gnome, and above the gnome, a pink chalk dialogue bubble that said, "Tried a gnome yet?" So when our waitress came over, she was stunning and petite and checked-out, in the way that beautiful people can be, especially when they're waiting to hear from their agent about the callback or whatever, and who am I to judge anyway? But anyway she comes over, and I'm trying to flirt a little because it'll be fun to joke about it with Kelly later, but also I'm genuinely confused, so I point to the drawing of the gnome and say, "Hey, what's a gnome?" And she thinks for a second, goes and checks with the bartender, and then comes back and says, "It's a mythical creature, sort of like a dwarf."

So, yeah. I figured Ava would have a better explanation of what espresso steam entailed, but then I decided to let it remain a mystery, at least for the time being. I don't need to know everything.

When I got back to the Birch—it might just have been "Birch"—
Jimmer was eating a fruit plate and watching SportsCenter. The
room was about the size of my apartment, with a long entryway, a
sitting room, a large master bedroom, and a gigantic bathroom. The
bathroom had a soaking tub like a lap pool and a showerhead with
settings for "deluge," "mist," and "pummel," the latter of which you
could use to strip paint. The sinks were accessorized with soap from
Singapore and tubes of pink Hudson Valley lotions and these rough
little pumice stones from Maui.

This Birch was better than the Becket Birches. This was a wellness
source I could get behind.

"You're on the couch, my friend," said Jimmer, which was fine
with me because it was a really nice couch, and it pulled out. I
suppose we could have called for a cot, and I half wanted to, because
it would probably be the coolest cot I'd ever seen, but I didn't push it.

"Jimmer," I said, sitting down next to him and spearing a piece of
cantaloupe with a knife. "This is badass."

He didn't take his eyes from the screen. Around the fruit plate
were various electronics: a tablet, two phones, a laptop.

"Can I, uh, contribute?" I asked, hoping my tone would convey
the complicated sincerity of the offer.

Jimmer waved it off.

"Don't worry about it."

I looked around the room. It was pretty gorgeous. Blacks and
neutrals. Exposed wood. Two flat screens that I could see. A bouquet
of flowers on the desk and a bowl of fruit on the coffee table. I felt

slightly destabilized, like you might feel if you got onto the wrong chairlift and had a few minutes to contemplate all the black diamonds between you and the lodge.

"Jimmer, this must cost a fortune."

He shrugged.

"I think so. We have it for the week. But, see, we don't pay a fortune for it."

"Why don't we pay a fortune for it?" I asked, cautious about the "we."

"We don't pay a fortune for it because they know I'll stay here more than once. And I'll tell my friends—my tech friends—and they'll stay here more than once. So the rate we get is about half of the rack rate, and that gets billed to the LLC anyway. Business expense, tax write-off. Not a whole lot more than your standard Four Seasons."

I tried to follow along.

"Business expense?"

"There are some kids at MIT doing neat stuff with nanotech. You have to see it to believe it. So I'll go see it. And then I'm going to speak at some dinner they're organizing. Pick up a small honorarium. Flight was on miles. If we invest, this whole trip will probably net positive."

He searched through the fruit plate for remaining honeydew and, not finding any, took a grape.

"It's a weird thing about wealth," he said. "The more of it you have, the less you sort of need it."

I nodded. SportsCenter went to commercial.

I was finding it hard not to be jealous of him, of his distraction and forward focus, his ease with this sort of life. So I tried to join him in it.

"Sment," I said. I'd gotten good results with that one before.

Jimmer confirmed that the SportsCenter he was about to watch was a repeat of the one that had just concluded, and put the TV on mute.

"Yeah," he said. "Sment. Wild."

"So, like, how'd you come up with that?"

Jimmer shrugged like it was a story he told a lot.

"Started at Caltech. We were doing some research on a DARPA grant, looking at mammalian olfactory receptors and their connection to memory and cognitive function. We began to try and emulate what people were doing with sound and visuals."

I nodded as though I understood.

"The initial applications were weaponized," he said, ducking his head back toward the fruit plate.

"Weaponized smells?" I asked. "Like, uh, what?" The answer seemed obvious, so I said it. "Farts?"

Jimmer grinned at the fruit.

"That is, in fact, where our research started. Not farts, but sulfur, other unsettling odors. Depressing odors. Stuff they might use offensively, or as part of a psychological campaign."

"What's a depressing odor?"

Jimmer shrugged.

"The data suggests asphalt. Industrial cleaner, like you smell in offices. Dead skin cells. Some people smell depressing. Unsanitary deep-fryers, although research is mixed on those. For certain subjects, the smell of an unsanitary deep-fryer works on a whole other level. Pizza has a surprising Q score. Imagine being confined for some period of time, and the only thing you can smell is pizza, but you can't have any. You'd go nuts. Seriously. You should see the chimpanzees. Or imagine you're on a battlefield, and all you smell is pizza, and then the pizza smell turns to bad eggs, and then back to pizza, and then back to bad eggs. Right? You might just want to call it a day."

"So, what?" I asked, nodding. "You pump these smells in over the Internet and depress your enemy to death?"

"Well," said Jimmer. "We don't do that, but certain arms of the government might. You need to have the right sort of receptors on the host device. Like, your laptop has speakers, you can hear music. But that tech will follow pretty fast once we get the application right. Future laptops, tablets, phones, cars, planes, they'll all have these little nodes that emit scent. We call them 'Petals,' of course. That's trademarked."

I started to frown, because I felt like I'd identified a flaw in that logic, but then reined it in since probably a hundred really smart people had already mentioned it, and it had been addressed. In that light, I reworded my query.

"So, is this just a military thing?"

Jimmer shook his head, the softball right in his PR wheelhouse.

"That's the really interesting thing. So, when we first started, we thought military, covert ops, detention centers. And that's where the funding was initially—Guantanamo-type places. But then we started to see some really interesting overlaps with cognitive thinking and modern human bandwidth. I mean, the associations between olfactory stimuli and cognitive functions like memory and reason and desire are pretty well documented. But our research suggested a more profound link. Like, when I was young, I always wanted to be cremated, right? As a logical proposition, any environmentally conscious person can't justify taking up a plot of land for the foreseeable future just for a grave, right? They're not making more land, and they are making more people. It won't work. So I was like, cremate me and spread my ashes fifty percent around the Lions Gate at Tanglewood, twenty-five percent at the old Boston Garden, twenty percent on the cliffs of Big Sur, and five percent in the Stanford women's soccer locker room. Pretty standard stuff, right? But our research was interesting. Turns out, when people imagine their own deaths they opt for cremation, but when you ask their survivors what the survivors would choose for the deceased, cremation or burial, the question causes all sorts of anxiety. And the anxiety isn't around the idea of a loved one's death. We control for that. The anxiety for the survivors is about being able to locate the deceased, physically, mentally, emotionally. The benefit of a physical memorial, like a grave, is that it frees the survivors from having to devote cognitive space to the memory of the departed. If you know where to find someone, then you're free to lose them. If we know Uncle Walt is buried back in Queens, you know, we can go about our lives, function better, not worry about having to remember him. Right? His grave isn't going anywhere."

I nodded along. Jimmer was cruising.

"Right. So what we found is that when we could isolate and replicate certain scents, the subjects for whom these scents represented certain triggers were able to in effect store their associations in digital form, let them go, know they were safe, and free up huge amounts of cognitive space. Like, they would have a file on their computer where they could store gigabytes of their childhood, their parents, their travels, their great loves and triumphs and heartbreaks. Like an online photo album, except that the olfactory associations just blow the doors off the visual ones. You know, you see a picture, and you see the picture. But the smell of your dead mom's apple pie comes wafting into the room, or your grandfather's after-shave, and you are fucking bawling. And you know where to find it, whenever you want. No need to carry it around."

"Wow," I said. "Shit is nuts."

Jimmer reached for the remote.

"I know," he said. "Cool, right?"

"What happens if your computer dies?"

Jimmer paused.

"Like, what?" he said. "Like the hard drive is fried?"

"Sure," I said. "Yeah."

"Well, there's the cloud, and there are the Sment servers. But, yeah, I guess you could be theoretically fucked if you don't back up. Might be awesome, though. You might have to start fresh, revert to IRL stimuli."

"Well," I said. "That's not the worst thing in the world."

Jimmer nodded. "Seriously, pal. You should see the folks for whom we've itemized trigger scents. They're like zephyrs. They move through life with no friction. They know where the shit is if they need it."

I leaned back on the couch. Jimmer's forward focus was making me feel like I'd wasted my life.

"So, is there like a library of the world's smells? Do I have a smell?"

Jimmer laughed.

"You certainly do have a smell, but yeah, we're in the process of smell-mining. I mean, there are certain basic elements—we call them 'smelements,' trademarked—that once you get them, you can combine to replicate pretty closely any other scent. But you know how it is, right? The thing sort of hinges on having the exact match—if you walk in a room and there's a smell that's almost like your baby blanket, it doesn't do anything. Almost doesn't cut it. So there are personalizing applications that we're working on."

He stood up.

"Speaking of which, I have a couple of e-mails I need to deal with. You good out here?"

I stood up as well.

"Yeah, sure."

Jimmer collected his electronics.

"Great."

He looked up at me.

"It's really great to see you. Brings back memories."

He paused, thought for a second.

"Like, actual memories."

I regretted all that nascent jealousy in a second.

"You too, buddy," I said. We hugged, briefly but enough.

"It's really good of you to come all the way out here to help with Chick," I said. "Kid's kind of a mess."

Jimmer looked away and chuckled.

"I hear."

"I have a plan, though," I said. "To straighten him out."

Jimmer nodded.

"Good to hear," he said, extending a hand to me. "Whatever I can do to help."

"All right, pal," I said, slapping him five. "Smell you later."

The joke went unacknowledged. Jimmer went into the master and slid the heavy doors closed. I pushed the coffee table away and folded out the couch bed that was wider and had better sheets than my bed in Boston. I stripped down to my shorts and slid under the covers. The gang was all assembled. We had until Monday to put things in place. I would dream the architecture of a solution, a way it would all work out.

In the morning I brushed and picked my teeth with an obsidian courtesy toothbrush and scalded myself under the torrential showerhead. I used the courtesy lavender-thyme shampoo and conditioner and the courtesy oatmeal body scrub. I shaved and rubbed pink courtesy Rhinebeck lotion onto my skin. I padded around in a thick robe and thick slippers and felt moisturized in the best ways.

At 7:45, the double doors of the master bedroom were still closed. I eased them apart a hands-width and looked in on a bed the diameter of which exceeded my view. Jimmer lay surrounded by pillows, a mask over his eyes, a meringue of duvet enveloping his lower half.

"Yo," I said.

He lifted his head slightly, did not remove the mask.

"We have to be at Welcoming in fifteen minutes."

Jimmer put his head back down and pulled the duvet cover up to his chin. "I don't have to do anything I don't want to do."

Could that be true? It sounded sort of revolutionary.

All I had to wear were my work clothes from Friday, a blue pinstripe suit and a smelly white shirt, but in the hall closet I found two sets of Head-Connect sweat clothes, one in earthen brown and one in vanilla. Pants, shorts, pullovers, and T-shirts, each emblazoned with a stylized evergreen. One set fit me nearly perfectly. On the floor of the closet were two pairs of bespoke cross-trainers, each stuffed with monogrammed socks. All that from a palm print?

I suited up and headed out.

I passed through the lobby and cut across the rotary to the Fleur-de-Lys mansion proper. The morning sky was pale and cold, but the sweatshirt was thicker than it seemed and had a cavernous hood. The material felt like a sort of elfin technology, magical, like those innocuous little flatbreads that sustained Frodo et al. on the march to Mordor. Eight or nine other people were crossing to the main building, all hooded against the chill, our outfits suggesting the start of some sort of conclave.

In the entryway of the main building, a big man with olive skin stood behind a wheeled cart, handing out coffee and juice. I took both. We were a baker's dozen in all, four corporate types yawning and slouching, three slender Asian men whispering in Cantonese, a minor movie star recently busted for drunk driving, what looked like a well-heeled mother-daughter pair, the luminous Vishy Shetty, an assistant who looked like a non–hi def version of Vishy Shetty, and me.

Ava Winston stood inconspicuously off to the side, a tablet under her arm. I felt bad about sort of lying to her, and caught her eye in an attempt to incept some sort of bonhomie. She was too busy taking attendance to care.

"Jimmer?" she mouthed at me, gesturing subtly around the room.

I shrugged, folded my hands to the side of my face.

Ava frowned and made a note on her tablet.

The entry foyer of the mansion was open and octagonal and seemed faithfully restored, at least based on the pictures we'd seen so long ago in Florence Banish's files. It rose straight up to a rotunda and had acoustics so refined that the smallest bell, rung to announce guests or mealtimes, carried throughout the mansion. Here was the hallway to the back ballroom. There was the landing on which Guy Van Nest stood with his rifle. We'd walked in the door through which the rhino had exited. Above us was a massive chandelier, environmentally retrofitted.

At eight sharp, the man behind the juice bar strode to the center of the marble floor. He was wide but smooth, his movements fluid like Shamu. He raised his hands to the sky.

"I am present and I am connected," he said in a baritone loud enough to ripple the coffee in our cups.

We all looked at him. Was this a coup? Vishy Shetty turned the corners of her mouth down and bent toward her assistant.

The man lowered his hands to us and smiled. His teeth were perfect.

"Welcome, all, to Head-Connect. We are present. We are connected."

He nodded to us. We nodded back, because what were we supposed to do?

"How is your coffee?" he asked. He had an accent I couldn't place. Something world-weary but generous.

We nodded again, some people offering more verbal assurances.

"I am glad," the man said. "I am also glad that it is the last coffee you will have during your stay here."

Fewer verbal assurances.

"I am Arvindo Blanc, Welcoming-Coordinator here at Head-Connect. What we do now will set the metrics, lay the foundation, and plot the blueprint for the rest of your time with us."

He raised his right hand and extended his pointer.

"And the rest of your life."

There was a murmur of appreciation for the dramatics, so flawlessly executed. Vishy Shetty took out her cell phone.

"Enjoy this last bit of caffeine. This last 'fix.' You won't need it anymore. No more fixing. Nothing to fix. A cycle of dependence is a thing of your past. In a moment, you will begin your Welcoming, which will include a full physical and cognitive audit.

The process is, of course, entirely voluntary, but we feel strongly that the success of your life-matrix depends on your candid and honest participation."

He drew the last word out to its full five syllables.

He gestured to doors at the sides of the foyer.

"Ladies will pass through to my left and gentlemen to my right. First, though, we ask our guests for a small deposit."

He looked around the room, a smile on his face. Then he waved his hands reassuringly.

"No, no money. Put your wallets away. Money is a four-letter word now. We ask only for a deposit of vice, hindrances, negative energy. We will hold these items for you in our Vice Safe. There they will remain throughout your stay here at Head-Connect, and upon checkout, you can choose to pick them up." He smiled even more widely. "Or leave them behind."

He swept his arms theatrically and heretofore invisible staffers opened a side door onto a small room. Within it, I could see a desk, a chair, and the large hinged door of a safe.

There was some mild snickering from the assembly. Arvindo Blanc smiled indulgently.

"Our Vice Safe has been in residence for over one hundred years here at Fleur-de-Lys," Arvindo Blanc said. "It has held a century of secrets."

He stepped aside dramatically.

"At your leisure."

We all froze for a moment, not sure what to do, milking our last coffee for the grounds. Inside the room, small cards—the sort that might identify seating arrangements at a wedding—were fanned out on the desk, near an ornate pen.

Nobody moved.

"You want us to write down our vices on cards?" said one of the corporate types, a tall man with an executive's paunch. "And then leave them in the safe?"

Arvindo Blanc smiled benevolently.

"Leave them atop the Vice Safe. I will deposit them. They will be deposited."

"How do we know you won't use them against us in some way?"

"To the contrary. You must know we will," said Blanc. "Letting go is an essential pre-step of our process here at Head-Connect."

Ava Winston piped in from across the room.

"There are, of course, significant financial and legal protections ensuring the confidentiality of Welcoming information, and indeed all information relating to our guests' time here at Head-Connect."

Blanc nodded, then walked into the side room and lifted one card up, like a host, and touched it to his forehead. He closed his eyes and appeared, momentarily, to be entirely still. Then he opened his eyes, lowered the card, and held it out toward the safe, letting it drop like a leaf onto the solid top.

"And so," he said. "We are present and we are connected."

He stepped back into the foyer and stood along the wall, a surfer Buddha. Totoro.

The process was simple enough. You entered the room, sat at the pale wood desk, wrote your vices on a card, put that in an envelope, and left it in a wooden box on top of the safe.

The minor movie star went first, entered the small room, sat with the pen and note card, shrugged, and wrote for what had to be five minutes. Apparently he was committed. The corporate types crowded in next, together. I could hear murmurs about mission statements, about working to live, about creating a culture that actualized. Bullshit like that.

Mother and daughter followed. They went in together, but sat with the cards one at a time, and I could see the daughter staring at her mother when she wrote.

Vishy Shetty was next, gliding with her assistant across the vestibule. At the last second, Vishy Shetty gestured, a look, a slight raise of a forebearing finger, for her assistant to wait outside. The assistant blinked at her as though waiting for a command prompt and stood in the open doorway, blocking our view of Vishy Shetty. Despite the assistant's efforts, I could see through the crook in her arm as Vishy Shetty slid something from her sweatshirt pouch into an envelope, wrote something on the accompanying card, and deposited them both on top of the safe. The assistant caught me spying and gave me a look like she'd cut me.

The Asian cohort went next. They'd been quiet in the foyer, but once they got into the little salon with the safe, we could hear all sorts of chatter. It appeared they were collaborating on a statement but couldn't decide who would do the drafting. When they came back out, two were frowning and one smiling widely.

I stepped over to the small room and looked back at Arvindo Blanc.

"Don't wait up," I said. Gave him a grin.

He just blinked at me, a long languorous blink. I looked around the foyer, but everyone else was gone except for the minor movie star, who clenched a fist in solidarity before following Ava Winston off to Welcoming,

I entered the room.

The safe was real, just as Chick had said. About 5 feet tall and at least 3 feet across, 4-inch walls of gray steel on thick clawed feet. The words "Cary Safe Co." were inscribed on its heavy front. I took out a note card and thought about my vices. Sloth. Gluttony. Avarice. How many more were there? Loyalty. Hah. What did people say when asked in job interviews for their biggest flaws? I took the pen and wrote *I tend to take on too much responsibility* on the notecard. I folded it into an envelope and dropped it into the wooden box. Arvindo Blanc was still out in the foyer, but he had his back to me and everybody else had left. Something that Ava'd said the night before came back, and I tried to turn the great safe's front handle toward the floor.

The handle didn't budge.

I tried turning it up. Still nothing.

This was a problem. A locked safe solved nothing, confirmed nothing.

I gave the handle a final tug.

The heavy door swung open with only token resistance.

I took a quick look out to confirm that nobody was watching, and then rifled the safe.

It had one central compartment, with notches along the inside edges for what must once have been shelves. There were no shelves in it now. Instead, on the bottom, there was a stack of wooden boxes, identical to the one above, each full of sealed envelopes. Here for the taking, the vices of the one-percent, or at least the ones they felt comfortable acknowledging. How boring would those be?

I felt the interior walls to confirm that there were no hidden drawers, and if there were, they remained hidden.

That was it.

I closed the door, got up, and returned to the foyer. Arvindo Blanc smiled at me and gestured toward the morning rays flooding through the rotunda.

"Brother sun is here," he said. "But he is always here."

I gave him the thumbs up and walked through my *M* door. Whatever it takes, pal. I suppose I should have felt disappointed. We'd found the safe, and it was empty. But I didn't, not at all. I felt relieved, relaxed, a load off my back. Jimmer was still asleep, probably, and Unsie was getting ready for work, and Chick was in a cold lockup up at the Berkshire House of Correction until Monday, but he was okay. There were no ghosts here at Fleur-de-Lys, nothing to chase except a better self.

I felt ready to enjoy a good workout, a biomass analysis, and a sea-cucumber colonic, if that's what the day held in store for me. And if not, that was fine too.

❧

Kelly and I met in law school in Washington, D.C. She was the daughter of lawyers and seemed to know what she was getting into. I was the son of teachers and took the LSAT because my college roommates were taking it. In first-year legal theory class, Kelly and I had been in a study group together, and I'd made her laugh by confusing the con law theorist Ronald Dworkin with one of the dwarves who accompanies Bilbo Baggins to the Lonely Mountain. She thought I was kidding.

Kelly was from California, a place I'd been only once before, but which had nonetheless shaped my identity growing up. I was a Magic Johnson fan, and Massachusetts, of course, was Celtics territory. I grew up at the tail end of the Big Three era, Bird, McHale and Parish. Magic's struggles in the early '80s playoffs—the Tragic Johnson days—were over by the time I started following him, and even with Jordan ascendant, Earvin Johnson was my man. Like Magic, I wasn't a great shooter, and my dribble was a little high, but I could see the court. Inglewood, the Fabulous Forum, Pat Riley's hair, the celebrities in the crowd—that was where I belonged.

I caught a lot of shit from the CYC kids, from old George Harvey, from pretty much anyone who found out there was a Lakers fan in their midst.

"Get your ass on the block," George Harvey would yell at me, his testicles swinging in his sweats, whenever I tried to bring the ball up court.

"None of that razzle-dazzle shit," he'd say when I'd throw a behind-the-back pass.

I practiced those passes for hours, and after Magic announced his HIV diagnosis, I practiced them even more.

And then along came Kelly, raised in Sherman Oaks, schooled at UCLA, knew her way around an earthquake and a seven-lane highway.

"What are you doing in the Northeast?" I'd asked her, as if maybe she'd just gotten lost.

She'd shrugged, said something about wanting to see the Old Country, the Atlantic, the vertical cities along the coast. She wanted a history that didn't exist out west. Twist my arm, right? When I got the job in Boston, Cradle of the Revolution, I asked her to come with me and she said yes. I showed her Plymouth and Salem and the Old North Church. We ate lobster and sat in traffic on the Cape, ate cannoli and stood in crowds in the North End. And then the Red Sox and the Bruins and the Pats kept winning, and the autumns did their thing, hot cider and pumpkins and hills that looked like piles of Skittles. I bought her a scarf, told her all my stories. We started weekending in the Berkshires. I figured we had her. I figured that the hooks were set, that, like the rest of us, she was here for the duration.

After she left, I had a dream about Magic Johnson. In the dream, it was early 1992, I was something like eight years old, and Magic had just gone on *Arsenio* to talk about his HIV. Some network guys decided that they would cast Magic in a remake of the *Captain America* TV series, but nobody had thought to adjust the wardrobe to fit a 6'8" guy instead of the regular-sized guy who'd previously played the role. So Magic Johnson is running around on a train loaded with explosives, battling bad guys, in a super tight red, white, and blue bodysuit that rides way up at his ankles and wrists. He's got the hood on, with the little gold wings on the sides, and whenever it's time for him to say a line, he just disregards the script entirely and looks at the camera and flashes that huge smile he has and says, "Man, I'm Captain America Man." And the studio audience roars anyway.

❧

At Welcoming, a squadron of Head-Connect techs weighed us and pinched us and quizzed us about our diet and work life. My tech's name was Tudd. Like Judd but with a *T*. Tudd was my age, maybe, it was hard to tell, with thin blond hair and ripped arms sticking out of a tight polo shirt. He used instruments that looked like pliers on my stomach. He asked me how much fish I ate and whether it was farmed or line-caught. He made me do math in my head. He asked me if I spoke French. He asked me how far I jogged and at what pace. He asked me to touch my toes, stand on one foot, and jump straight up in the air. In high school I could dunk. I told Tudd that, and he seemed skeptical.

"It's hard to stay in shape when you're living a sedentary lifestyle," he said. He said that in the first forty-five seconds of our session.

Tudd asked me how long I was staying at Head-Connect. I said the weekend. He seemed concerned.

"You could use a month," he said. "At least."

"People stay here for a month?"

He nodded.

"Some people live here. We have residents."

I must have looked skeptical, because then he said, "It's also a state of mind."

Tudd walked me through the gym, open floor plan, all the resistance machines, gleaming chrome and padded benches. A couple of dozen people were in there, moving from machine to machine, some guests but some staff too, differentiated by how well their workout clothes fit and how casually they approached the machinery. I wanted to find a bench press, do some Paleolithic grunting.

"No free weights," Tudd said. "We promote a holistic approach. Resistance from within, overcome from within."

"But what if I don't put up much resistance?" I asked.

Tudd looked me over.

"You are putting up a lot of resistance already, Mr. Johansson."

I wasn't sure if that was a slam or a come-on or some sort of spa wisdom, so I just rolled with it.

Tudd took me through twelve machines, and on each one I felt like I could have tripled the resistance he was recommending, and at the end of the twelve I could barely remember my name.

"So this will be your routine for the week," Tudd said. "Once in the morning, once in the afternoon, with aerobics and Bikram yoga and meditation in the middle."

I was clutching at a cup of water.

"That is from a spring in Vermont," Tudd said. "They also make our cheese. And our outdoor attire."

"Who does?" I asked.

"Vermont," he said.

He walked me over to the services desk and handed me off to a small, attractive African-American woman.

"He should have the salt rub," Tudd said, and the African-American woman nodded and pecked at a tablet.

"And here is your personalized menu," Tudd said, handing me a piece of paper folded into thirds. My hands were sweaty and shaking.

"Don't worry about it," Tudd said, taking the paper back. "I've uploaded it already. You can find it on any of our monitors, under guest services. Have a good massage and I will check back with you in a bit."

He clapped me on the shoulder. His hand felt like wood.

"Good Welcoming."

I nodded. I wasn't sure if we were supposed to be pals now. Hard to be pals with a guy who has just kneaded your liver.

I was sort of looking forward to the massage, because I was sore as shit, but also because, you know, all bets are off with a massage, right? Probably not, but I always wondered about that. Then the pretty African-American woman passed me off to a rash-looking and substantially older Italian man named Fulvio who had me lie down naked on hot wood slats while he played trance music and spread this sticky mix of salt, nettles, and Vaseline all over me. He had hands like pliers.

"Do you have a cat?" Fulvio asked me as he ground the salt-nettle mix into my upper thighs.

I said no.

"A salt rub is like being licked head to toe by a giant cat," he said. "Like a panther. A panther bath."

I stayed silent. I was pretty sure he was breaching protocol.

Fulvio rubbed and flexed and squeezed me so hard that I felt like a baseball glove. He bundled my junk up into a towel and shoved it brusquely away while working on my hip sockets. He put really hot rocks on my spine and the backs of my knees. I wanted to say something, or cry, but you can't, can you? It felt like that would be surrendering. Plus, Fulvio kept saying, "Is good, no?" and once I got into the habit of agreeing I couldn't stop. After an hour, a sponge bath, and several realigned vertebrae, he helped me up from the table. I felt woozy.

"Now," he said. "Eucalyptus steam and plenty of water today. We removed a great number of toxins from your system."

He sort of hugged me into a standing position and took me by the arm. I felt like I might collapse. What if the toxins were the only thing holding me together?

Fulvio gave me a thick white robe and led me through a short hallway to the showers.

The men's clubhouse was lined with gleaming oak lockers and mirrored vanities. A few other guests were in there, in various stages of undress, ruddy cheeks and limp appendages, but still seemingly more comfortable with their bodies than I was. I wondered how long it'd been since their Welcoming. Elixirs crowded the sinks, oils and hair creams and mouthwash. I washed my mouth out with a green liquid that tasted like parsley. I stripped down to a towel and put my robe and sweat clothes into an open locker. I showered with more oatmeal scrub. I checked my eyes—were they less bloodshot? Was my skin more resilient? Maybe.

The caldaria were accessible via a tiled corridor down a short flight of stairs at the back of the showers, and walking through it I got the sense that I was underground, that perhaps the corridor linked the new Head-Connect wings with the older Fleur-de-Lys mansion. I climbed up an equal number of steps at the end of the corridor and emerged in a small hallway with doors on either side. The doors were glass and heavy and behind them nothing was visible but steam. Each one had a description written on a slate by the entrance. Peering in, I sensed that there were other people around. Hard to see, but I could feel them, sort of. Steam rooms made me a little uneasy. You could never be sure what was going on in them. When I got to the entrance to the eucalyptus room, I grabbed another towel and kept walking.

The hallway bent around to the left, and after about 10 yards I passed a slate advising that I was now in a mixed-gender area and should be clothed accordingly. The hall merged into a room about half the size of a gymnasium, a wide oval with windows that curved out onto the back lawn of Fleur-de-Lys, the apple orchards and old dirt roads that bisected the woods. The effect was of a ballroom, or the bridge of a starship. Along the edges of the room were statues, eunuchs and satyrs and nymphs and stuff, probably scavenged from the woods when Head-Connect moved in. The lighting was subdued, and in the center of the room were two bubbling whirlpools, each around 12 feet across. Between them was a rectangular pool, grave-like in size, which was so cold that when I dipped my toe in I almost squealed. The lights from these three pools played around on the low ceiling of the room, sliding and resolving, as if that were the surface and the room itself was underwater.

My towels were warm and soft, and I sat on a bench near the windows for a moment. I was alone. There was no sound except for the bubbling of the pools. The room felt tranquil, almost sacred, the innermost boiler of the whole enterprise, powering the lights and ovens and lesser cores of the system with a steady flow of steam. Through the bank of windows, I could see a string of cross-country skiers vanish on the thin powder into the distant tree line. An arrow of geese, silent to me, flew north beneath the clouds. It would be nice to stay here for a year, I thought, get really healthy, impress Ava. Best Tudd in some competition. Go into that cold dip pool. Replace all my toxins with wheatgrass or mother's milk. I just had to invent something that everyone in the world would buy.

I stood up to return to the lockers, slightly ashamed to have been gifted with such luxury and to want more of it. I commiserated with a bust of Apollo and turned back toward the passageway.

And there, in a wall alcove by the side of the corridor, was the horn of the great beast Guy Van Nest had shot in the woods.

It stood point up, a polished black spike, fastened to a marble base and lit from above. I looked around the bath room. There were other alcoves, with other displays—a cricket bat, a timepiece, a taxidermy egret by the far wall. At least I hoped it was taxidermy. Egrets were sneaky fuckers. None of them had labels, but I had no doubt that this was the horn from the safe, the horn of the rhino. You ever catch a bat in your house, and it looks exactly like a bat? Like, the moment you see it, you know that you have always known just what a bat would look like? The horn was that way. There was no mistaking. It looked brutal, potent, prehistoric. My testosterone rose a couple of clicks just looking at it.

Guy Van Nest, I thought. Damn, kid.

❧

The Head-Connect dining room was in the main building, in a high-ceilinged wing opposite where we'd done our Welcoming. There were only eight tables, each big enough to seat four people, and guests dined in forty-five minute shifts. The dining room staff, which was dressed in a sort of elegant casual, circled solicitously through the area. The clattering from the open kitchen was so rhythmic that it might have been recorded.

I rushed in during the 11:30 seating. My own seating was not for another twenty minutes, but I had to tell Jimmer what I'd seen. The dining room was nearly empty. A couple of silverbacks in gray sweatsuits sat in the corner eating wedges of papaya like corn on the cob. They looked like producers. A large woman was consulting what might've been a treaty. Jimmer was lingering at a small four-top across the room with Vishy Shetty and her assistant. When I tried to cross to him, a Head-Connect staff member stepped up to thwart me.

"Mr. Johansson, sir," she said, another helper of indeterminate age and indeterminate motive. "We aren't expecting you yet. Sustenance is highly individualized, and the kitchen has not prepped for you. Can I offer you a smoothie while you wait?"

I shrugged her off.

"Not eating." I said. "Just here to talk."

She looked momentarily taken aback, as if I were there to talk to her. Jimmer turned in his seat as I crossed, and the helper took the opportunity to vanish.

"My man," he said, getting up to meet me with a slap and a half-hug. "Sit. Sup."

He gestured to the table where Vishy Shetty and her assistant smiled high-caliber smiles. Vishy Shetty had enormous sunglasses propped on her hair and was spearing a blueberry in a fruit cup, eating daintily, almost guiltily. Her assistant palmed an iPhone.

"This is Miriam and her sister Joanne. They're from Sydney," he said. "Not really, but that's the cover we've all agreed to acknowledge. Cool?"

I shrugged. Neither Vishy Shetty nor her assistant acknowledged it.

"Hey," I said to Jimmer. "Can I speak with you for a minute?"

Jimmer sat back down.

"Of course," he said. "Sup?"

He smiled at his little wordplay.

"Privately, I mean." I looked at Vishy Shetty and her assistant. "No offense."

Their eyes flickered for an instant, in a way that suggested it would be nearly impossible for me to offend them. They existed beyond a membrane. Vishy Shetty's eyes were so big that she was hard to look at. You know how it is with really beautiful women, like they're so beautiful that when you look at them, you can't think straight? Like that. I couldn't look at Vishy Shetty, and I could barely look at her assistant.

Jimmer seemed immune. Maybe he was beyond the membrane as well.

"Sure," he said. "Let me just finish my espresso here, and this lovely piece of hake."

He moved his fork like a wand over a flaky filet and set it aside. The filet was untouched. The espresso he finished.

"Delicious," he said.

"How'd you get that?" I asked, momentarily distracted by the caffeine. "Dude said there was no coffee."

Jimmer looked over the room.

"I'm running this bitch. That's my operating agreement."

He stood up.

"They just try and discourage you from asking. Pardon me, ladies," he said, winking to Vishy Shetty and her assistant. "I'll see you later today, I hope."

Vishy Shetty flashed what appeared to be a genuine smile, brief and demure. Her assistant refocused on the iPhone.

"Do you know who that is?" Jimmer asked when we were out of earshot.

I nodded, even though at that point I didn't really know. She was somebody. That much was clear.

"Have you seen those pics?"

On that one, I shook my head no. We stepped outside of the main house and into the cold midday sun. The sky looked like snow.

"Listen, Jimmer," I said, checking the immediate vicinity for helpers. We were clear. "You know what's going on with Chick, right? Unsie told you?"

Jimmer stamped at the pea-stoned drive and put his sunglasses on.

"A little. Not much, actually."

"You know about the rhino, though, right? That's why we're here?"

Jimmer stopped stamping and looked up at me. He smiled.

"Well, that's why you're here."

"What do you mean?"

"What do you mean, 'what do you mean'?" Jimmer said, pointing with his chin. "Look, look at this luxurious place. Look at these beautiful people around us. Look, behind those doors are some of the finest spa services available to mankind."

"The rhino, Jimmer. He's been searching for it since forever."

Jimmer turned back to me and took his sunglasses off. He seemed embarrassed to be dealing with this conversation, to be dipping back into the muck.

"The rhino," he snorted. "Please. I get that there is this quest, which I might find ridiculous. I love the guy, love him to death. But I don't, like, own a rhino farm yet. I can't deliver whatever it is he's chasing. And what do you think would happen if I could?"

He bent at the waist and stamped his feet, then straightened up again.

"I don't think I have the power to change whatever path he's on. I can support him and invite him to join me on my path. I can encourage him to make good choices. I can also walk away. That's it. Those are the limits of my powers."

He paused.

"Yours too, you know."

"But then what did you come all this way for, if you're not here to help him?"

"Who says I came to help him, Pete?" he said, a slight inflection on "him."

Now it was my turn to be embarrassed, if I was reading him right. I assumed I was.

"Well, look, I appreciate that. I appreciate that you came here to help me out. I'm doing okay, and the best way that you can help me is to help me help Chick."

Jimmer looked skeptical.

"Okay," he said. "Let's just play that out. I mean, we're already here, and as you correctly noted, that's not accidental. You look around, you do your little investigation, and then what?"

I accepted the condescension as the price of his time. Condescension I could handle. Besides, I had something to show him.

"Now we're getting somewhere," I said, heading toward the spa. "First, come with me."

"She's pretty, right?" Jimmer said as we semi-snuck back down the steam room corridor to the baths.

"Who?"

"Vishy Shetty."

"Uh, pretty isn't the word I'd use."

Looking at Vishy Shetty was like looking at the sun, she was so pretty.

"Smart too. She's made some bad choices, though," said Jimmer. "I think she's wounded."

"Oh, I see," I said. "You'll help her, but you won't help me?"

"You're not that pretty," he said.

We were in the baths. They were empty. Bubble shadows flickered on the white ceiling. Outside, a snow flurry was falling. I maneuvered Jimmer so that his back was to the rhino horn, sight lines clear, the alcove free from shadows. Optics were critical.

"Stop," I said. "Before you get too far along on this little Bollywood escapade, look at that."

I pointed behind him.

Jimmer turned, focused, stared. Crossed the baths and stood before it. The thing was black as coffee, part weapon and part crown.

"Wow," he said after a minute. "You win. That's badass."

"I know, right?" I said. "That's what he's after."

Jimmer looked appraisingly at it.

"Well, he's not going to get it."

I was quiet. That sounded a little more definitive a little more quickly than I had been prepared for him to be.

"Any ideas?" I asked.

"Ideas?"

"Yeah. I mean, I never even thought this thing existed. Chick was sure, though. He thought it was in the Vice Safe, but I guess they moved it down here."

"Look," Jimmer said. "Do you know how much this thing is worth?"

I shrugged. Jimmer ran the back side of the nail of his pointer finger from the horn's base to the tip of its spike.

"It's worth a shitload. Like mid-six figures shitload."

"Seriously?" I said. "Thing's a hundred years old."

"Yeah, that probably makes it more valuable. If Chickie screws around with this thing, he won't be looking at probation. You're talking grand larceny. I mean, there's the historical angle, the preservationist stuff, and whatever that's worth. But if Head-Connect is smart, they're valuing this thing by the gram."

I frowned.

"What do you mean?"

"For insurance purposes. Dudes believe these horns have magical properties. That's why the poaching is so bad. They think they can cure illness, restore your virility, that sort of stuff. They grind the things up and pop them like Alka-Seltzer."

Guy Van Nest, Gable's first holistic healer. Probably also explained why Head-Connect was fetishizing it down by the baths. At these prices, a little voodoo couldn't hurt.

"Goddamn, man," I said. "What are we going to tell Chickie?"

Jimmer snorted at me.

"Nice try," he said. "Look, you didn't think this thing existed, right?"

I nodded.

"So why not just let it continue to . . . not . . . exist?"

"You mean lie to him?"

Jimmer grimaced like I was a particularly disappointing child.

"You know what will happen. You can say you checked the safe and it was empty. Leave it at that. Maybe then he can let go of it, get himself straight."

We heard voices coming down the corridor from the steam rooms. The corporate types, exploring from the sound of it. I folded my arms and blew through my cheeks. Jimmer walked over to me.

"Dude," he said. "Do whatever you think you need to do."

He clapped me on the shoulder.

"Just, you know, consider the repercussions before you do it, okay?"

He checked his watch and wiggled his shoulders.

"I have a date with a yoga class. Loosen up the old chakras."

He headed for the corridor back to the spa.

"See you back at the room, okay?"

I nodded to him. He raised his eyebrows at me.

"Okay?" he said again.

"Okay," I said.

He smiled.

"Make good choices."

The corporate types emerged from the corridor, three men and a woman swaddled in white robes. The men were red-cheeked and damp, laughing. The woman trailed them, dry, a little slow, eyeing the hot tubs skeptically.

They nodded at us and fanned out across the baths, emitting various sounds of wonder. One of them approached the egret, regarded it closely, seemed to sniff at it. Jimmer took the opportunity to drift back out of the room.

"What's that?" said another, looking at the horn. "A tusk?"

They had circled back to the center of the room, around the hot tubs.

"This is what I'm talking about," said the third, a heavyset fellow in his fifties, probably. "A soak tub. None of that eucalyptus business."

"What's that?" the birdwatcher asked, standing at the edge of the cold dip pool.

"That's an ice plunge," said the heavyset dude. "They got one of these at the club down on Necker. You don't want none of that, unless you want your balls back up in your belly."

He laughed, and the other two men joined him. The woman hesitated for just a second, just long enough to compel the rest to acknowledge her. Then she laughed too, indulgent with a hint of derision, and the rest of them stopped.

It was time for lunch.

I wandered back up to the dining room. Six of the tables were filled. Some guests I recognized—the movie star, talking to himself, the Asian trio, the mother and daughter. The others seemed looser, more relaxed. At the entrance, Tudd appeared and put his hand on my shoulder.

"Welcome, Mr. Johansson, to Sustenance at Head-Connect."

He led me to an empty table. The utensils were silver. The linens were starched. A personalized menu lay on my place. My name was written across the top in some midcentury font. Beneath it was an abbreviated list of my vitals—age, height and weight, body mass, length of stay, a series of codes I couldn't decipher. On the back was a schedule of my workout times and a place for me to write in the elective activities I'd chosen.

"Jesus," I said.

"No grace here at Head-Connect," said Tudd. "We're nondenominational. We do, however, promote conscious eating. We find that even in sustenance, it is imperative to take purpose and proportionality into account."

I looked at the list again.

"I got to tell you, man. This is a depressing way to start lunch."

Tudd smiled.

"Exactly," he said. "But let me check with you again at the end of your stay, see then whether you're depressed."

He stood up.

"Now please excuse me. Should you have questions, just ask any helper. I will see you for your afternoon workout."

He smiled at me and left.

As soon as he'd cleared the dining room, a young woman brought beets, thick and bleeding on a white plate. Coral salt. A thimbleful of yak butter. I looked at the menu again. Lunch was three courses. The beets were followed by Kale-Smoke over Dorado, which sounded more like a Western than an entree, then sorbet with cilantro foam.

"Excuse me," I said to her as she set the plate down.

She was young, a kid. A healthy glow to her cheeks. There was something vaguely Canadian about her.

I picked up the menu. Under my name, in the list of abbreviations, I pointed to one of the numbers I didn't understand, an abbreviation that read ".382 bvo."

"What's this one?" I asked, and put my finger to it.

The young woman looked where I was pointing and squinted her eyes. Then she smiled meekly and begged off.

"Sorry," she said, shrugging. "I'm afraid I can't. Sorry."

"Is everything all right?" asked Ava Winston, who'd slipped in behind me.

I turned in my chair.

Ava nodded to the server, who excused herself. I motioned for Ava to sit.

"What's this number?" I asked Ava, pointing at it again.

She looked.

"I could tell you, but then I'd have to kill you," she said.

"You don't know, do you?"

She smiled.

"I do know."

"You don't."

"I do too, and if you're not careful I will tell you. What was it again?"

I showed her.

"Hmm," she said, wrinkling her nose. "That explains a lot."

She held that pose for a second, then laughed.

"Don't worry about it. We'll have it up by the end of the week."

I couldn't tell if this was bullshit or not.

"Dude, come on," I said, and she slapped her leg and laughed. She was a lot prettier than I remembered.

I cut into my beets.

"I hope these will help," I said.

She chuckled and looked at the plate.

"Nowhere to go but up," she said, and laughed a little more.

"Wow," I said, lifting my fork.

She calmed herself and looked around the dining room.

"I have to do the rounds," she said. "Everything good so far?"

I nodded, chewing. The beets were pretty great, actually.

"Where was Jimmer this morning?"

I swallowed.

"Jimmer's in his own world."

She nodded. "We get that a lot. How about you? How's Tudd treating you?"

"Dude is killing me."

She smiled.

"I assigned him especially for you, Pete. You'll thank me later."

It was nice talking to her. We had an old bond, a shared history, but this interaction felt independent of that. It felt natural, unfettered, modern. Would she be busting on me in this vaguely flirtatious way if I was a complete stranger? I liked to think so. This is what attractive, well-adjusted people do.

"Let me thank you tonight," I said. "Buy you a drink?"

Ava's eyes sparkled a little bit, but then she pursed her lips. "No alcohol on campus. And certainly no fraternizing with the guests."

"No alcohol?"

She shook her head.

"And no caffeine?"

She raised an eyebrow.

"Well, that one's negotiable. But generally speaking we limit that stuff. It's important to walk the walk, you know? Solidarity."

I showed her my menu again.

"Do you have one of these?"

She pointed to her head.

"Mine's all up here."

"Tell me something, Ava," I said, playing out the hand. "Are you, like, incredibly healthy?"

She snorted, endearingly.

"Well, I still have my weaknesses, Pete So Handsome. But let's focus on you."

She stood up to leave.

"So no on the drink, then?"

I clicked my teeth like she didn't know what she was missing.

"You're still that guy, aren't you?" she said. But she was smiling.

I gave her my best Han Solo.

"And then some."

Ava Winston shook her head, a kind of nonverbal "please." I was playing to my strength, frustrating but irresistible. Seemed to be getting it half right.

She sighed.

"Enjoy your lunch, Mr. Johansson."

She walked off to check in with another table. I didn't even try not to watch her.

I finished my lunch and checked my schedule. I had a couple of hours before my next date with Tudd and nothing on the calendar. The options were numerous: Nordic in the back woods, entry-level aikido, mindfulness meditation, a documentary on the Rarámuri Indians of Mexico, who could run for three days straight. I walked up the pebbled path to the guest wings, considering a nap.

It felt good to flirt with Ava Winston. Surprising, but good. Good to focus on the future. She was fun. She knew where I came from, and came from the same place, sort of. But she'd transcended it, gotten herself here, which technically was the same place but different. This place had helped her. I revved up my inner Jimmer. Look at this beautiful establishment. Look at this attention to self-realization, this focus on what tomorrow could be. Look at these women who knew our measurements and accepted them. Was it not wonderful?

I thought of Chickie in his cold lockup. If I could get him here, would it help? No. If I brought him here, if he kept digging around, he'd find out about the horn, and then he'd never let it go.

I ran through the other options. Let's say we just told Head-Connect the whole story. Let's say I got a sit-down with Arvindo Blanc or Tudd or whoever was pulling the strings in Nevada and explained how my high school buddy really wanted to return their mid-six-figure artifact to the unmapped woodland because that's where he thought it belonged. Would they indulge us? What if we offered to replace the horn with something of equal value?

Hah.

What if I just let the thing go? As Jimmer said, let it cease to exist. Could it just not exist, even though I'd seen it? Wouldn't that be better?

That would be better.

I entered the guest wing and saw the movie star and the mother-daughter hustling across the lobby. The movie star looked at me. I nodded to him.

"Beginners aikido?" he said, pointing to a hallway that led to some distant studio. "About to start."

"Yeah," I said, turning to follow along. "Cool."

"Tell the story," Jimmer said. "The one about the Beechers."

It was later in the day. Jimmer, Unsie, and I were sitting at one of the Heirloom's round tables with Vishy Shetty and her assistant and the minor movie star and the Asian guys and a couple of regulars, telling ghost stories. Popcorn from a shallow bowl was scattered like sawdust across the table. Ginny Archey brushed kernels aside and set down a cold pitcher of beer.

"I know that one," Ginny said. "I hate that one."

Jimmer smiled. He'd sprung Vishy Shetty from Head-Connect on the premise that he'd show her Edith Wharton's estate, a small chateau called the Mount, hidden at the end of a long path through the woods. A famous American director with an India fetish had recently announced his intention to do a remake of *The Age of Innocence*, and Vishy Shetty was eyeing it as her comeback vehicle.

Jimmer knew all that because Jimmer knew everything. He had two phones and eight screens on him at all times.

We'd all worked at the Mount as kids before we got jobs at Tanglewood, and then, later, at the Red Lion Inn, parking cars for the garden tours on the thousand-degree summer days. Menial service jobs in which we tried to hide our scorn for the tourists and they tried to hide their scorn for us. Once, on a particularly humid afternoon, an ice-cream vendor drove in the main gates and wound his way down the dirt road to the concession stand, and forgot to latch his rear door after the delivery, so the door swung open on the way out and—would you believe it?—a box of Dove Bars fell through. Forty-eight of them, vanilla dipped in chocolate, retailing at the concession for four bucks a pop. A gift from God. Chickie found the box just outside the main gate, lying on the side of the road. We ate them all.

Showing Vishy Shetty (and her assistant) Edith Wharton's estate took about fifteen minutes, as it was only a mile down the road from Head-Connect and closed in the winter. The Mount was famous for its gardens and its ghosts, but the gardens lay fallow in March and the ghosts didn't answer doorbells, so after a few minutes stamping around in the cold, Jimmer pitched our guests an oral history of the county's haunting, complete with local color and beer, as a tool to assist Vishy Shetty's nascent character study. Vishy Shetty appeared reluctant until Jimmer also promised to let her check out his phone. The others leapt at the jailbreak, even though they'd been at Head-Connect less than twenty-four hours.

I poured a golden curl of beer into my tilted mug, letting an inch-high head form at the top of the glass and drift down the sides. The mug sat on the table, and I held it at arm's length, nestled between my fingers, debating. It was Saturday evening. I'd worked out twice, filled a small notebook with observations about Master Ueshiba's "way of unifying," and washed my quinoa salad down with pomegranate-infused bubble tea. Ava Winston was giving a presentation on winter revenue streams in the back offices, and Tudd was texting me about a moonlight snowshoe class he thought I'd enjoy. But it seemed best to pace this transition, so when Jimmer asked me to skip out with them, I said sure.

Gable had plenty of ghost stories to choose from, dating back centuries, and every couple of years a new one seemed to pop up. Ginny Archey had already told the one about the glowing gravestone on October Mountain; the stone marked the burial site of an early Becket settler named Hand, a man shot for assaulting his neighbor's wife. The night he faced the squad was a muggy night. A vengeful crowd bayed in the square, while across town the neighbor's wife was in the sheriff's office recanting. Turns out they were lovers. As Hand stood blindfolded, a huge clap of thunder had split the sky, and rain started to fall in thick sheets. The crowd began to riot, and the sergeant at arms, having not heard from the sheriff, ordered five men with four bullets to fire. The muskets flashed like lightning, and Hand was no more. Now, on stormy summer nights, kids who went up there to park swore his headstone lit up like a lantern.

Between you and me, though, it was just headlights. The road through October Mountain dipped and curved, and at one spot near the burial grounds, your high beams could split two trees and light up a tablet 50 yards away. Especially if it was wet. Everything else was a tale passed down through generations of boys trying to get to second base.

It'd never worked, either.

There were other tales, newer ones, less utilitarian, like Kristin Sparrow swearing that water goblins wrapped their green fingers around her sister's ankles in the cold depths of Otis Pond, and Bud Park's claim that something unseen had pushed him to turn his shotgun on himself in his West Normanton tree blind three falls ago. Bud Park had lost his left ear and some of the sensation in his hands, and had stumbled out of the woods swearing that he wasn't suicidal.

"I think maybe those spirits came out of a bottle," Ginny Archey had snorted at that one, echoing the consensus at the time that Park was ambushed not by anything supernatural but by the dovetailing influences of an impending divorce and Johnnie Walker Red. Still, it got added to the list.

Unsie had started to tell the one about the hard men of North Ford who drank themselves stupid every Thursday so that when they walked home they wouldn't see the ghosts of the kids who died in a factory fire in 1911, but he stopped himself. That wasn't a fun one. Which left the Beecher story. It had a lot going for it, a historical distance, some nice touches, a relatively respectable denouement, and our crowd was hanging on each word. When folks like Vishy Shetty start throwing their charisma at you, it's hard not to get caught up.

I wrapped my hand around my mug and brought the beer to my lips for a long swallow. Truth be told, I hated these stories. They were exhausting. But I told them anyway.

"You know how over by Ventfort, in the woods behind Fred Carter's place, by the old road, there's that big old foundation in the ground. That was the Beecher estate back in the 1910s or so."

I had the table already. Even the Asian guys were listening.

"Well, so, Augustus Beecher is looking for a summer home for his family away from New York City. He has a young wife and a baby on the way and he's feeling pretty flush with money from his family's import-export business. So he starts building this big house up here in the woods. Place is a palace, marble floors, oak walls, lots of curtains and drapes. Two pianos. And they're just about finished in the spring of 1914, getting ready to spend the summer up here. Augustus's wife is from Montreal, and she's eight months pregnant, and she wants to get into the country and away from the city as soon as she can."

I took another sip of my beer. Nobody else spoke.

"But then the war starts, the Beechers aren't positioned right. They start losing business. Augustus has expensive taste, MC Hammer taste, and likes to play the ponies. Pretty soon, he's in trouble. He starts looking for a quick score, and you know how that is."

You know how that is.

It was windy and cold out and the sun was long behind the whistling hills.

"So he's looking for a quick score to get him out of the hole he's in, but he keeps making it worse and worse, and then he's in real long-term, poorhouse trouble. So he starts thinking about selling the house up here, but who's going to buy a big place out in the woods in that economy? Nobody, that's who. And Augustus knows it. So one day in the late spring, he tells his wife that he's going to come up to the country to see a guy about the horses—they have horses—and he rides up in his car. It's a rainy day, and it takes forever to get here, but Augustus is pretty desperate at this point. It's dark when he finally gets into town and drives up the old road to his house. The house is just about done, there's only some final shingling left to do on the stable, and Augustus stands in the driveway looking at the house and imagining the summers up here with his family. He doesn't go in—he can't bear it. But he takes a gasoline canister from his car and pours the gas around the house—along the porch, and the walls. He splashes some up onto the eaves. Then he stands back and tosses on a match. The house is insured and Augustus figures the insurance money will get him out of debt. Nobody but his wife knows where he is, and the house is at the end of a long driveway where nobody can see it. Augustus figures he can drive back to the city that night."

I shifted, looking down at the beer. The Asian guys were leaning forward in their seats. Unsie put a hand to his brow. Jimmer was smiling—he knew what was coming.

"So old Augustus is standing there watching as the flames start to crawl up the sides of his house, and pretty soon the whole thing's burning pretty good—there was a lot of wood, and I guess the finishing stuff they used back then was sort of an accelerant—and Augustus looks up into the second floor window . . . and there's his wife."

Vishy Shetty gasped. Her assistant gasped. The Asian guys looked at each other. Had they heard that right?

The minor movie star said, "Duuuude."

I paused, poured more beer into my mug, picked up a handful of popcorn and tossed it back into the dish.

"There's his wife, trying to open the window, but it's locked and I guess with the smoke or the construction she couldn't get it open."

Ginny Archey excused herself and went back to the bar.

"And she's pregnant," Vishy Shetty said quietly.

"And she's pregnant, right," I said.

The detail was a fixture of the story. You had to say it. But now it felt sort of obscene.

"Turns out she took the train up to surprise old Augustus, and with the weather and the roads, she got here ahead of him. She goes to their new house, sets up in the master bedroom and falls asleep. When she wakes up, the house is on fire. She looks out the window, and there's her husband standing in the driveway, looking up at her."

"So Augustus, you know, he pretty much loses it there in the driveway, watching his wife at the window, and he runs into the burning house after her. But the ceiling collapses and the house burns to the ground and they never get out."

Vishy Shetty's impossibly wide eyes got wider and I thought she might cry. But she also might have been acting.

I took a sip of my beer and continued.

"And then one night about fifteen years ago, Chief Winston—you know his mom was a Beecher—he's out walking his dog down the old road by that foundation, and the dog starts barking and tears off into the woods and Chief Winston gets real scared and he can't say why—he says it's just this heaviness, this feeling of *something* that he can't see, can't name, and then the moon shines through the trees and he sees someone standing on the old road just in front of him. He says he's scared like you wouldn't believe, and he just stands there, and the person doesn't move, and it's all dark and shadowy and Chief Winston swears he hears someone whispering to him, whispering right in his ear, words he can't understand. And, you know, because he's a cop, he says, 'This is the police, who's there?' But then the moon goes behind a cloud and he can't see the person anymore."

The minor movie star's beer mug slipped in his hand and sloshed onto the table. He barely noticed.

"And when the moon comes back out, there's nobody on the trail."

I sat back, a little disgusted, a little triumphant. A sad task performed flawlessly.

"What were the words?" asked Vishy Shetty.

"You really want to know?" I asked.

The entire table nodded.

"*Il brule*," I said. "That's French for *it burns*."

There was a long silence. Then the lead Asian guy started to shake his head a little, and then the three of them got up and went to the men's room together. Vishy Shetty whispered something to her assistant, and the woman nodded and started pecking on a tablet.

Jimmer stood up and clapped.

"So good!" he said, heading to the bar. "Who wants another round?"

Vishy Shetty went with him. The minor movie star wiped at his spilled beer, which was dripping down onto his jeans. I looked over at Unsie, and he smiled sadly at me. All this death, all this fetish. I wished I could use it, could type it up, monetize it, rather than just carry it around for parties.

"How's Sara?" I asked.

He smiled, a real smile this time, turning a corner.

"Good. Big as a house. Don't tell her I said that. Cranky. But it's good."

"You good?"

"Yeah, man," he said. "I'm really good. Looking forward to"—exhale, shrug—"the baby. All of it."

I grinned at him. He grinned back.

"I'm happy for you, man," I said. "You think she'd have my baby?"

"Who?" Unsie said. "Sara?"

I nodded.

He wrinkled his nose.

"I can ask her."

Jimmer came back to the table with his hands full of tequila.

"Who's up for a shot?" he asked. Vishy Shetty looked up from her assistant's tablet and started to raise her hand.

"I shouldn't," she said. "But."

Her assistant whispered at her. She lowered her hand.

"I won't."

The minor movie star looked like he was at the top of a long flight of stairs.

"I'm gonna option that story," he said, reaching for the tequila. Vishy Shetty gave her assistant a quick glance.

I shrugged. "That's an option."

My phone buzzed in my pocket. I looked at it. Unsie looked at me.

"Chick," I said, standing up. I downed Vishy Shetty's tequila and grabbed another one for the call.

Outside, I took a deep breath and lifted the phone to my ear.

"Guy," I said.

He was amped.

"Guy!" he said. "What's going on?"

"Nothing. Up at the Heirloom, talking about you. You okay?"

"Yeah, sure. Bored. Gonna get out Monday, I think."

"Hey, guess who's here?"

"Who's there?"

"Jimmer."

"Jimmer? Holy shit! What's he doing here?"

"Came to see us," I said. "And guess where he's staying?"

"Where?"

"Fleur-de-Lys."

"No shit!"

I nodded, even though I was talking on the phone.

"Yep," I said. "And I'm staying with him."

Then I felt stupid for telling him. It just came out.

"Yeah?" he said, then paused. "So, can you sneak me in?"

I picked up the second shot and held it to my lips. It smelled like turpentine. The pool secretary at my office had a wooden sign on her desk that said "Be the Change You Want to See in the World."

I knocked the shot back. It burned.

"Chick," I said. "It's not there."

And like that, the deceit was done.

"Huh?" he said.

"The safe is there, you were right. I got inside it. It's empty."

Chick was silent on the other end. I forced myself to think about a future of stability, forward motion, employment.

"Swear to God, Chick," I said, flinching even as I said it. "I checked all inside it. The horn's not there."

The tequila began dissolving the lining of my stomach.

"Chick?"

I could hear a sigh on his end.

"Come on, man," I said. I tried to sell it, but it sounded fraudulent even to me. "Listen, it's a good thing, right? We've seen it through?"

Long pause.

"Nah, guy. Not a good thing for me."

"Hey," I said. "Jimmer's here, and we can hang on Monday, put something new together for ourselves."

"Right," he said. He sounded hollow.

I started scrambling.

"Let's just get to spring. Couple more weeks. Spring comes, we'll go out and look for the rhino again. Maybe Jimmer's got some technology that we can use."

Chickie was quiet.

"Chick?" I said. "Guy?"

"Yeah," he said.

"Chick," I said. "I'm sorry."

"Yeah," he said, again. He sounded almost like he was crying. "Hey, it's cool. I got to go."

"Come on, man," I said. "We'll figure something else out."

"Yeah." Again. "Gotta go."

"Okay. See you Monday morning, right?"

"Right."

The line went dead.

I got really nervous and hit redial on the incoming number. Some random cop at the house of correction answered and identified himself as the duty sergeant. I said I was a friend of Philip Benecik.

"You mean Chickie?" he said.

"Yeah," I said. "Keep an eye on him?"

"No problem," he said. "He's sitting about 15 feet from me."

I heard a muffled conversation.

"He says he'll see you soon."

I touched off my phone and vomited into the bushes.

❧

Jimmer called a Head-Connect van to come and pick us up. Tudd was at the wheel.

"What is this?" he asked, looking askance at the Heirloom's beer signs as we piled into the van. I just shook my head. I smelled like vomit. The minor movie star smelled like beer. Vishy Shetty sat with Jimmer, while her assistant crouched behind them and frowned. The three Asian guys ducked their heads and huddled in the back, pretending not to understand anything.

"Unsustainable," said Tudd.

Between me and the movie star, the van reeked. Tudd turned the car down the hill toward Fleur-de-Lys, shaking his head. In a moment, we were out of town, trees and shadows on either side.

We passed a flower shop, and the smell of lilacs wafted through. I couldn't smell my vomit anymore, if I kept my mouth shut and breathed through my nose. I couldn't smell anything but the flowers.

It was after ten on a Saturday night. It was March. There were no flower shops on Bramble.

Jimmer was holding up his phone, which glowed. A small black tab, shaped like the thin curling lip of a rose, grew from the tip.

"It's a prototype," he said.

Sunday was a wash. Jimmer slept late, then went looking for Vishy Shetty. I ate my granola. I swam in the lap pool and stretched in the heat of the Bikram studio. By way of penance, I let Tudd drag me on a snowshoe excursion into the back woods, our wide titanium robo-steps crunching on the hard snow. We walked far enough that I could just make out, through the denuded trees, the chimneys of my old neighborhood, the pylons of a broken-down dock.

I called my office and left a message for the pool secretary, saying I had to be in court on Monday out in the Berkshires and I wouldn't be in for a couple of days. Law firms were weird places—emergencies arose, nobody knew what you were doing from day to day, and if you said you were in court, you were basically unimpeachable. Plus, I'd been busting my ass all week and had some goodwill banked. I called the house of correction and got the duty sergeant again, but when I asked to speak with Chickie, the sergeant said he couldn't talk.

At lunch, I was staring at a ginger turkey burger with a side of kimchi when Ava Winston stopped by.

"How is it?" she asked.

I shrugged.

She sat down.

"I heard about your little excursion last night."

"Wasn't my idea," I said, taking a bite of the burger to buy some time.

"The Heirloom? Really?"

"Talk to Jimmer," I said through the food.

She frowned.

"Well, one of our guests checked out today, a week early."

I'd seen the minor movie star wheeling his bags to a Town Car that morning.

I shrugged again.

"He say why?"

"He said he had to get back to his career," she said. "He was trying to get sober here."

"Wasn't trying that hard," I said.

"That's not even close to funny," she said. "Look, I can't tell what's going on with you, but I hope you'll respect what people are doing here. What we're doing here."

I put down my turkey burger and considered it. The bun was whole wheat and topped with flaxseeds. The ginger peeked out from under, tart and pink and translucent, like the tongue, or the foot, of some bivalve. Thing was delicious.

"Dude," I said.

She looked at me.

"Dude?"

"Ava. I respect what you're doing here."

She looked suspicious.

"What are you doing here?" I asked.

I thought it was funny. She didn't. She stood up to leave, her jaw tight.

"Wait," I said.

Fucking Chickie.

"You don't even know. I'm trying. I'm trying really hard to hold a bunch of things together. I'm a goddamn Trapper Keeper."

She was unamused.

"I am really trying."

"Well try harder," she said, a drill sergeant, a motivator. Her eyes flared. "Or hold less. I mean,"—she bent aggressively toward me, spoke in a harsh whisper—"goddamn it. Grow up."

She looked around the dining room, unnerved by her own profanity.

"No more nonsense, all right?"

A defensive sort of resentment welled up inside me. Nonsense? Grow up? What was she, my mother? You want to see nonsense? A bunch of rich people in sweat clothes picking at their blackberries and trying to stop the hands of time. A grown man named Tudd hovering somewhere nearby, with skates, probably. This whole fucking ridiculous enterprise. Nevadan snake-oil merchants cleaving like barnacles to the hull of this shiny sinking ship.

"Right, no more nonsense, yeah," I said coldly, picking up my ginger turkey burger on a wheat bun with flaxseeds. "Now, sorry, but I have to finish this because I have a hot fucking stone massage in twenty minutes."

Ava flushed. I couldn't tell if it was authentic or another tool of the trade.

"You know," she said, leaning in. "When we were kids, I really liked you. You could've had a shot too, but you were never serious. You were too busy off with your friends, hiding, screwing around."

She bit off the last two words, then stood as if to move around the dining room, check on other guests. But she didn't. She just walked out.

Goddamn. I mean, this—this Head-Connect bullshit, this rhino-horn stuff—this wasn't even my thing. I'm busting my ass to make things work smoothly around here, to pull these various idiots along, and I'm going to get treated this way?

You know what, fuck that. I should just leave them all to their own devices. See how they like it then.

I actually did have a hot stone massage on the schedule, and to tell you the truth, I'd been looking forward to it. I finished my ginger turkey burger and tried to use some of my new mindfulness techniques to calm down. I filled my mind with the taste of the kimchi. Tart, fermented. Greenish. Everything was green. A good color. A color of growth. I started to feel better. I'd lied to Chick, but it was okay because it was going to help him. Chick's arraignment would happen tomorrow, and after that we'd get together with Jimmer and Unsie, get all sorted out. Just like old times. I'd lied to Ava Winston, and then used profanity with her, but it was okay because she was tough-loving me. She could handle it. Plus, I had a shot with her in high school and she had some nice calves. They were long and supple, like aubergines, which were not green but purple, purple calves propelling her across the taupe carpets of Head-Connect. I was a good guy. I tried. I replaced the image of kimchi in my mind with the image of Ava's supple purple calves and sat with that image, turning it around and around in my head until I felt calmer. Then I went to my massage.

At 7 A.M. on Monday morning, I dressed in my suit and drove up to the Knots, parked in the hard salt-stained lot of the house of correction, and escorted myself through the adjacent front doors of Berkshire Superior Court. The courthouse was gray stone, a three-story building that fronted East Street. Its front doors funneled visitors past metal detectors and sleepy cops. At bigger courthouses, there was sometimes a special expedited entrance for attorneys, and all you had to do was flash your bar card and you could skip the line. Sheepish defendants, forlorn girlfriends and toddlers, all waiting to be screened. They'd stare at you—the attorney—with a mix of avarice and contempt.

Berkshire Superior was a small enough courthouse, though, that we all entered through the front. I'd never been there before, but when I was a kid we used to drive by it all the time on the way to a rye-bread bakery my dad liked out on East Street. The courthouse was the sort of steady, permanent structure around which municipalities coalesce. City hall was a block away. The public library was across the street. The house of correction backed it up. In the courtyard, a bronze pioneer named Frankfort Knot stood atop a stone column and grimly surveyed the roundabout.

I nodded to the guards and slipped my keys, phone, and bar card into a plastic tray for inspection. The metal detectors beeped for my belt, the younger of the two guards performed a disengaged wanding, and I was through. It was a lot easier to get into a court of law than it was to get into Head-Connect. A caramel-colored guy behind me got more scrutiny, possibly because he was wearing a Jets parka.

The ground floor was a warren of offices and administrative cubbies, middle-aged women and men in uniform who clicked across the marble floors like stagehands in the wings of a theater. I checked the docket and climbed the two flights of stairs to Courtroom 5, the Honorable James T. Ralph presiding.

You walk into a courtroom for the morning docket, and it's like walking into the least happy prom you've ever been to. The tension is thick. Half the people are there for the first and, they hope, but also secretly doubt, last time. They don't know what's going on. The other half are regulars who know the drill and are trying to work an angle. Every head turns to see who you are, to see whether you're their exonerator, and then turns back to their private worries.

I walked in and stood to the side near the doors, behind the rows of wooden benches. The real estate you claim in a church when you get there late, if you're an ambivalent churchgoer, where you can sneak out before the Eucharist. Back when we used to go to church regularly, my dad would always angle to stand at the back, my mom always trying to push us up into the pews.

The courtroom had a smell. A bouquet. Floors mopped nightly with something industrial, flop sweat in the benches, dust on the portraits. Jimmer and Unsie were meeting me. Ava Winston was already there, in a front row on the left, flanked by Head-Connect honchos and Chief Grevantz, who, from what I could see, looked just about the same as he had a decade and a half earlier, at least from the neck up. The rest of the gallery was filled with lawyers, families, defendants.

I took a seat toward the back.

When I went to court on civil matters, the first thing I did upon entering the room was to check in with the clerk. That way the court would know who was present and which cases could be productively called. The clerk, who was usually but not always a woman, was the queen of the courtroom chessboard—she could make or break you, get you a delay, push an angry judge on to other matters. I'd always made it a point to compliment her on something at check-in. Nails, blouse, anything. Earrings. It didn't matter. Courthouse staff cultivation was actually one of my primary skill sets.

Inside the well, the clerk and a series of lawyers in functional suits shuffled papers back and forth. A young woman sat at the prosecution table with a large stack of files next to her. An older man sat at the defense table, balding on top, gray hair long in the back and tied into a ponytail. He wore the cheap suit, flowery tie, and jaundiced righteousness of the public defender.

"All rise," said the bailiff, an older officer with a cowboy mustache. A door opened behind the bench, and Judge Ralph moved quickly through it and up to his seat. He was an ungainly man, moose-like, with broad shoulders and a monstrous head atop what appeared, even with the robe, to be a thin base. He didn't look up, but set his glasses on his nose and dug into a stack of files before him, the glamour of the arraignment docket, the ebb and flow of process.

"Let's see what we have here today," he said, seemingly to himself. He sounded almost amused.

The clerk began calling cases, strings of numbers, sometimes with a name appended. The crimes of the Commonwealth. There were forty-six sets of numbers on the docket list pinned to the bulletin board outside the courtroom, three pages of lined paper. One after the other, defendants appeared, either through a side door that led to the waiting cell or by standing when their number was called and moving sheepishly into the well. The ones who had been sitting in the gallery seemed far more uncomfortable than the ones camping out in the waiting cell. Charges were announced by citation to penal code—possession, intent to distribute, battery, criminal trespassing. The young prosecutor barely shuffling through the files, the public defender consulting briefly with his clients before offering up a plea and a proposed trial date. Judge Ralph consulted a calendar, engaged in a Vulcan mind-meld with his clerk, and sent the accused on their ways. The whole process, when it worked smoothly, when the defendants kept their mouth shut and nodded, took thirty seconds. By my count, about two-thirds of the defendants were released pending a trial date, most of which would be voided later after a plea bargain.

Jimmer and Unsie slid into the bench next to me.

"Anything yet?" Jimmer asked. He was checking his phone.

I shook my head.

"Nah," I said, eyeing Jimmer's phone nervously.

I knew a lawyer who'd been checking his phone in a courtroom gallery once and got reamed by a sharp-eyed judge. Ever since, I'd left mine in my briefcase, powered down. Indeed, most courtrooms required it.

Jimmer didn't seem to care.

The clerk called the next case.

"Docket number 12-0936. People v. LaBeau."

Elvis LaBeau walked out of the holding cell, shaggy and shifty. Looking like he'd slept in his clothes, which of course he had.

Possession with intent to distribute. Swift arraignment. Not guilty plea. Ordered to return in three weeks for further proceedings.

LaBeau nodded to the judge, barely acknowledged the public defender, and headed back through the side door for processing. On the way out, he looked over the gallery and saw me. His face darkened and he ducked away.

"Docket number 12-0938. People v. Benecik."

The side door swung open again and seemed to pause there. I could hear a mechanical clattering, and then Chickie rolled haltingly through the door in a wheelchair. Two side bailiffs endeavored to clear a path for him. He looked like shit, pale and weak, barely following the proceedings. The chair made it as far as the jury box, but couldn't fit between the box and the defense table. At that point, Chick stood up and spread his arms, as if a miracle had occurred.

"That's a Snoop move," he said, speaking to the bailiffs but loud enough for the gallery to hear.

What a fucking dope. Why does he get to do this stuff? Got a grin out of one of the bailiffs too.

He took his place next to the public defender and turned his head toward the gallery, acknowledging it with a cool nod.

The clerk read the charges. Criminal trespass. Breaking and entering with intent. Larceny. Resisting arrest.

"Larceny?" I whispered to Unsie.

"The ladder," he said.

In the front row, Ava Winston leaned forward and whispered to the public defender, who then signaled for the prosecutor.

"Your Honor," the public defender said. "I'm informed by a representative of the property in question that they have little interest in pursuing the trespass or B & E charges and would support a plea to lesser charges in exchange for a restraining order."

Judge Ralph looked down over his glasses, the smooth orchestration of his arraignment docket now unsettled.

"Sorry?" he asked. "A representative of whom?"

The public defender tensed.

"The defendant here is accused of trespassing on, and breaking into, the Head-Connect property down in Gable on Thursday night. A representative of Head-Connect is here today," he said, nodding at Ava Winston. "And has informed me that Head-Connect doesn't have much interest in pursuing charges based on that conduct."

"Oh really," said Judge Ralph. "Head-Connect doesn't care about the trespassing?"

Jimmer nudged me.

"People don't understand how it works," he whispered, smiling.

I got the sense that Judge Ralph probably did know how it worked, that Jimmer was maybe over-exalting his new clarity, but I waited to see what would happen.

Judge Ralph now took on the visage of a condor, looming over the bar. The public defender slid to the side and exposed Ava.

"You can speak," said Judge Ralph.

God bless her, Ava Winston stood right up and spoke.

"Thank you, Your Honor," she said. "My name is Ava Winston. I'm an executive at Head-Connect and can represent to the court that, while Head-Connect takes the defendant's behavior and guest security very seriously, it does not see much benefit in a drawn-out public process and would prefer to handle the matter privately, perhaps with a small assist from the court."

She took a deep breath.

"We don't need him to go to jail. We just want him to keep off the property," she said, almost sadly, looking at Chickie.

Chick's head dipped.

"That still leaves the larceny and resisting," said the prosecutor.

Judge Ralph looked at all the parties before him. Each had handled its tasks competently. He dipped into the files before him.

"It says here that this defendant has priors, including . . . several relating to the property in question," he said, looking up. He focused on Chick. It might have been the first time he'd looked at a defendant that morning.

"What about it, then?" he said to Chick. "Well, let's back up. I guess we can't ask for a plea until we've sorted out the charges."

"I did it," said Chick. "I'm your man. If that's what you mean. I'll plead guilty. Not like it wasn't me."

The public defender put a hand on Chick's arm.

"Well, let's hold on for a second," he said.

Chick looked to Ava and hung his head.

"Sorry," he said.

She lowered her eyes. Chick looked down the row to Chief Grevantz, and then back around to the three of us in the gallery. His eyes lit up for a second when he saw Jimmer, but tamped down just as quickly.

Judge Ralph looked at Chick.

"Slow down a second, young man," he said. "Now, listen. I appreciate whatever it is you're trying to cop to here, but I'm not inclined to dismiss a case until I understand what it is that I'm dismissing. I'm ordering you to return in two weeks for sentencing on what I assume your counsel and the prosecution will present as a misdemeanor trespass matter. And at that time, I'll be inclined to order you to stay away from the property in question in perpetuity and make restitution in the amount of,"—he checked his file— "well, whatever the going rate is for a ladder, reserving the court's ability to reinstate the more serious charges if necessary."

Chickie shrugged.

"Perpetuity's a long time," he said. "But it's cool."

Judge Ralph smile-frowned at him. "We'll see. Until then, you are ordered not to come within 500 feet of the property."

Judge Ralph leaned forward.

"Is that an order that you think you'll be able to comply with?"

Chick exhaled and nodded.

"Yeah," he said. "I'm done with all of it."

I felt both happy and sad at the same time.

Judge Ralph held his pose for a second, and then shifted back to his files.

"I hope so," he said, moving on to the next case.

We waited for Chickie at the heavy side door of the house of corrections. It was cold. Steam rose from the Styrofoam cups Jimmer had gotten at the Dunkin' Donuts across the street. Through the reinforced glass we could see Chick walking out of processing, talking with Elvis LaBeau, although probably nobody recognized him but me. LaBeau looked up ahead and saw us, made a face, and squirreled himself off down another hallway. Chick shuffled on toward us. For a guy who had seemingly just dodged a felony charge, he was pretty blasé.

"Fellas," he said when he pushed through the door.

Jimmer got the first hug, then Uns clapped him on the back.

"Yeah, yeah," said Chick, and by the time he got to me it felt a little perfunctory.

"Well that was exciting," said Jimmer. "You know California misses you. You ought to come back."

Chick laughed a little bit and looked at the ground.

"Yeah," he said. "Maybe."

He looked up at the gray sky.

"Warmer than this place, right?"

"Hella warmer," said Jimmer, employing some sort of vernacular.

We stamped our feet on the steps for a second.

"So," Jimmer said. "What's next on the agenda?"

I looked at Chickie. He was staring vacantly off into Knotsford. It was all I could do not to reach out and shake him.

"Breakfast?" I said.

Unsie had already eaten, steel-cut oats, probably, with a side of pinecone, and after some more hugs he headed back over the hill to open up Asgard. Jimmer, Chick, and I went across the rotary to a place called the Shammy, a greasy spoon where the cops ate in the morning, drank after work, and vice versa. We slid into a booth. Chick and I ordered pancakes and Jimmer negotiated an egg-white omelet.

"What's your schedule?" I asked Jimmer once the food came.

"Flying out Friday," Jimmer said. "I have to go to Boston today for some meetings, but I'll be back in town Wednesday."

Jimmer reached for his pocket and pulled out a jewel-like wafer.

"Let me get your cell," he said to Chick. "I'll call when I'm back."

Chick picked at his pancakes.

"My cell?" he asked. "Nah, I'm out. Don't have to go back."

Jimmer looked at him. "Your cell phone."

"Oh," Chick said. Usually he smiled at his own goofiness, but not this time. "Don't have one."

Jimmer frowned.

"Had one, but it broke," Chick said. "I think I landed on it when I fell off the roof. Doesn't matter."

"Well, you need a phone," Jimmer said. "You can't get by without a phone."

"How did we make do for centuries?" asked Chickie. At least he was listening.

"Not efficiently," said Jimmer. "And just try getting by now without one."

Jimmer reached into his other pocket.

"Take this one," he said, sliding a slightly less jewel-like version of his phone across the table. "It's an older model. Use it until you get a new one, or Wednesday, whatever comes first."

Chick looked at it noncommittally. Jimmer pushed it closer to him.

"Don't lose it," he said. "Now, where are you staying?"

Chick shrugged.

"You're welcome to stay in my room at the spa," Jimmer said. "With Pete."

"He can't," I said.

Jimmer looked confused. What force was there that could contradict his plans? Then he blushed, laughed sarcastically.

"Right! Shit. That's right. The long arm of the law. I'm sure we can get around that, though. Just say you're with me."

In Jimmer's world, that could probably work.

"It's no problem," Chick said, sliding Jimmer's backup phone into his pocket. "I can crash with some friends."

"Who?" I asked. "LaBeau?"

Chickie shrugged, wouldn't look at me. He pushed his untouched plate away.

"Don't worry about it," he said.

"Let's just go back to the Horse Head," I said.

Jimmer raised his eyebrows at that. Chick did too. They were mocking my suggestion, and even though I knew Jimmer was on my side and just trying to connect with Chick, it pissed me off.

"I'm fine, dude," Chick said.

"You're fine?" I asked. "You don't have a phone."

Chick held up Jimmer's backup phone. I went on.

"You don't have a car. You were just arraigned." Drawing out "arraigned" into a three-word bit.

"I don't need a car," Chick said. "I'm fine."

Stupid fucking fucker.

"How are you fine?" I asked, raising my voice a little. "Seriously. How?"

Jimmer raised his hands from his omelet.

"Okay," he said. "We're all adults here."

I pointed to Chick.

"He's not an adult," I said. "He needs to go back to the Birches. Or give me my money back."

Chick tossed his fork down and pushed out of the booth, heading for the door. A couple of cops watched us over their bacon, more amused than alarmed. They were on break.

I went after him. Caught him on the sidewalk.

"Dude," I said, grabbing him by the shoulder. He swung back toward me and put two hands into my chest, a short, sharp shove. Seemed like it took most of the energy he had.

"Get the fuck off me," he hissed.

I grabbed the sleeve of his coat and wouldn't let go.

"Pete," he said, his voice shaking. His eyes were black. We'd fought once before, when we were about fourteen. I don't even remember why. He'd thrown a rock at me, hit me in the ear. I'd thrown one back at him, hit him in the shoe. He'd kicked my ass. Back then he fought all in, like a wild animal. But I'd filled out since then. And my aim had improved.

"Where are you going?" I said.

"Let go of me."

"Where are you going?"

He shook his arm.

"Let. Go."

"If I let go, will you come back in?"

I don't even know what it was about anymore. We are supposed to grow up, take responsibility for ourselves. Make choices. I felt like I'd been doing a pretty decent job of that over the years. Or maybe not. Depends on who you asked. All I knew right then was, here's this guy, my oldest friend, who'd walked a path right next to me and still managed to get lost. But we'd been together, and were together again. And now he was walking away.

"Will you come back in?"

I knew he wouldn't.

"Stop," he said. "Just . . . stop."

He looked at me like he couldn't stand it.

"I don't want your help anymore. You can't help."

Felt like a slap. Maybe to him too, because he looked away fast.

"There's nothing to help with," he said.

I let go. He looked down, then turned away.

"Of course there is," I said. I shouted it, actually, my voice cracking a little, surprised by the rush of emotion. "Just wait a second."

But he didn't wait. He walked on, up the sidewalk, shuffling, then breaking into a little mini-trot, only to stop and shuffle again, around a corner and into the north side of the Knots.

I thought about running after him. I was pretty sure I could catch up, pin him down, hold him there until . . . what? Until spring?

"Let him go," Jimmer said from behind me. "Let him cool off. He'll come back around in a bit."

I shook my head.

"I don't know, man," I said.

"What's going to happen?" said Jimmer. "He's a big boy. He's got to do it himself. And you don't know, maybe he will. Dude has circumnavigated the globe, right? He probably can handle the Knots."

I looked off in the direction of where Chick had turned, then back at Jimmer. Four-leaf clovers and green top hats stuck to the window of the Shammy.

I dug my hands into my pockets and shivered.

"What if he can't?" I said.

Jimmer checked his watch.

"Well, if he can't, he can't," he said. "Uh, listen."

I looked at him. He had somewhere to be.

Right, of course.

I had somewhere to be too. We were adults. There were limits. I took one last look down the sidewalk, toward the swallowing stones of the polis.

"Let's go," I said.

We drove back to Gable, the Escalade purring down Route 20 and past the glory of the Knotsford-Gable Road. Jimmer had his tablet out and glanced up only occasionally, fully engaged in whatever was happening with his e-mails or his chats or whatever. It was like the virtual and the real worlds were reversed for him. When we passed the Horse Head, I looked over with what I hoped would feel like disinterest but instead just felt sort of forced. The parking lot was empty and there was no way Chickie could've gotten there already on foot.

Shake it off. Move forward.

At the Head-Connect gates, the security officer waved us through after a semi-cursory inspection, Jimmer barely acknowledging him. The pebbles crunched organically under our wheels, a pleasant, indulgent sound, and the young mystery valets swung our doors open before we'd even stopped moving. Welcome back, they said, smiling perfect, healthy smiles, wearing sweatshirts and light gloves beneath the entry portico's heat lamps. The lobby smelled of pine and wood-smoke, but only mildly so, only enough to suggest a hike, or perhaps a massage, or an instructional lecture about pine and wood-smoke and their significance in Native American aromatherapy. We were a world away from the industrial cleaners of Courtroom 5.

Vishy Shetty, the most beautiful woman in maybe the whole world, rose from a banquette under a chiaroscuro painting of a landscape, or perhaps it was just a window.

"Hello," she said, her voice flowing like cursive, nodding to me but clearly speaking to Jimmer.

He put his tablet down and smiled at her. Her assistant was nowhere to be seen.

"Ready?" he asked.

She smiled what appeared to be a genuine smile.

He held his arm out for her. She picked up a flowing, white parka, glided across the carpet, and placed her arm in his.

"Back on Wednesday," Jimmer said to me. "You have your key, right?"

I nodded. Outside, one of the valets pulled up in a black BMW 7 Series. Jimmer escorted Vishy Shetty to the rear passenger-side door, which another of the valets had already opened. Then Jimmer came back to me.

"You're all right, right?"

I thought about it for a second and was pleasantly surprised at the result. I nodded.

"I feel good."

Jimmer smiled.

"Good!"

He headed around to the far-side passenger door.

"Keep me posted," he called to me, flashing the finger-and-thumb sign for a phone that no longer existed in his world. I made a pistol hand at him, and he got in.

I watched as he spoke quickly with the valet in the driver's seat, who then pecked at a dashboard navigator. In the back, Jimmer had already leaned over to Vishy Shetty and was holding his magic tablet up in his palms. A small petal protruded from the speaker port. Vishy Shetty looked over at him, and then, as the BMW pulled away, she closed her eyes, breathed in deeply, and vanished.

I looked around the entrance, where people hustled without seeming to rush. Valets stacked skis in a rack near the doors. Sweaty guests wiped their sneakers on luxurious honey-colored bristle mats. The oxygen bar. The kombucha tureen. Lunch shifts would be starting in a half-hour. There was always a next thing, a better way. I looked for Ava Winston, but didn't see her. Then I did, coming through an administrative door behind the front desk. She was wearing the same skirt-suit she'd worn in court, looking down at a folder of papers and heading to her guest services desk.

I moved on the diagonal to cut her off, positioning myself so as to present what I hoped would be a knee-buckling contrapposto. My idea, sort of formed but unrefined, was both to thank her and get her to see what a responsible figure I could cut in a suit. Thank her because, while I was sure plenty of public relation considerations had gone into Head-Connect's decision to chill out on the felony counts, I suspected that Ava Winston could have sent someone else. Get her to check me out because, forsaken by Chickie, I felt surprisingly unencumbered. I felt ready to embrace a more forward-thinking mindset, and perhaps embrace Ava Winston in the process.

I stood near the end of the front desk, the point at which she would come around the corner and leave the protection of the mahogany bar, or cedar, or whatever it was, and cut across the open ocean of carpet. I considered a hand-in-the-pocket move, a casual lean, a raised open palm.

Instead, it was Ava who employed the raised open palm, her left hand, flat and empty, shutting me down before I'd even begun to speak. Swear to God for a second I thought she might be high-fiving me, and I was just glad I'd gone with the hand-in-the-pocket thing and couldn't recover in time. She brushed by, never taking in the tight knot of my tie, the cut of my jib. I watched as she moved efficiently across the lobby, engaged a guest just as the guest required engagement, solved a problem, and sat down at her desk, poised and proper. She'd never even looked at me.

Didn't matter. I'd known enough girls over the years that I could tell when one of them was fighting a losing battle. Methinks thou dost protest too much, Ava Winston. There'll be world enough and time for us. Right after my wrap.

Around four o'clock, I tried Jimmer's old phone, the one he'd loaned to Chick. No answer. I left a message and tried Chick's cell, but that just got me a "no longer in service" recording. I rang the Horse Head to see if he'd checked in there, but they said not. I asked if they'd had any new guests register that day, and they got paranoid and hung up.

I was trying real hard not to look back. Chickie had my number, knew I was here. He could get in touch with me whenever he wanted. But he didn't want to, and I should be taking that as some sort of message—to let go, to enjoy my quinoa salad and dandelion–ancient grain crostini, to appreciate the promise of tomorrow's buckwheat cleanse.

I went looking for him at eight.

First to the Heirloom, where Ginny Archey was tending the wounds of the Monday night crowd. Tim-Rick Golack sat at the bar, nursing a grapefruit juice and watching the Celtics lose to the Heat on a screen in the corner. Some of the corporate crowd from Head-Connect were clustered around a booth at the back, heads together, apparently bidding adieu to their boondoggle with a couple of pitchers of Sam Adams. They shrunk when they saw me, as if I was an emissary from the spa or, worse, from their own HR department, checking up on the value-add. I gave them the eyes-on-you sign.

"Seen him?" I asked Ginny.

She shook her head no, looked over at Tim-Rick.

"He's probably with my brother," he said.

"I hope not," I said, looking at Tim-Rick meaningfully, and added, "for both their sakes."

Tim-Rick met my look, not confrontationally but knowingly.

"Me too," he said, and he sounded sincere.

"You know how I can get hold of your brother?" I asked.

Tim-Rick shrugged.

"No," he said, and turned back to his grapefruit juice.

I left and drove up to the Horse Head. The parking lot was empty. The rooms, all twenty of them, were dark. I parked and sat in the Escalade for a second. I tried the numbers I had for Chick again, then went over to the front desk.

Bowhunter was in the back, came out grudgingly when I rang the desk bell.

"You get anyone checking in here tonight? A young guy, my age, blond, with a beard? Last name Benecik?"

He looked at me like I was crazy.

"What do I look like?" he said.

"You look like a man who could use forty bucks," I said, taking out my wallet. I wrote my cell number on a card and put it on the desk with two twenties.

"Call that number if he checks in," I said.

Bowhunter took the cash and looked at the card.

"What's this about?" he asked, buying in.

"I'm afraid I can't tell you that," I said. "Just call that number if he checks in. Do you understand?"

He nodded. I turned to go.

"And do not engage him."

Bowhunter's chin quivered, and he nodded. He'd been deputized.

The streets around St. Eustace were empty and dark. I swung the Escalade over around KMC, but couldn't see anything there either. I tried a number for an Elvis LaBeau in Dalton, but it was his dad and it didn't sound like they were close.

The moon was fat and yellow in the black sky, a patchwork of clouds around it. I drove back to Head-Connect, rolled up to security.

"Listen," I said to the guard, whose name, I knew by now, was also Pete. "Listen, Pete. Were you working Thursday night, when all that stuff went down with the trespasser?"

Pete nodded. We were old buddies by now. Two Petes.

"Well, keep an eye out for him. He's actually a friend of mine who's having a hard time these days, and if he comes back around—I don't think he will—I'd appreciate it if you'd let me know."

Pete the guard narrowed his eyes.

"Well, Mr. Johansson, obviously we have protocols in place for something like that."

We were no longer two Petes.

"Oh, you do? Cool," I said, nodding, trying to salvage the page I wanted to think we were both on. "Okay, then. Have a good night."

They have protocols. I don't have protocols. They're security guards. I'm just a guy.

This is stupid.

I rolled back up the long drive, leaving the night town and its salty streets behind me. Halfway up, I passed Tudd leading a moonlight snowshoe expedition. Two newcomers, the mother-daughter, one of the Asians. Come with us, he said through my rolled-down window, so I dropped the car with a valet and did.

The woods were lit by the moon and utterly silent. We clomped along in our snowshoes, the snow at this point a hard shell, beaten down by the cold, compressed by previous explorers into a resentful crust. We followed a winding path until it ended at the Magic Meadow, an ancient lawn of tractor-mowed fields, enclosed on all sides by the forest, hidden from the roads and town surrounding it. My father had taken us sledding there as kids, Chick, Jimmer, all of us packing onto plastic shells and toboggans for the long drift down a knoll to the edge of the distant woods. The air had the tang of nearby wildlife, deer asleep in the groves, raccoons foraging along the creek beds.

"Powder tomorrow," Tudd said in his vague accent. "Good for the skiing."

"Isn't it late for snow?" asked the mother of the mother-daughter pair.

Tudd shrugged.

"Every winter is different. Last year, very little snow. This year, a good winter."

"I think it's almost over," I said. "Right?"

Tudd shrugged again and looked to the sky.

"Famous last words."

We crossed the meadow, shoes crunching through the crust, the snow frozen on tall grass and brook reeds, like gravel underfoot. I walked next to the Asian man, toward the back, as Tudd led the others through the bent boughs of a passage at the edge of the meadow, back onto the trails to Head-Connect. Many of the marble statues from the heyday of Forsyth Van Nest had remained in the woods when Fleur-de-Lys went under, and the Head-Connect designers were smart enough to leave them there. Now the statues whispered to each other in their ghostly winter tongue, pale torsos and bare breasts and bearded heads, seraphim, blank eyes. You want to know what a gnome is, they could tell you. That and more.

In a half-hour, the lights from the spa's rear entrance began to glow through the trees, a spaceship, a boat in the fog, and we were back.

We unhooked our snowshoes and passed them to Tudd for storage. The mother-daughter team hustled off down the residential corridors toward their room. The mother looked older, but not in a bad way, and the daughter looked taller. She held her mother's hand in the hallway. The rest of us stood around, basking in the warmth and sense of ennoblement that a winter night's hike can evoke. Like we'd just survived something, communally. Nobody went down. Nobody got left behind.

Tudd clapped me on my shoulders and pointed toward a rolling cart set up just inside the spa's rear entryway.

"There is soup," he said, almost giggling. He was a happy guy after stuff like this. "Carrot-ginger, good after a cold hike. And the saunas are open."

He gathered the snowshoes and, whistling, headed back out the door.

I ladled some soup into a paper cup and sipped it like espresso. It did taste revivifying. Made me feel like a large, healthy rabbit, just back from a trip to Mr. McGregor's microgreens. I needed to go to my room—Jimmer's room—and pack my stuff up. Get organized. Read through some briefs I'd brought out on Friday. Answer some e-mails or something. At some point soon I needed to get back to Boston, back to work. This hearing ruse wouldn't work for more than a day or so.

I went instead to the nearly empty lobby and searched for Ava Winston, who was probably, I hoped, getting off work. She was standing by the edge of her desk, stacking papers on top of each other. She looked up and saw me coming, a look like the end of a long day had just gotten both longer and less predictable.

I walked up to her and looked around quickly. The oxygen bar was clear. The kombucha tureen was moldering silently. There were some attendants at the front desk, but they wouldn't activate unless a guest approached.

So I kissed her, full on the mouth. Right there in the lobby.

She made a noise of surprise and pushed me away. And damn I thought I might have misjudged things.

"Come with me," she said, pulling me down a side hallway. "Please."

I went with her, beginning to formulate an apology for what now felt less like a scene from *Say Anything* and instead maybe a little like assault.

We entered the corridor. She wheeled on me and punched me in the arm. Hard.

"Asshole!" she hissed.

But then she kissed me back, just as hard as the punch.

I'm not going to tell you how the rest of the night unfolded, because I'm a gentleman and I think some things should stay private, at least while they still have potential, but let's just say that when I woke up, alone and late for my 8:30 shiatsu, I could see clearly the benefits, from an emotional and physical standpoint, of a career in high-end health services. I lay in the big bed in Jimmer's suite, its high-thread-count sheets wrinkled and buffeted and whispering whenever I moved my arms, and tried to meditate on the night's events. The things said and done, the promises implicit in them. The flexibility. How staggeringly rested I felt.

We didn't do it, if that's what you're wondering. Didn't seem that big of a deal. I mean, yeah, I took a wide turn around third and sort of juked toward the plate a little bit, but I wasn't going anywhere and she knew it. I didn't need to go anywhere. That was the feeling. Which was good because I'd have been out by a mile. Instead, I could just hold off, play it cool, see a few more pitches. It was a good game, once I apologized for kissing her like that, explained myself as best I could. It had the potential to be a classic.

I hadn't hooked up with anyone besides Kelly in probably four years, if you don't count some mild grinding with a temp paralegal in a broom closet at our firm's Fourth of July/End of Fiscal Year Party during the summer I was an intern. She was now, as I understood it, studying to be a physician's assistant in Quincy. Kelly had been in California; it was before we'd gotten serious and moved in together, and there'd been an open bar. It wasn't much of a transgression, as transgressions go, although I think the paralegal might have been engaged at the time. As for Kelly herself, and the tacit disloyalty the past ten hours might suggest, well, not sure. We weren't exactly staying in touch. Feeling I got was that we were over. She'd set her social media platforms to private, and for all I knew she was clubbing on Melrose, backstroking toward the grotto at the Playboy Mansion, whatever the single kids do on the Westside.

Probably not.

Anyway. I wasn't exactly wracked with guilt, and whatever betrayals were there to dwell on, they felt vague and diffuse. Maybe I should have been dwelling on them more.

I tried that for a second.

Nope, too much. I switched gears and thought about breakfast. Steel-rolled oats? With fresh goji berries? Don't mind if I do. What was a high thread count anyway? A thousand? My hair had a high thread count. Maybe that's why I was so handsome. I moved my arms and legs against the sheets like I was making a very expensive snow angel. My arm was sore from where Ava'd punched me, but the rest of me felt like a million bucks, give or take.

My phone rang from a pants pocket draped over the back of a chair.

I considered three possibilities, maybe four, as I fished it out. But it was the fifth—Jimmer.

"Are you in the big bed?" he asked.

I stopped moving my arms.

"How did you know that?" I asked.

"Dude," he said. "I would kick your ass if you were not in the big bed. Nice, right?"

I sank back into a pillow. Were the pillows Egyptian and the duvet down? Or the other way around?

"Yeah. Very nice."

I considered telling him about Ava. Instead, I asked him about Vishy Shetty.

"Sweet girl," he said. "Very spiritual."

"You're just saying that because she's Indian."

"She's Indian?"

I could hear someone in the background.

"Is she there?"

"No," Jimmer lied. "She wants to know if you've seen Neena."

"Who's Neena?"

"Joanne. Her sister. You know. The minder."

"Nope," I said.

I could hear Jimmer speaking to someone, Vishy, in the background. Then he was back to me.

"Vishy thinks she's following us."

"Really?"

"Yeah, really. She's on someone's payroll. The studio, the tabloids. We're not sure which. Don't sweat it."

I rolled over and looked out the window. The pale winter light was seeping through the shades, high cloud cover, grays and whites.

"How was your conference?" I asked.

More laughing in the background.

"Good. Some really cool stuff."

"Like what?" I asked. Sounded interesting. Progressive. I liked to stay on the cutting edge.

"Uh, one of these kids is pitching a sort of web search-and-destroy program, like it would hunt through the Internet and delete stuff. But not wholesale slaughter, like a virus. Targeted killings."

I didn't really get why computer people used such violent language.

"The Internet sounds like a scary place."

"It is," said Jimmer. "It is. I mean, it's not if you know how to stay ahead of it. Which is why we're interested in this start-up."

"Weaponizing again?"

"Well, yeah," he said, sounding a little defensive. "But the real widespread applications aren't martial. Or maybe it's the other way around—like a Sun Tzu thing. Maybe all applications are martial. Anyway, for example, and, you know, this is confidential, right? I mean, I'm not worried about you, but keep this stuff to yourself, obviously? In the spa? At breakfast. Who knows who is lurking around? Loose lips sink ships and all that."

"Yeah, yeah," I said. "Just hold on a minute while I get off the other line with my broker."

It only took Jimmer a second to laugh.

"Right. That's not funny. No, but there are all kinds of applications for this stuff. If it works. Like imagine you could program an app to search the web and remove any mention of your name. Shit, every job applicant with a Twitter account would use it. It's like that movie, the one with that guy, *Eternal Sunshine*? Right? Erasing memories. Except instead of working on your own brain, this thing would work on the web."

I had a vague sense that this sort of thing would be monumental for a certain kind of person engaged in a certain kind of lifestyle, but for me it was sort of remote. I mean, wouldn't people just repost stuff? Wouldn't the truth of what someone said or did remain in the world, whether or not anyone could find it online? But I could also see that both Jimmer and Vishy Shetty were people of this new world, future people, and that for them this sort of thing was probably like growing a pair of wings.

"And you know what they call it?"

I did not know what they called it.

"They call it Webster. Which sucks. But we're gonna call it WolfSpidr. No *e*. Because we prowl the web."

"Wolf spiders don't prowl webs," I said. I was really scared of spiders, and thus knew a great deal about them.

"Doesn't matter," said Jimmer. "Because it sounds fucking awesome. No *e*."

I couldn't argue with that, and searched my mind for another topic, one to which I could contribute without betraying the trust of Ava Winston.

Oh yeah, one leapt to mind.

"Hey," I said, the obvious cloudbank drifting over me after a half-day of sunshine. "Have you heard from Chickie?"

"Um," Jimmer said, and I could feel the effort it was taking him to switch gears. "No. You?"

"Nope. I don't know where he is. I tried him a few times yesterday and went looking for him last night."

"Where'd you look?"

"The usual. The Knots."

"You worried?"

Was I worried? I hadn't been, until now.

"Maybe a little, I guess."

"Shoulda called me," said Jimmer. "I can track him."

I could hear Jimmer put his phone down and then the snap and crackle of nails on a laptop.

"He's in Sink City," said Jimmer. "Downtown."

I could hear Jimmer's voice drop as he said it. Only one reason for Chick to be in Sink City and it wasn't a good one.

"How do you know that?" I asked.

"My phone," Jimmer said. "Of course."

I sat up on the edge of the bed.

"Sink City, huh?" I said. "You can't give me an address, can you?"

Jimmer sounded almost embarrassed.

"Sorry. I told you it was an older phone."

"Listen," I said, checking my watch. It was closing in on 9 A.M. "Can you check again at eleven and let me know? If he's not headed back here, I'm going to go get him."

231

"Uh, yeah," said Jimmer. "I guess. But call him first. He'll see that it's you. Maybe that'll get him headed in your direction."

"Cool," I said. "Thanks."

Jimmer clicked off.

I went down to the massage salon and sat through an unproductive shiatsu. Fulvio seemed concerned.

"You are very tense," he said. "Would you like a wrap?"

"No," I said. "But let's wrap this up." Punning because it felt frivolous and I could use some frivolity.

I threw a towel across my shoulders and headed for the caldaria, determined to lose myself in the eucalyptus fog. But when I opened the door and the steam started floating out at me, reaching for me, I closed it right back up. That steam seemed to represent something. I pushed through a side door for some fresh air but wound up in a service corridor behind the public spaces of the spa, where large wheeled baskets sat piled with towels, the ubiquitous white towels, the currency of resort living. The corridor was warm and smelled of laundry and old sweat. An almost alkaline smell, something I figured Head-Connect might consider using in its brochures—give us a month and we'll turn you into a battery. Machines scrubbed and tumbled around a corner. I could hear the chirps and groans of the laundrywomen at the machines, the upbeat industry of immigrants. I leaned against the wall and let the steam cool on my skin.

In the end, it was the smell that did it. It took me back to the locker rooms of the CYC, to Coach Harvey shouting at us, to the practice courts where Chick and I would drain foul shots for hours. And then back further, something deeper, my dad, home from his own Monday night pickup games, his North Gable Variety T-shirt wrung out and hanging on the bathtub rail, of him coming into my room and leaning over me and kissing my cheek, sweaty and flushed, and how only then, with the home complete, could I fall asleep.

I went back to the room and checked my watch. It was only 9:45, but fuck it. Sink City, the Venice of Western New England. It was on the way back to Boston.

I started to pack.

Ava Winston was in the lobby, escorting a guest from check-in to facilities, when I came through.

"Good morning, Mr. Johansson," she said, blushing slightly and releasing the guest at her elbow into the down-spa current. She was dressed in her occupational finery and her golden hair was pulled back and I could just tell from 4 feet away that it would smell like lavender if I could get close enough. "I understand we missed you at Sustenance this morning."

I smiled and looked at my feet in a way that I hoped would be endearing. We stood there for a second, and then Ava noticed the shoulder bag I was carrying.

"I thought you were staying until Friday," she said, her face betraying little besides a slight widening of her eyes.

"Yeah," I said. "I need to get back to Boston and take care of some things. But I'll be back tomorrow. Or the weekend."

She raised her eyebrows slightly, still trying to maintain her balance. I checked the lobby and then leaned in very quickly and kissed her on the cheek.

Ava's hands started to come up, either in protest or in reciprocation, but she reined them back in and straightened herself up.

"You can't keep doing that," she whispered, and I got the sense that she was serious.

But I was serious too.

"Seriously," I said, to let her know how serious I was. "I'll be back."

She looked at me for a long moment, her eyes going from wide to narrow, and I was a little glad we were in public. But then she sort of shimmered and the façade was maintained.

"Well, thank you for staying with us," she said. "We look forward to seeing you again."

Then she turned on her heel and headed to her desk.

"I'll be back," I said a third time, as she walked away, third time means I mean it, but I might as well have been talking to myself.

I hit the Pike hard with a bear claw and a cup of Dunkin' Donuts coffee. The Pike was always better for leaving, downhill and fast, none of that sappy hill-town kitsch to slow you. Thirty miles of straight road between exits, Gare to Westfield, and another seven to 91, which would take me to Sink City. I took a slug of the coffee, which was impossibly sweet and hot, it was to coffee what gin was to water, and every nerve in my body jolted awake. I passed through the toll and set the truck to cruise. The Berkshires were behind me in a flash. Come like a virus, leave like an exorcism.

The plan was to hit Sink City and track down Chickie, talk some sense into him or turn him in, maybe even take him to Boston with me until he could clean up. Confess everything to everyone, wrap us all up in a nurturing environment. That would be ideal. Chick could sleep on the couch, meet some new people, watch college basketball with me at the bar on the corner. It'd be like the dorm we'd never shared. I could put a sock on the doorknob when Ava came over.

The Pike intersected 91 at the bottom of a long defile, shortly after it crossed the gorge between Russell and Westfield. The Westfield River sloughed along beneath, on its way to join the mightier Connecticut, these rivers with their dead mills dotting the banks like the Pioneer Valley equivalent of the Berkshire cottages. The salmon were gone from the Connecticut, which was dammed up in a half dozen places by coastal industrialists, routed through canals, processing plants, turbines. Up to the north, some of the factory towns were rising from their ruins, Turners and Greenfield and Shelburne, beckoning artists and manufacturers and young families with their converted mills and their lantern festivals. But the central valley was still beleaguered, and Sink City was its sacrificial heart.

I pulled over at a lookout on 91 and got out of the truck. You could see the whole place from here. There were the church spires and bell towers and Sink City's immense town hall, the distant fields and water towers. I looked out over the Flatgate Mall, the first of its kind in western Massachusetts, which must have seemed like such a good idea when they built it back in the early '80s but then choked the retail life out of the downtown, leaving behind a blasted cityscape of bars and barber shops and boarded-up warehouses. You could see the good bones of the place, the brownstones, the regal corpses of the factories, the two canals cutting through the eastern edge of the metropolis. You could see what was possible if they could begin to lure the bohemians down to weed the medians and colonize the firetraps, join forces with the children of the immigrant population and the Olde Sinkers hanging on to the hillsides. If they could come together to imagine a future. A Portland, even a Portsmouth, with mixed-use developments and galleries and maybe some rebooted manufacturing. A place where you could get microbrews and a butchered pig and some textiles along the wooded edges of the river. You could get those things now, actually, but few people were ballsy enough to do it. So instead, they were building a casino, which would no doubt solve everything.

I got back in the truck and headed down into the city. Past Monsta Kuts and the Nines and O'Hara's, past the convalescent homes and nursing homes and graveyards for those too tired to move south. Past the derelict lots and the kids loitering on corners at 11:15 on a Tuesday, just trying to make it through the day. Down to the flats by the river, the urban frontier, where a handful of pioneers were digging in and renovating an enormous mill project. There was a children's museum there, and, surprisingly, the National Volleyball Hall of Fame, less gaudy and less popular than its roundball sibling to the south. Outside the children's museum was the empty bed of a water sculpture, dry since 1984.

I pulled over near city hall and tried Chick's numbers again. No answer. I was about to call Jimmer, see if he could work his tech magic and get any more precise on coordinates, when I spotted a purple Trans Am parked up the block, near the massive bell tower of the congregational church.

I swung around and came by it from behind.

Nobody in the back seat. One person in the driver's seat. I looped around again and parked, walking quickly up toward the passenger side. The sidewalk was cracked and stained and I had my Head-Connect sweatshirt hood up over my head. The door handle was cold but snapped open when I pulled.

I jumped into the passenger seat. Elvis LaBeau, behind the wheel, jerked awake with a start.

"Oh, shit," he said, when he recognized me.

I looked at him like a dad who'd caught his son coming in after curfew.

"What do you have to say for yourself?" I asked.

LaBeau looked fleetingly at the glove compartment, but whatever was in it he wasn't dumb enough to go for. Instead, he sat still in the driver's seat, appearing to calculate the odds that, even in Sink City, a public beating would be tolerated. After a second he rubbed his eyes.

"You try saying no to him," he said.

"Where is he?"

LaBeau gestured with his head toward the bell tower.

"Up there," he said. "Listen, I didn't seek him out or anything. He came to me, said he had nowhere else to go."

That stung.

"I kept Robbie out of the loop, if that matters to you."

"Don't matter to me," I said, even though it did. I felt like I should present a hard front. It's easier to open a fist than to make one, something like that. "I'll bust that motherfucker up."

"Yeah, well, I'd be careful about that," LaBeau said, gesturing to the church. "You got a weak link here. And Robbie, between you and me, is still hoping for a happy ending with his brother. That high school shit. He might see Chick's head as a peace offering."

"For who? Tim-Rick?"

LaBeau shrugged.

"Just saying. He'll take the dude's money, but you don't really want to give him a reason to go tribal."

"He knows what would happen, though, right?"

LaBeau shrugged again.

"You going to be around full time then?"

He wasn't stupid, Elvis LaBeau. He knew what was up.

"Tim-Rick's over it."

"Tim-Rick tell you that?"

"Yeah, he did. He's moved on, so if Robbie is hoping for some reconciliation, Chick isn't the way to go about it."

"Maybe get Tim-Rick to tell him that."

I sat steaming. These assholes and their stupid games. This old bullshit. I would kick all their asses.

"Tim-Rick. What a stupid name, anyway."

"Robbie told me that it's two names."

"No shit."

"No. Like, it's the names of two people combined. Their mom was pregnant with twins, but only one made it. She couldn't choose, so she combined the names."

That struck me as a terrible idea, and I didn't give much of a shit about Tim-Rick Golack.

"That's fucked up, man."

LaBeau raised his eyebrows.

"Weird the shit people will tell you when they're high."

We both sat there for a second. I imagine we were thinking the same thing, wondering what it would be like to carry your dead brother's name around for your whole life.

Enough with that shit. I checked my watch and looked up at the bell tower.

"What's he doing in there?"

LaBeau shrugged.

"Getting high, or coming down, probably. Dude's been high since last night."

"Where were you last night?"

"The Knots. Came out here this morning because last night your boy said if I didn't drive him he was going to hitchhike. He was in no shape to hitchhike."

"What's he on? Oxy?"

LaBeau nodded. "Among other things. He's an addict, man."

"No shit," I said. "And what the fuck are you doing to help?"

He looked at me.

"What do you want? I'm an addict too."

He looked down at his hands. Opiates were coming in like rot out here.

"Shit. I took him in, let him crash. Dude has a fucking *tent*. It's freezing out. I drove his ass here so he didn't freeze to death. I'm the one sitting here waiting on him."

He reached into his coat pocket, but all that came out were his keys.

"I don't need this shit, dude. You want him, you got him," Elvis LaBeau said, and put the keys in the ignition. He was making a pretty good point. "Call the cops. Turn us in. You'd be doing me a favor."

"Fine," I said. "Go home. I'll take care of this."

For a minute, I didn't get out and he didn't start the car. The two of us, we deserved each other.

Then I opened the door and stepped out onto the asphalt. Behind me, the Trans Am coughed to life, and LaBeau was gone before I'd crossed the street.

I checked the nave and the chancel, the narthex and the pulpit, a whole catechistic vocab coming back after fifteen years away. No Chick. The church was dark and quiet, votives flickering within a side grotto, velvet confessionals gossiping to each other. The rug swallowed my footfalls and I moved up to the choir. From the balcony, the empty wood of the pews shone in the cold late morning.

I found him at the top of the bell tower, in a small round room with a high ceiling from which the Sanctus hung. He was slumped silently on a bench, hands in the pockets of a light coat, passed out or asleep. His breath made clouds in the open-windowed room. His beard looked rough and his skin was pasty.

I sat next to him and waited for him to wake up.

So, yeah, sure, a bell tower again. I felt it, the symbolism, the events from half a life ago, half our lives anyway, the way you wonder, as you always do, in that useless way, how things might have been different if things had been different. But, and I'll be honest here, I was also thinking about Ava and Boston and my job and my life and all the things that did not involve my drug-addicted friend breathing unevenly on the bench next to me. Like my other, non-drug-addicted friends. And my new familiarity with yoga. And my weight, which was down about 5 pounds since last week and was beginning to seem scalable. All these things. And about how I would share them with Chickie when he woke up, and he would see what I was seeing and might offer an insight or two that changed the way I saw them, or propose some vaguely outlandish but nonetheless thrilling alteration. And he would do so with a smile and genuine fellowship. And we would wind up laughing.

And then the Sanctus bell rang, thunderclaps in the small room, because it was noon.

Chickie snorted and swallowed and his chin fell forward. He opened his eyes, which were bleary and unfocused. I sat there, waiting. The bells went on forever.

When they stopped, he shook his head and looked over.

"Where are we?" he said.

"Sink City. The bell tower," I said.

The words seemed to drip into his ears and leech their way to his cortex. Then he lifted his hand and put it out onto mine.

"Sorry," he said. "To make you come all this way."

I shrugged.

"I had to be here anyway," I said.

Chick smiled. The best smile ever.

"Sorry about," he said, tilting his head in a way that I figured meant storming out of breakfast.

I nodded. "Me too."

Glad that was cleared up. We sat there for a minute.

"What are we doing here?" I asked.

"I was about to ask you the same thing."

I looked around the cold, stone room. This was fun. But silly.

"I hooked up with Ava Winston," I said. I felt bad about it for a second, and then didn't.

Chick smiled again and tapped my palm.

"I was hoping you'd say that," he said. "She's a sweetheart."

I nodded, more to myself than him.

"Listen, your ride left. I'm going back to Boston to pick up some things and get sorted out. Come stay with me?"

Chick breathed out into the cold air. For a minute he was quiet. Then he shook his head.

"Naah," he said. "I don't think that would be a good idea."

I looked at him.

"What do you mean?"

"I'm not going to Boston. Appreciate it, but no."

"Well," I said. "What are you going to do instead?"

Chick looked around at the empty room and tried to smile again, but it was weak.

"Doing it, I'm afraid."

"What?" I said, looking for a corner into which to spit the words but not finding one because it was a round tower. It was good too, because the last time I'd pressed too hard he'd split on me. I tried to modulate my delivery accordingly. "Get high and pass out?"

"I know it's not exactly ambitious," he said. "It's not what you or the other guys would do. But my options are limited."

I didn't know what to say, so I just sat there. Eventually I thought of something.

"Why'd you even call?" I asked. "When you got back. Why even call me if all you planned to do was fall down a hole?"

Chick shrugged.

"I knew you'd come."

Broke my heart.

"I guess I shouldn't have," he added. "I didn't mean to fuck up your stuff."

"No, man," I said. "Are you kidding? It's been great."

He laughed at that.

"Look," he said, straightening out his back and grimacing. "Let it go. Just let this all go."

He stood up.

"We're in different places, Pete."

I hated it when he called me by my name. It was never good.

"That's probably obvious," he said. "Don't take this the wrong way, but sometimes I don't even know if we're still friends. I mean, you know? Maybe we're just guys who went through some shit together as kids."

Dude was just flat-out throwing bombs.

He turned and walked out of the bell tower room, down the long, narrow stairs toward the choir. I followed, because what else was I going to do? In the narthex, where the latecomers would huddle during Mass, hoping to sneak over to a pew during a break in the homily, I dipped my finger in the holy water, blessed myself out of habit. Also it seemed like a good idea.

Chick slid toward the open door, moments from vanishing again.

"Where are you going to stay?" I asked him.

He didn't answer, just kept limping toward the cold city. He looked like a ghost on the skids.

I felt the clock ticking. What were the odds here? Chick was one pill away from an overdose and didn't seem to care. Jimmer wouldn't be hanging around for too much longer, and Unsie was ready to wash his hands, sensibly, of the lot of us. I could just go back out to Boston, act like the past week and a half had never happened. Let all this stuff go. Look up that paralegal-turned-physician's-assistant, see how her engagement had worked out.

Wait for the call saying Chick was in the hospital, or jail. Or worse.

Goddamn. It wouldn't even take much for things to break right. It was close already. I mean, there was Ava, and whatever that was, but promising, no? Ava and my new interest in probiotics and stretching and soon, soon, it would be spring. Jimmer was in love and Unsie was about to be a dad. March was the most dangerous month, the swing season, cold snaps still lurking and the occasional storm and then suddenly spring and it was light longer and the earth was wet and the creeks and lakes were thawed and you could get a glimpse of a distant summer. The trees woke up and the flowers returned. Chick said he didn't want my help, but I knew he did. Or even if he didn't want it, he needed it. If I could just get him through these next few weeks, just make it to April, everything would be okay. I mean, shit, Christ rose in April. We could too.

Fuck it.

"Okay, fine," I called after him. "You win."

He stopped in the doorway. I took a deep breath.

"About the rhino. The horn. You were right," I said.

He turned around and looked back at me.

"It's there," I said. "At Fleur-de-Lys."

Nothing happened for a second. Then he raised his hands like touchdown.

He was only mildly upset about the lying. Almost like he got it, got why I would lie. "Really?" he kept asking. He would ask, and then laugh, and then ask again. He wanted to know where it was, how it was displayed, whether, after all these years, it still looked sharp.

We were sitting in the Escalade, still in Sink City. The street was mildly alive, a lunch crowd braving the wind for a smoke or a slice of pepperoni. Clouds were massing to the southeast, late winter checking its tank. The forecast called for snow.

I told him what I could remember, which was everything. Three feet, almost, curved like a scimitar, black and gray as if charred. I told him about the whirlpool room where the horn sat shining in its niche, about how the room opened up onto the rolling back lawn. I also told him what Jimmer had said, about the value of the thing, both in real and in historical terms, what Jimmer'd said about the class of felony it represented.

"What we'll do, then, is wait until the heat dies down, then we can save some money and spend a weekend there," I said. "I'll show it to you then."

Chick looked at me like I was crazy.

"Or we could go tonight," he said.

"We can't go tonight," I said. "You can't go near the property yet. You'd go to jail."

"I'd only go to jail if I got caught, which I won't. And don't you still have a room there tonight?"

That was true, actually.

"So you go in, I hide in the truck, we go see the horn. Then we leave. That sounds pretty simple."

It did sound simple. Too simple.

"It sounds too simple," I said. "They're keeping an eye out for you. The guards are on, like, DEFCON 2. They wand the cars. Plus, you can't get to the spa area without walking through the lobby, which is where Ava and all the front desk people are. They'd recognize you."

Chickie sat and thought.

"If I could get to the back of the tub room, then I could just come through a window or something."

I shook my head.

"Those windows are locked. It's winter."

Chick nodded.

"We need someone on the inside."

He looked at me.

I was scrambling.

"Nope. Here's an alternative. We talk to Ava, explain what they have in there, why we want it, she shows it to us, lets us spend some time with it, and then takes it from there. Maybe she puts the horn in a place of honor."

I thought about Ava's face if I showed up with Chick and explained that my weekend there had all been part of a ruse to infiltrate Head-Connect's inner sanctums and then raid them.

"We can't do that to her," Chick said. "Plus, she'd never go for it."

He was right on both counts.

"It's got to be us," he said. "We're the ones who know. We're the ones who've always known. These fucking thieves. Think about what they did to that thing, that poor scared bastard. They used him for their own amusement. Then he fights back and they cut his horn off."

Yeah, I thought, nodding. That would suck.

"Least the rhino was already dead, though, right?" I said. "When they took the horn?"

Chick shook his head.

"Yeah, cuz the dude fucking shot it."

He was feeling it, feeling the truth.

"A thousand sins, going back all the way," he said. "They've all led us to here."

He looked out the window at the warehouses of east Sink City, then back at me. He smacked his hand against his thigh.

"We are the avengers. We're the wrath."

He gave me a righteous look, then broke into a smile.

"Shit," I said. "And here I thought we were just a couple of guys who went through some shit together as kids."

Chick smiled wider.

"We only went through it together because we're friends."

At this point it was too late, but I took a last shot at mitigation.

"Listen, we cannot steal the horn. And by 'we,' I mean you. That's real trouble, long-term trouble. I need you to work with me on this. There are people, people with resources. Maybe we should call, like, the Sierra Club, or PETA. Get them to come in and take up the cause. Or the *Franchise*. They'd do it."

Chick looked out the window. I wasn't sure if he was listening. I was parked at a corner and we could see down a rolling avenue across the canals to long brick warehouses. Most of the windows were boarded up, but some of them weren't, and the glass looked new, and some of the doors showed signs of fresh paint. Maybe it was possible. Sink City by its bootstraps.

But maybe I was projecting.

"So, how about this?" I said. "I go in, you meet me at the back of the building. I show you the horn. Then we leave. We leave, we call in the reinforcements, make a big deal out of it with the newspapers, human interest stuff, get them to, like, find the rhino, excavate it or something, do a whole ceremony. A nice thing. Head-Connect has the money for that. They could spin it, make it marketing. Can you get behind that?"

Chick was still looking down the avenue.

"That would take months," he said.

"You're right. Months of sobriety too. But it'll be spring, at least. Not too hot. Blossoms and shit. And then in the summer we can hang out with Unsie, hit the Bowl, go canoeing."

Chick took a deep breath and looked out the front window. He seemed to resign himself to something. Then he nodded.

"That sounds good, man."

"Right?"

He nodded.

I nodded back.

"So we're good? We're going to do this?"

He nodded again.

He was nodding too much.

"Guy, I need to hear you say it."

"We're good," he said. "We're going to do this."

Now we were getting somewhere. I reached out and tapped him on the knee.

"Keep it together," he said.

He slept most of the ride back. I took the Pike again. This was no time for introspection, this was time for focus. In and out. No hassle. I called my office. This time, one of the partners got on the phone. Don Huey, who was a big deal at Huey Huckle, especially since Bill Huckle was dead.

"What's going on, Mr. Johansson?" he said.

It took me a minute to figure out who it was, and then to tame my sense of being betrayed by my assistant. I rarely heard Don Huey speak. I'd once stood next to him at the urinals in the men's room and came away convinced I'd pissed on his shoes, but after a few minutes of reflection I concluded that it was unlikely.

"Mr. Huey," I said. "Nice to speak with you."

"It's nice to speak with you too," Don Huey said. "I understand that you're out in western Massachusetts?"

I nodded reflexively. "That's right."

"Never liked western Massachusetts," Don Huey said. "Prefer the Cape."

That's what everybody in Boston said.

"It's God's country out here," I said. "We should open an office."

Don Huey snorted, apparently a connoisseur of gallows humor.

"Maybe we will," he said. "Tell me, what specifically brings you out there? I understand there was a hearing on Monday?"

"Yeah," I said. "Uh, it's the Van Nest estate."

I let that hang. I wasn't sure how well Don Huey knew the open matters in the office, or if he knew that the Van Nest estate was not one of them.

"How did the hearing go?"

I felt like I was talking to a spider.

"Went pretty well," I said. "We have some work to do, but things look good."

"Will you be in the office tomorrow?"

"Yeah, I think so. I'd hoped to be back today but some things came up," I said, as vaguely as I thought might be tolerated. "Should be back by noon."

"Well, listen," said Don Huey, a pleasant enough spider but a spider all the same. "I suspect a large part of this is bullshit, but I'm going to let it ride. I'd like you to stop by my office, though, when you get here tomorrow at noon, so I can get a clearer picture."

Someone once told me that the way to survive in a law firm was that whenever a partner asked you a question, any question, you should say, "The answer is twelve," firmly and with enthusiasm.

"No problem," I said. "Twelve it is."

Don Huey hung up and I considered the pretty distinct possibility that I was less than twenty-four hours away from losing the only real job I'd ever had. My link to a world that was starting to effervesce. I looked over at Chickie, who was asleep against the window. We had crossed the gorge and were climbing back up into the hills. It wasn't yet five, but behind us, the Pioneer Valley was already darkening. Clouds were coming up the Hudson, off to the south, bringing snow. The east was still clear.

❧

Chick was still asleep when we got into Gable, so I drove uptown and parked between Asgard and the Heirloom, which felt sort of like the poles of a dilemma—the alpha and omega, the future and the past. Too much? Yeah, I thought so too. And just then who walks out of the Heirloom but Tim-Rick Golack, both of him.

I rolled down my window.

"What's up, buttercup?" I said.

It felt weird talking to him, like talking to someone who's sick, whose prognosis has circulated.

Tim-Rick came over and peered into the truck.

"Ah," he said. "The prodigal son returns."

"Me or him?" I asked.

Tim-Rick just smirked.

"What'd you do, tranquilize him?"

I looked at Chick, whose head had sunk into the collar of his coat.

"Hit him with the truck," I said. "You want to get some shots in?"

Tim-Rick smiled.

"Nah. I'll wait until he wakes up."

"Might be a while."

"Is he high?"

I shook my head.

"Not this time."

We were having an actual conversation.

"How's Ginny?"

Tim-Rick looked back at the Heirloom.

"She's good. I think. She doesn't tell me much."

"Smart lady," I said.

He shrugged and turned his collar up against the snow, which had started to fall.

"I don't want to know much, actually. Less the better. The details make me nervous."

He shifted gears, looked up into the flakes.

"This weather's badass. Almost spring, though."

I nodded. That seemed like a promising thought, a safe thought. Couldn't quite let the heavier stuff go, though.

"So, like, are you in a good place now?" I asked. I don't know why I asked it. I guess it just felt like I could. He did seem like he was in a good place, relatively speaking, and I was interested in how he'd gotten there. I could use the info for Chick, maybe.

Tim-Rick shrugged. "Pretty good, I guess."

"You burying hatchets?"

He looked at Chick.

"In anyone I can," he said, but he was smiling.

"How'd you get there? In a good place?"

Tim-Rick sort of squinted at me. It felt like he was wondering what I knew, how much and from where. Like he was weighing his openness. He waited a second, then shrugged.

"Time. Effort. Love of a good woman, maybe."

I must have looked doubtful, because he followed up fast.

"And therapy," he said. "A lot of therapy. You should look into it."

"Let's not get carried away," I said, trying to convey some sort of jocularity.

Chick snorted next to me and raised his head. I checked on him, seemed like he was waking up. I turned back to Tim-Rick.

"Listen, dude. I hope things work out for you. Really."

He looked at me for a second. Then he laughed.

"Appreciate it," he said, shaking his head. "I guess."

He kicked the front tire of the Escalade and looked at the darkening sky.

"If I was you I'd hit the road."

And with that he walked away.

❧

Chick and I drove up the dead-end street on which we'd lived as kids and parked at the top, where the houses met the forest and trailheads snaked off into the woods. Near the road, a big sugar maple wore a skirt of buckets. We sat in the truck. I sipped Gable's version of bodega coffee, a latte with foliage drawn into the foam. Chick had pounded the espresso I bought him. He was distracted, twitchy, his knees bouncing like they used to do before basketball games.

"You remember the way?" I asked.

"Shit yeah," Chick said. "Back of my hand."

I went over the plan. Give me an hour. Come through the woods. At eight I'll be in the tub room. I'll open one of the windows. You'll come in, commune with the rhino spirit, then leave. Eyes only. We meet back here and crash at the Horse Head.

The snow was coming down hard, thick flakes falling like stars, and I gave Chick my Head-Connect sweatshirt to wear under his thin black coat. He pulled the hood up. The woods were quiet, the snow starting to dampen everything. I looked around the old neighborhood. I imagined us in our homes, little kids with the world ahead of us, sitting around the dining room table, staring at our broccoli, our mothers staring at us.

"Remember Mrs. Dangle?" I asked, looking at the little cottage next to the space where Chick's house used to be. "Remember how she'd yell at us on Halloween?"

Chick laughed a little.

"She hit me with a wooden spoon once, right on my knuckles."

"Her grandson threw a rock at me once," I said. "Because I called him a granddangle."

"I remember that. I thought it was because you called him Nussbaum."

"That was his name," I said.

"Yeah, but you called him Nussbaum Nussbaum. That's when he picked up the rock."

He was right. I'd forgotten that, and still couldn't remember why I'd done it in the first place, except that the kid was a year older than us and a jackass.

Chick got out of the Escalade. He looked down the trail, a white path through the woods. Augustus Beecher's woods. His white hood blended with the snowfall and it almost looked like a headless jacket standing in the trees. Then he turned back around and reached out to give me a fist bump.

"One hour," he said. "Stay low. Don't stop moving."

He smiled his big smile. His eyes were bright. It just made me more nervous.

"You got to stay with me on this, right?" I said, giving him my serious look. "I'm putting my neck out for you."

"Float like a bumblebee," he said, winking at me. "Sting like a . . . something."

Then he jogged off down the path, through the trees, through the snow, and vanished.

❧

I waited for a few minutes, staring into the whiteness where he'd been, and then drove back down Scrimshaw, out onto Bramble, around the 4 miles to the main entrance to Fleur-de-Lys.

Security Pete waved me down.

"No sign of him, Mr. Johansson," he said.

I projected blankness.

"Who?"

"Your friend, the trespasser."

Security Pete was smiling in a way that seemed to convey both bemusement and condescension, as though I were a child who'd asked him to keep an eye out for the Easter Bunny. They had protocols. Easter Bunny wasn't getting through. Nothing like that could ever happen here.

Fuck these guys.

"Well," I said. "I'm sure he'll be along presently."

I smiled at him to let him know I was joking.

He gave me a little faux salute and wanded my truck with his flashlight, and then I was through. I rolled up slowly, the black pines and barren hardwoods dark and forbidding. They seemed closer than they'd been before, like they were encroaching. Maybe it was the snow. It was falling heavily now. Chickie was out there somewhere, slip-crunching his way through the Magic Meadow, maybe, or maybe already inside the Head-Connect perimeter.

The valet guys took the truck away before it occurred to me to ask them to keep it close, maybe even keep it running, in case we needed to make a getaway. They seemed oblivious, but studiously so? Were they already onto us? Were there microphones in their ears, two-ways in their fleece cuffs? I consoled myself with the thought that there were lengths to which we simply couldn't go. Chick was already taking a ridiculous risk, a risk that I was enabling, and if he got caught he'd be looking at a very angry judge. And I'd be looking at a very angry Ava Winston, if indeed I got the chance to look at her again.

The plan. Show him the horn, send him on his way, involve some third parties, get on with our lives.

It might work.

It was never going to work.

It was never going to work and I was an idiot for believing otherwise. All that rah-rah stuff, all the team building, the buying in. We were fucked. I should walk back down the drive, escort Security Pete to the tub room, and turn us both in. Chick would get some time in some facility, maybe kick his bad habits. I could go back to my life. It would almost be an act of charity. I should do that. I should.

But nope.

I walked into the lobby. It was late and Ava Winston was not at her desk. I checked my watch. Half an hour until rendezvous.

"Welcome back, Mr. Johansson," said a voice behind me. I turned. It was Tudd, red-cheeked and bright-eyed. He clapped me on the back. "No hike this evening due to snow. But we can swim."

That sounded great.

"Maybe," I said. "I need to check my schedule."

Tudd nodded in a way that managed to express both deference and disapproval.

"We will hope to see you," he said, but he didn't walk away. He just sort of stood there.

"Okay then," I said. "I'll go check."

Tudd was making me even more nervous. I left him and walked down the hall toward the guest rooms. In Jimmer's room,

I changed out of my winter coat and into less conspicuous attire. I'd given Chick my sweatshirt but still had the pants, roomy and warm. I put Jimmer's sweatshirt on, he'd left it there, of course. I slipped my feet into the pair of sneakers housekeeping kept placing in the closets. Jimmer's sweatshirt was tight, but maybe not as tight as it would've been last week? Because I was levelling up. Or had been, before this bad, bad decision.

I checked the hallway and headed off toward the spa.

The long corridor empty. The gymnasium and yoga studios full and distracted. The spa attendants with the lotus flowers and towel baskets stood behind desks, demure and accommodating. The caldaria, who knows? Steams were thick. I caught vague floral and earthen smells, something southwestern maybe. Couldn't see inside. I walked down the back corridor to the tub room, lit like a Turkish cistern, the twin whirlpools roiling like Scylla and Charybdis, the dip pool a green grave. Aqueous shadows rolled on the ceiling. The egret, forever sharp-eyed. The horn shining like an Elvish blade in a Tolkien book. Elvish LaBeau.

Man, we're all over the place.

Ava Winston in her guest services uniform was standing at the windows, pointing out to three women in plush robes how the back lawns rolled down to a distant glen that had once stabled the horses. She turned when I walked in and, when she saw me, the look on her face—surprise, a secret thrill—broke my heart for the second time since noon.

"Pete . . . Mr. Johansson," she said, a smile spreading beyond her control. "So nice to have you back."

Fuckety fuck.

The three women—brass blond, in their fifties but toned, wearing rocks that would just tear their hands up at yoga, I could tell them that—looked at me with the conspiratorial warmth of the wealthy. We're all strangers wearing bathrobes, the look said, but it's okay because that's just how you roll when you're this goddamn rich.

"Isn't this wonderful?" the tallest of the three said, her face a Picasso, gesturing with a thin hand around the tub room.

I looked at Ava.

"It sure is," I said, and I felt like she knew what I was trying to say because she sort of blushed.

"Here for a soak, Mr. Johansson?" she said when she'd recovered. "Or are you braving the frigid depths?"

I scanned the curved bank of windows behind them, but couldn't see anything.

"Uh, not sure," I said. "That cold dip looks a little intimidating."

"I bet all the men say that," said the Picasso, and her companions laughed.

Ava looked at her quickly.

"Actually, it's wonderful for your circulation, and many people find it remarkably invigorating after a soak in one of the baths." She looked at me. "You should try it. Be brave."

I nodded, smiled.

"We'll see," I said. Then I gave the Picasso and her companions a sideways look. "The temptation is strong."

I laughed and the ladies laughed with me. They were eating it up. We stood there for a moment, engaged in about three different mental communications at once, and then Ava said, "Okay. So let's continue to the studios."

The three women nodded at me as Ava led them toward the hallway to resume their tour of the facilities. On the way past, the Picasso touched my arm.

"Do let us know how it is," she said.

I patted her on the hand.

"You'll be the first," I said, giving her the full Handsome. It was the role I was born to play.

The ladies laughed again, our little charm theater an unexpected perk of the tour, and headed on toward the studios. Ava Winston followed them. She was beaming. Because I still got it.

"Enjoy your soak, Mr. Johansson," she said, flashing me an unprofessional smile as she moved around the corner, and I swear to you she was nearly sashaying. "I'll catch you later."

I gave them a few minutes, paced, tried to look idle and innocent lest there were cameras behind mirrors, other guests still submerged. I didn't see any, but then you wouldn't, would you? I peered at the egret, a proud bird doomed to spend its afterlife down here in the tub room, inspecting a parade of stretch marks and keratoses. Or was it a heron? Heron, egret. What was the difference? Poor bird probably dealt with that its whole life, and now even in the Hereafter. I egret to inform you that I am a heron.

Nah, it was an egret, I decided. Herons were blue.

I had a sudden idea of what could happen next, an idea that I could unloose the horn from its marble base, stash it in the waistband of my sweatpants, like a sword or something, and saunter right out through the lobby of Head-Connect. Draw Ava aside and give her the opportunity to say, "Is that a rhino horn in your sweatpants or are you just happy to see me?" Even if she didn't actually say it. Just give her the opportunity. She'd get it. She'd smile and her eyes would sparkle and that'd be something. Then I'd explain everything to her, turn the thing in and let the proper authorities handle it.

That would be a good outcome. I could look at Chickie and shrug.

I picked up the marble base.

The horn felt solid and smooth. Someone had used a laminate on it, and it shone in the lamps. It was lighter than I expected, like a piece of driftwood. I put one hand on the inside curve at the bottom and the other along the base and rattled it slightly. It was affixed with a screw. When I turned it, it began coming loose, and before I could really think about what I was doing, I was holding it in my hands. Homoerotic as shit, for sure, but I was relatively secure in my sexuality. And the thing was wicked.

I heard a tap on the windows.

I threw a towel over the horn. Put it in the crease of one of the Adirondack chairs along the wall. Meandered over to the hallway entrance and peered down in each direction. Nobody there.

The tapping became more insistent.

I slow-strolled to the windows, head on a swivel. When I was a few feet away, I broke into a trot.

Chick was barely visible against the glare from the interior lights. I had to lean up to the edge of the glass and cup my hands around my eyes to see him, and then he was right there, inches away. He'd shed his dark windbreaker and had the hood of my Head-Connect sweatshirt pulled up against the snow. One hand was buried in the sweatshirt's kangaroo pouch, and with the other he was giving me a vigorous thumbs-up. I flashed him one back. I motioned for him to wait, pointed behind me, went to the chair where the horn lay swaddled, picked it up, and brought it to the window. The black tip peeked out like a newborn.

I watched Chickie's eyes settle on it, focus, widen.

That sort of felt like maybe it should have been enough, Chick peering through the fancy glass, seeing what he came to see, seeing that it was real. Beyond that, if this little excursion went any further, there were about ten ways for it to end and nine of them were bad.

But who are we kidding? He was coming in, and I was letting him.

I met him at one set of the French doors that opened onto the back lawn. They were dead-bolted. I put the horn down, twisted the lock counterclockwise. The doors wouldn't budge. Chick pointed up to the top of the door frame, where, lo and behold, there was an additional bolt. I slid the brass knob down, and then reached to the floor to free the identical lock there. These were nice doors. Summer doors. They had faux-antique lattices but you could tell that the glass was a straight-up twenty-first-century thermal shield, double-layered, and that the insulation was tight. When I tugged on the handles, they swung open like an airlock. In warmer weather, Head-Connectors would walk out through these doors onto the manicured lawns beyond. They'd breathe deeply, their skin pink and tender from a soak, their muscles tingling, alive, present, the rolling lawn as new a world as they might hope, at that point, to be offered.

But it was winter, and the doors opened with a gust and a confetti of snow.

Chick dragged himself in and I pushed the doors closed behind him.

"Been out there for half an hour," he said, his lips blue and quivering. "I thought they'd never leave."

I started to help dust him off, stopped, and then started again. He was an icicle.

"Shhh," I whispered.

I pushed him toward one of the two corners of the room, where the wide bay met the flat interior walls. He kicked off his boots. He wasn't wearing any socks.

"Dude," I said.

He pointed to his feet.

"Can't feel them."

"Why aren't you wearing socks?"

He just shrugged. I gestured to the hot tubs. He plodded over, like a man walking on blocks, and before I could stop him, stepped into the cold dip pool.

"Shee-zus!" he said, hopping back out.

I tried not to laugh. Wasn't like I liked seeing him in pain. Wasn't even funny. It was just that my nerves were tight and that cold dip pool scared me.

"Thought you couldn't feel them."

He hopped over to one of the whirlpools and stepped into it up to his knees. His arms were spread out, the fear on his face replaced with relief.

"Ahhh," he said.

His whole body seemed to shiver.

"Any time now," I said, and went to check the hallways again. They were empty.

He was sitting on the edge of the hot tub now, dipping his raw hands in and squeezing them into fists.

"Where's it at?" he said.

I brought the horn over. He reached up for it.

"Eyes only," I said. "Right?"

Chick stood up slowly, lifting his pink feet tenderly out of the water. His eyes looked watery. He dried his hands on his sweatshirt.

"Come on," he said. "What's the worst that could happen?"

So I handed it to him.

He unwrapped it.

I tried to be still. It wasn't easy. My adrenaline was flowing, every muscle in my body saying hurry up, let's go, there's not much time, but trying really hard to let the moment play itself out. The success of the whole endeavor seemed to depend on not rushing it.

Chick just stood quietly, holding the horn. Looking at it. Then he started giggling.

"Right?" he said. "Right?"

I couldn't help myself.

"I know," I said. "Shit is nuts."

He reached his free hand out. I hooked him up with the five. For a second we'd won.

Then we heard footsteps up the hallway that led to the women's lockers. We both looked up.

"Shit," I hissed at Chick.

He looked at the hall, looked at me, his eyes went comically wide. We were about to be caught, and nothing could have delighted him more.

"Put it back," I said, and tried to mean it. But he just stood there. His mouth formed an *O*.

I went to him and grabbed the horn, hustled it over to the alcove, and gave it a couple quick turns. It was listing, but we could deal with that later. I pointed at him, and then at the door, a stern point that I was planning on employing as a parent.

"Shoes," I said. "Hide."

He nodded obediently and hustled over to slip his boots over his still-wet toes. Then he pointed at the horn and raised his shoulders.

"Do not," I said.

He sort of feinted toward the horn, still smiling. Like, I'm not doing this, but I'm doing it.

"Nobody'll know," he said.

"Guy," I said, and even as I said it I felt like screaming, because the stakes were so fucking high. How could he not see how high they were? "I am not joking."

He looked back at me, grinning that stupid grin. Then something else crept into his look, and it was hard not to see an apology there, an apology I pretended I didn't understand. He looked at the horn, and then at the French doors, then again at me. And I could've grabbed him, taken him down. I had him by probably eighty pounds and I hadn't been sleeping on a cot. But I didn't.

The noise in the hall was getting closer. I looked at him. I knew exactly what was going to happen.

"Guy," I said again, raising a warning finger. "Please."

Chick smiled at me, and now there was nothing in the smile but him. All that time, gone in a blink.

"You know I love you, right?" Chick said.

And I did. And that was that.

Anyway, there was really no place to hide.

I stepped into the hallway.

"Hi," said Ava.

She was alone, still only halfway to the baths, walking back from depositing the biddies in the salon. She looked at me. I was still wearing the sweats and sneakers. "Umm, not going in?"

"Ava," I said as she got closer. I tried to smile but it felt weird and I can't imagine how it looked.

She glanced back down the hallway and put her hand on my arm. We stood together for a moment. I thought about trying to kiss her again, both because I wanted to and also, mainly, if the truth be told, as a distraction, but that seemed too cynical even for my playbook.

She continued around the corner to the tub room and looked around. I waited in the hallway, contemplating a dash.

"Why's it so cold in here?" she said.

I walked after her.

She stood in the empty room, rubbing her arms. She walked over to look at the windows, still all locked. She stopped at the doors I'd opened earlier and stared at a wet spot on the floor, where some dogged snow was still melting.

"I, uh, opened those," I said, following her eyes to the doors.

The absence of suspicion in the look she gave me. Man, nobody should have to go through that.

I pressed on.

"Just needed some air," I said. "I, uh, think the quinoa didn't agree with me."

Her eyes brightened and she grinned a little bit and said "Trouble in Marrakesh?" and for an instant I could see what could have been a future of comfort between us, the whole thing, quips and romps and rolls and courtship and then rolling right through the head colds and bad breath of domesticity, the times when we weren't at our best but it was okay, the tykes, the mortgage, the eventual orphaning and bleeding and wizening of age. I could see it all play out, rolling forward into the invisible future like a carpet in a cloudless sky. I thought to myself I could marry this girl. But then she looked past me, behind me, to the niche in the wall that I already knew was bare, and her bright eyes widened and then hardened, and as fast as I saw that particular dream, I saw just as clearly the dying of it. And it was almost a relief.

"What the . . . " she said, and blew past me on her titanium calves, to the wall, to the alcove, where the marble base for the horn now stood empty and upturned, the affixing screw in its center snapped off. I didn't even need to turn around to know it.

I was going to say something, but there wasn't much point, so I just stood there in that stupid room in those stupid plush sweats and those stupid sneakers as she looked around again. Now she regarded it professionally, unburdened of tenderness, taking in the French doors, the puddle, my dry hair, my false grin. What I would have said, if asked, if it would have made any difference, was something like, "Who's gonna help this kid but me?"

Which, you know, that's it in a nutshell.

Ava looked at me, and for a second her face crumbled like when your parents tell you that they're separating, that irredeemable moment, but then she pulled it together and cleared her throat and unhooked the walkie-talkie from her belt.

"Get out of here," she said.

I should have kissed her when I had the chance.

Ava's broadcast, which I heard as I headed up the hallway, past the steam rooms and through the spa, set several things in motion. A number of the helpers, including Tudd, materialized in the spa. Three of them escorted me to a side office. Arvindo Blanc floated down the sloped path from the main house wearing something that looked like a GORE-TEX kimono. He stopped me and said "Brother son, moon and stars," and then handed me off to the heretofore unseen head of security, a decidedly unhealthy-looking troll named Crevis, who asked me to wait in a windowless room behind the reception desk while he called the police. A few guests milled in the lobby, apparently attracted by sudden vibes of activity more than by the sound of any alarm, of which there was none. Walking with Crevis, who stood slightly behind me, close enough to grab my arm but otherwise apart, I spied the mother-daughter duo, the mother looking worried, the daughter looking interested. I spied the minor movie star, back from wherever, who gave me a nod. I did not spy Ava.

"What's your name again?" asked Crevis.

"They call me Handsome," I said.

The room where I waited was maybe one of the only places at Head-Connect that was not aesthetically soothing. It was more of a sensory-deprivation chamber. There was a folding card table, one of those metal ones, and a corresponding folding chair. There was a trashcan in the corner with a single Dunkin' Donuts coffee cup inside. Against one wall was a worn leather couch. On the opposite wall, someone had hung a poster for Head-Connect Nevada, which looked like a Quonset hut on Mars. Nobody asked me if I wanted water or ginseng or anything. Nobody came at all. I just sat there in Jimmer's too-small sweatshirt, which I was growing to hate, so I took it off and threw it in the corner.

I didn't even mind what Chick had done, not too much. At least it was done, and what's done is done, finally. It was hard to even feel surprised. I'm sure he'd weighed the consequences beforehand, maybe. Maybe he really believed nobody would connect us, and maybe they wouldn't have if it hadn't been Ava who came in. At least not right away. It probably would have taken some time, and by then we'd have figured something out. That's probably what he thought.

Or maybe he just saw one shot at this thing he felt he needed to do and figured I'd understand, which, sitting there, I sort of did. I mean, I'd given it to him.

I also felt no compulsion to protect him anymore, something else I'm sure he'd anticipated.

There was a knock on the door, like at the doctor's office, and then Crevis came in with Chief Grevantz.

We nodded to each other, the way you do.

"What's going on?" Crevis said, sitting on the couch.

Chief Grevantz stood across from my chair, arms folded, archetypically authoritative. He was wearing a great winterish cop coat, sort of a variation on the jackets we'd get in high school when we'd win our division, fleece lined and shiny sleeves. His hat had snow on the brim.

I cleared my throat.

"Well, see," I said. "There was once this rhino."

I told them most of the story, the shorter version. I tried to make it personal for Grevantz, a nod to his younger self's police work and the kindness of his predecessor. I left out the part about the oxycodone, and left Jimmer and Unsie out of it. Of course, I didn't mention my brief interlude with Ava Winston, the resurrection of which, with time and reparations and such, I still hoped was possible. I didn't minimize my own role, but I did present myself in as sympathetic a way as I could manage, at one point emphasizing my own frustration with an arm-sweep from T-shirt to sneaker and a nod at "that stupid sweatshirt." This is not my uniform, I wanted to say. This is a costume I've been compelled by unseen forces to wear.

And I ended with a flourish.

"But I know where he's going," I said, raising my arms and smiling triumphantly.

"Old times, huh?" Chief Grevantz said from the front seat of his cruiser as we drove down away from the main building toward the gate.

I sat in the back and looked out the window at the snow-covered walk that ran parallel to the drive. I felt like I could make out footprints coming down from the main house. Who knew whether they were Chick's or someone else's. Halfway down, did they veer off toward the curtain of woods? Did they vanish into the steady snow?

We drove up Scrimshaw to the trailheads at the top. Grevantz got out and looked at the unmarked snow. A second cruiser pulled up behind us. There were only a couple other police cars in Gable, and one of those was still at Head-Connect. A good time to shoplift from the Foodtown.

I wasn't sure if I was under arrest, or if I was just sort of assisting in the investigation. I mean, I had participated in what might be looked at as a felony burglary, but I felt relatively comfortable with the story I could tell. Chick would vouch for me when they caught him, make it clear that I was just trying to help him see the thing, not steal it. We'd give it back, no harm no foul.

Still, I understood the basics of being an accessory. Which was sort of funny, because I'd never been able to accessorize for shit.

The back doors of the cruiser were locked, and I figured I'd wait until an opportune time to raise certain questions.

"He was coming this way," I said. I felt no guilt about it. It's not like this was a mystery. "He's probably already passed through. If I were you I'd check the Heirloom. Maybe the Horse Head."

Grevantz turned toward the back.

"The Horse Head?"

"I know, right?"

He shook his head. "Plus, it's what? Four miles away? In this snow that's a haul. Does he have access to a car?"

"I don't know about access," I said, thinking of Elvis LaBeau. "He doesn't have a car. He has a phone, though."

I could've told Grevantz about how Jimmer could locate people, but I decided to wait.

"Don't leave a car here," I said instead. "If he sees the car he'll just go somewhere else."

Grevantz left one of the cruisers by the trailheads anyway and drove up to the Heirloom, the snow blowing in eddies across the street outside. I stayed locked in the back and nodded to the few people who passed by, hats pulled low and collars popped, pantomiming a request to be released. Nobody took me up on it. But I was kidding anyway, sort of. Fuck 'em. If you can't laugh at yourself in the back of a cruiser, well then you're a sorry son of a bitch.

Grevantz came back out, shook his head.

"Nobody's seen him," he said.

We drove up to the Horse Head and parked outside the office.

"Let me do the talking," I said from the back seat.

"Stay here," said Grevantz, and went inside. After a minute, he came back out.

"Nothing," he said.

"He probably won't use his name. He'll be looking for me."

I thought that was true. It was true, wasn't it? Anyway, Grevantz wasn't listening. He was on the radio, talking to his dispatcher.

"It's going to get cold tonight," he said when he was done. "He'd better get somewhere fast."

"Let me stay here," I said, leaning forward toward the partition. "I'm not going anywhere. I can't go back to Head-Connect, right?

If Chick comes here, which he probably will, I'll get the horn, call you, done deal."

Grevantz turned in the seat to look back at me.

"You know that isn't how it's going to work, right?"

I slouched back onto the seat.

"Well, shit," I said. "I'm supposed to be in Boston by noon tomorrow. Is that going to be a problem?"

Grevantz shrugged.

"I suspect that it will very likely be a problem."

I looked out the window. The snow was coming down hard now. It was a long walk to the Horse Head, up Bramble and into town, and then up the hill on the Knotsford-Gable Road. The walk would be especially long if Chick was looking for me at the trailhead.

"We can track his phone," I said.

Grevantz looked back at me. I dug my own cell out of my sweatpants.

"This doesn't count as my phone call, right?" I asked.

"Just do it," he said.

I called Jimmer. He was still off somewhere with Vishy Shetty and didn't answer right away. I left a message with the basics and told him to do that thing he could do and let me know where Chick was as soon as possible.

Grevantz nodded appreciatively.

"We need a warrant for that sort of thing," he said.

"Welcome to the future," I said.

Grevantz started the car.

"Okay, look," he said. "You can come back with me and wait at the station of your own volition. Or I can arrest you. Up to you."

We went back to wait at the police station, which in Gable shares a brick building with the fire station, the town hall, and the ambulance bay. I really didn't want to be arrested. I felt like I should put that off as long as possible. It would not look good on my ethics forms. But it's not like I could go back to Fleur-de-Lys and crash in the big bed either. So I sat in a chair a few feet from the lockup and watched the snow pile up on the window ledge. There wasn't a ton of accumulation—maybe 8 or so inches—but the wind was snapping like a bed sheet. The lockup door was open and the only person in it was a pharmacist picked up at a DUI checkpoint, sobering up and panicking quietly. I shot the shit with some of the other officers, the older dudes I remembered, their handshakes firm and their faces weathered from traffic duty, and the younger guys still ironing their uniforms every morning. We talked about the town, new buildings, old scandals, the Shaunda Schoensteins of our youths, a few of which we even had in common.

Grevantz came and went, moving papers around, making phone calls. I couldn't tell if he was working on the Head-Connect thing or other stuff. It didn't seem like there could be too much else going on in town on a Tuesday night.

I looked at my watch. It was closing in on midnight. A junior officer came in shivering from the parking lot and spoke with Grevantz in the office. I walked to the door and they stopped, both looking at me with annoyance. I got the impression that I was making myself too at home.

"You check the Horse Head again?" I asked anyway.

Grevantz nodded.

"All right," I said. "Well, I'm going to go find him."

Grevantz stood up.

"No you're not. We have two cars already looking for him, as well as security at Fleur-de-Lys. He shows, we will pick him up. I'm not diverting resources to follow you around too."

"Dude, it's freezing out," I said, pointing to the thermometer suctioned to the outer window. I began to feel a seeping in my chest, like smoke, like the first sign of something really bad. "I'm going."

"You know what?" he said. "Sit the hell down."

I started to walk toward the door. Almost got there too, before three of them landed on me. You got to give it to cops, they can go from your buddy to your oppressor like that.

I spent the night in the lockup, the door closed. The pharmacist got picked up around 1 A.M. by a very disappointed-looking woman in a bathrobe whom I took to be his wife. Grevantz and most of the other officers went home a half-hour later, leaving only a young night watchman sitting at a dispatch desk. Every once in a while the radio would crackle and the officer would type into a computer. I closed my eyes at two and when I opened them it was five and Grevantz was back, at the door of the cell with keys. He looked sharp, his hair slick and his chin smooth and wet, like he'd gotten the full eight hours, a hot shower and a warm bowl of oats. Whatever he was doing, he was living right. By contrast, my back hurt like a mother and my mouth tasted like a sock.

"Come on," he said, motioning me toward his office. "Your friend Jimmer is on the phone."

Outside, the sky was still dark.

"Guy," I said, when I got to the receiver. "Where you at?"

Grevantz put the call on the speaker.

"I'm in Halifax," he said. "It's really early. Why are the police calling me? Do I want to know what's going on?"

"Halifax?" I said.

"Halifax," he said. "Don't worry about it. Listen, I just got my messages. I called you back. You didn't answer. Now I'm taking calls from the police? What's up?"

I decided to gloss over that one.

"Gotta find Chickie again," I said. "It's urgent."

I heard Jimmer sigh, and then type.

"Hold on," he said.

I looked up and saw Unsie coming in through the station's outer doors. He was wearing Thermolite leggings, a wool hat pulled down over his ears, and the patrician look of a man who did not frequent police stations. He spoke with the desk officer and then looked through the glass partitions to me and Chief Grevantz. We both nodded, and Unsie came through the interior doors. He started to say something, but Jimmer came back on the line and I raised a finger.

"Can't find him," he said, sounding confused. "Phone must be off. But hold on."

A second passed. I mouthed the word "sorry" at Unsie, who ignored it.

"Yeah, he was at Head-Connect at midnight," Jimmer said. "That's all I got."

"Where at Head-Connect?" I asked.

That fucker. I pictured the eucalyptus room, the enveloping steam. The big bed! Had he snuck back in? Had he ever actually left?

I bet he was eating my granola as we spoke.

"Can't say. In the future, when you all move to cities like reasonable people, we will be able to be more precise. Until then, you'll have to accept the tech that the sticks find acceptable."

"Thanks," I said. "Gotta go."

"Wait," said Jimmer.

But it was too late and I hung up on a multimillionaire.

✤

We loaded into a cruiser in the predawn cold. It was freezing out, and Grevantz let me borrow a police-issue overcoat. The snow was thin on the ground but blown high in the corners and pockets of the lot. We drove down to Fleur-de-Lys, where Security Pete gave me the side-eye and I gave him the finger. Unsie followed us in his Forester. The sun was pressing gently against the gray air to the east, a wall of cloud moving north. Security Pete made a call up to the administration, and by the time the valets were opening our doors—even mine!—Crevis and Arvindo Blanc were waiting at the front. New Age music piped softly into the lobby and a yoga class was about to let out of one of the studios, disgorging thirty or so sweaty one-percenters into the lobby. I looked toward Ava's desk but she wasn't there, and another Head-Connector was cocking his head solicitously toward her computer screen.

Crevis ushered us quickly into a side room, out of sight of the guests.

"He's not here," Crevis said. "We've searched all the common areas."

"Steam rooms?" I asked, and Crevis nodded.

"We've also checked Mr. O'Neill's suite," he said, looking pointedly at me.

"He had nothing to do with this," I said. "Chick's on a vision quest."

Arvindo Blanc nodded.

"Quests are sacred," he said.

"Shit yeah," I said.

Behind Arvindo Blanc, Crevis rolled his eyes.

Blanc continued. "I would like to hear the story of this animal," he said. "We found the horn in our Vice Safe, of course, but we assumed that there was some long-ago safari behind it."

Chief Grevantz interrupted.

"There might be time for that later," he said. "Right now, we need to search the property."

"Can you do it subtly?" asked Crevis.

We separated into pairs, Grevantz and me, Crevis and a junior officer, Tudd and another. A few of the valets joined us. Unsie strapped on a pair of cross-country skis and set off down a virgin trail on his own, his strokes as smooth and precise as a metronome. Tudd watched him go like I'd watched Ava, lust in his eyes, and broke out some compensatory snowshoes. We headed out into the woods.

The sun was up and starting to cut through the gloom, but it was still cold enough to freeze the hairs in my nose. Grevantz and I followed the trail that led out the back of Fleur-de-Lys and through the Magic Meadow to the top of Scrimshaw. The wind had blown hard in the meadow, and along its edges the drifts cut like half-pipes. In six weeks these fields would be covered with bluebells or bluebonnets or whatever the hell those flowers are called, but right now it was still rows of winter grass and cattail, the cold corduroy of March.

We hiked for thirty minutes. I buried my hands in my pockets and wondered whether Chick was up at the Horse Head, sleeping in, maybe hitching down to breakfast at Gina's. I thought about calling LaBeau, figured I'd try Chick one last time first. I borrowed my phone back and pressed the numbers, wrapping the sleeves of my sweatshirt around my exposed hands. The phone went straight to voicemail, then slipped from my swaddled fingers and fell into a pile of snow, and as I bent down to get it I heard Grevantz's walkie-talkie crackle, the sound like when you get soap in your ears, and the junior officer walking with Crevis say to come to the near side of the meadow, the side just over the rise and close to

Bramble, 300 yards away. I heard Grevantz ask if they needed an ambulance.

But I was already running.

Pick 'em up, put 'em down. The goldenrods and ice sheets cracked under my feet. My legs felt strong. My chest was a bellows. I crested the rise and could see down a straight, slight slope to the edge of the meadow, still two football fields distant. One, two, three people. Maybe more coming through the woods. Unsie was there, leaning on his skis. I let my legs go and my momentum carry me down the slope.

When I got closer, I could see that they were gathered around a spot just off the trail. A creek bed. A pair of sneakers attached to a pair of legs attached to a big white sweatshirt half in a stream. Someone tried to grab my arm but I gave them a little stutter-step and a swim move and then I was past and in the icy water, the cold dip, pulling him up, his face up, the icicles in his beard, and he was long gone. I could see it in his eyes.

My Chickie, my best bud.

I held him in my arms, the overcoat open and spreading around us like shade, and I ran through my options.

Slip a hot wire up his bent spine.

Whale on him like Rocky in the meat locker, hit him until his heart was so purple it beat again out of umbrage.

Press my warm forehead to his cold one, my pink lips to his blue ones. Lift his chin, as we once had, and just will it to be otherwise, will him back into this world.

As if, at that point, either of us had a choice.

Later, when they tested, they found all sorts of things in Chick's system. Oxycodone. Heroin, surprisingly. Other stuff I don't even know. They figured he must have had something on him, or already in him, when he ran, and that the drugs kicked in at about the same time as the cold, and that he just fell unconscious into the thin creek. I guess that made sense, but it didn't explain how he wound up where he did. This was the third time in a week he'd traveled these trails. He must have known where he was going. But this time he'd had the horn. Because I'd let him take it. I spent a while thinking about the things I should have done, whether I'd killed him, whether after all of it I'd wound up being an accessory not just to his crime but also to his death.

But that was later, and there on the edge of the Magic Meadow, as the sun finally started to break through and Chick dripped and stiffened in my arms, I just cried. I cried my fucking balls off. There's probably a prettier way to say it.

Don Huey was good enough to call me himself on Wednesday night. I didn't take the call. Finally got a hold of him on Thursday, when he told me I didn't need to come back. I told him not to worry about it. I had bigger fish to fry.

Friday I had a quick introductory meeting with a criminal defense attorney Unsie knew and Jimmer had offered to bankroll. Both of them felt responsible, I guess. But they shouldn't. The lawyer and I talked charges, plea options, the somewhat pressing issue of the location of the horn. Chick had not had it on him.

The weather cleared and Friday afternoon was soft and wet, a solid 40°F warmer than Tuesday night. Unsie and I went back out to the Magic Meadow with Chief Grevantz, tried to trace Chick's steps from the door of the spa to the side of the creek, the creek newish, a product of beaver dams and the disgorgements of the Head-Connect septic system. Somehow Chick had wound up on that weird edge of the meadow, far from the trailheads. If he could have just made it to Bramble, the sidewalk would have taken him into town, to the crowded Heirloom, to Asgard. To a pay phone, if he needed one. But he veered away from it and wound up in a no man's land of roots and bogs. We found a little cleared-out area, not too far from the meadow, that looked like a campsite. Little stones in a circle as if for a fire. Maybe he was planning on putting that tent up out here? Maybe he'd been staying out here for longer than I knew.

As for the horn, I like to tell myself that he finally figured out where the rhino lay buried, and had at long last made it whole. Head-Connect had sent several helpers into the woods, under the pretense of trail maintenance, to look for it. Squads of hooded trainers in duck boots and fleece. They were coming up empty-handed as well.

"Maybe they'll find it in the spring," Grevantz said as he called off our little expedition, but we all knew how that would work out.

They held the wake on Saturday at the Ripton Funeral Home next to St. Barney's. The line was around the block. Chick's mother came up from Florida and I couldn't look at her. She wanted a Mass at St. Barney's, and I was like fuck that, but nobody asked me, so my own mom drove down from Vermont to whisper in her ear and hold her up. She squeezed my arm but I was okay. I was done crying by the time everyone else started. Jimmer came back from Halifax, of course, with Vishy Shetty and her new assistant. His clothes were better than anyone else's, his girlfriend's tears were more glittery. I could feel him scanning the room in his grief, trying to understand it in a way that would become useful. Ginny Archey was there, her belly ripe and pendulous, tears streaming down her cheeks. It was a little alarming. In a month, her water would break while she was drawing a pint of Lost Sailor at the Heirloom and Tim-Rick would rush her up to Knotsford Medical Center, where she'd give birth to a healthy little guy they would name John, but whom Ginny would call Clubber because he was born with a Mohawk and thick gold chains around his neck. Kidding about the chains. But anyway her water hadn't broken yet, and from the way she was crying it looked like she had plenty to spare.

Tim-Rick was there, at her side, his own eyes red and wet maybe for the first time? Probably not, but still. People—Jimmer, Billy Glib, others—seemed to make it a point to embrace him, put the past down, move on united. Like it fucking mattered. I was so angry. The whole time. The church did what it does best in small towns, which is to collect and hold the grief of the community, and I just could not abide it. A young priest from St. Barney's moved through the crowd, offering comfort. He hadn't done anything, was probably a good guy, but I thought if this dude touches me I'll break his arm.

Ava stood off to the side of the room, holding hands with her dad. He was pretty openly teary, in a dignified way, and I couldn't see her eyes because she was wearing these huge glasses, but she had something shiny and bee-stung going on around her mouth. She wouldn't speak to me. Through the attorney, I'd heard that Head-Connect was considering keeping the whole thing quiet for PR purposes. Spas where they find a dead body in the woods tend to lose business. Apparently you can do that with money, make things disappear.

I'd heard Ava was transferring to the Nevada facility.

I looked around the room. There was Ms. J., our former vice principal, still terrifying in her seventies. On her arm was Ms. F. from middle school phys ed. They nodded to me, but I ducked them. The waitress from the breakfast place was there. Mooselike Judge Ralph, chagrinned and semi-anonymous out of his robes, hanging his head like he'd dropped the ball. And that couldn't be Coach Harvey, stooped and small, in a wrinkled suit and a crewcut. A hundred others I knew but felt compelled in my shame to try and unremember. Unsie stood by the casket, upright and forlorn. Soon he too would become a father, the springtime full of baby boys, and he and Sara would name their son Philip and call him that. People put their hands on his arm and he nodded to them solemnly. From where I stood, I could see Chick's face in profile, they'd shaved the stupid beard and he looked ten years younger. Which was just great. I couldn't bear to get closer than that.

I stuck it out for as long as I could, then shunted toward the door in a way that I hoped would get Ava to notice me. If she did she didn't let it register. The priest from St. Barney's passed by and his robes brushed my arm. He was clasped up with an octogenarian from our old paper routes, but gave me a sympathetic look over his shoulder.

Not having it, padre. Not. Having it. Take that kumbaya bullshit somewhere else.

I went out to the parking lot and sat in the Escalade. Maybe this was all meant to be. Maybe we never had a chance from the minute Bill Trivette sunk his teeth into Chick's soft shoulder up in the bell tower all those years ago. You know that serenity prayer, about having the serenity to accept the things one cannot change, the strength to change the things one can, and the wisdom to know the difference? What a stupid prayer. Here's something I believed. I believed that if I put my back into something, I could change it, whatever it was, and therefore I did not have to accept shit. Which is why, maybe, I rarely put my back into much. But I'd put my back into this, and here's what it got me.

An irreconcilable. A lightning-struck tree. A big hole in the space-time continuum.

Fuck it. Want to hear something that's not a prayer? In the law, there is no duty to rescue. If you see some random dude drowning in a lake, you don't have to jump in and try to save him. You can just stand there and watch him sink and the law won't judge you for it. But if you do jump in, then you have to perform your rescue well, or at least adequately. You can't swim out, pull the guy up from the depths, and drag him into the middle of a busy roadway where a car will hit him. It's not enough to try. If you try, you have to be competent. You can't make it worse.

I had to get out of there.

Alone in the parking lot, I started the Escalade, my remnant, my wild machine, and found I was nearly penned in by a police cruiser, a Datsun, and a hearse. There was some space between the Datsun and the hearse, and I eased into it, trying to get out, get anywhere else. I saw the Datsun roll a bit as my bumper pushed it. I backed up and cut the wheel, but this time, the hearse shuddered.

I pressed on the horn. Nobody came.

Cut the wheel the other way, backed up again. Heard a little crunch as I hit the cruiser. Honked the horn again. People began looking at me from the sidewalk. A few heads bent out of the funeral home doors.

And you know what? I stopped giving a shit. I moved forward again, pushing on the hearse. I cut the wheel *into* the hearse. I honked again, an extended blast, a one-fingered salute to all that piety and remorse and whatever else they were feeling in that fucking morgue. These fucking penitents. These ass-licking mules.

Only my grief is real.

Only I am entitled.

The engine growled. A fever set in. Those slumbering departed in the cemetery next door coughed in their sleep. But enough was enough. I wasn't about a resurrection anymore. I was about a takedown. And I hoped the people in the ground would understand.

I hit the gas and pushed the hearse until it slid forward and I had enough room to scrape the entire side of the Escalade on its chrome railings. It felt so good I did it again in reverse. A crowd came out of the funeral home and I gave zero fucks. I backed up and smacked the cruiser again, more forcefully, a 400-horsepower game of whack-a-mole, and then I was out, free, leaving more paint on the Datsun, and there was the lawn between me and St. Barneys, and I jumped the parking lot's curb and hit the gas, the dead grass turning to slurry under my tires. I cut a donut onto the lawn; we used to do that in the snowy parking lots in Chick's mom's Festiva, racing forward and pulling the e-brake and spinning in a wide arc while LL Cool J played *Mama Said Knock You Out* on the cassette deck. I guess there might have been some shouting somewhere behind me but I wasn't hearing it—I was doing the shouting now. An extended "Fuck!" sound, or something similarly enraged. A couple of months' worth of anger, frustration. Maybe it was more. I was carrying some shit around, be the first to admit it. But it doesn't change anything. Fuck all of this bullshit. I'm out. Done. And when the big day finally comes, when that last whistle blows and the corpses of the liars line up in parade, at least I won't be there. At least I'll know that.

I came out of my spin and then there was the bell tower, solid rock, right in front of me. I said, "What do you want to do?"—to the Escalade, I guess—and, you know, what do you expect a truck like that to say? It said storm the keep. It said make an impression. And I'd never heard a better idea. So we floored it, within the parameters of space and traction, and flew across the lawn and then the driveway that led to St. Barney's lot out in the back, and we aimed right for the corner of that bell tower, where the low foundation began to climb out of the gritty snowpack still piled up against it by January plows. And we hit that corner like a sock full of rocks at, I don't know, something fairly fast, maybe thirty or forty miles an hour, I don't really remember because it was a blur. And I didn't know until then that you could break your nose on an airbag, but you can, and I did, and the blood came out fast and thick all over the yoke of the bag and the white of my shirt and it was a second before I could get my bearings and try to back the Escalade up for another go, the bell tower being unscathed and, indeed, seemingly unimpressed. Like I gave a shit. Just you wait, bell tower. There's more coming your way. This baby's gonna start back up in a second.

But in that second, it was probably more than a second actually, the driver-side door swung open, and instead of a valet, which I'd sort of gotten used to, it was Chief Grevantz, with Unsie behind him, pulling me out onto the ground and then bending my arm behind my back on the wet walk. And when Grevantz lifted me up, cuffed this time, I could fully appreciate the crowd that had gathered around St. Barney's, two hundred people at least, a good showing, some crying more, some frowning. Moans and disapproval. The earnest man of God looked deeply concerned. I bequeath this to you, all you sons of bitches. A veritable New England jubilee. You're all welcome.

Chief Grevantz led me through the crowd toward his damaged cruiser, pretty roughly I must say. I must have looked like a monster, blood stained and wild-eyed, not so handsome this time, but I gathered my monster wits enough that as we passed Ms. J., I remembered the fish we'd emancipated from the abandoned mini-golf and how she was grateful to her anonymous benefactors and I said to her, shouted I guess, "It was us! Remember? It was us!"

She looked like she was about to cry, and even in my state I couldn't bear that.

So I looked away, and shouted "Captain America!," just to keep us all off balance.

"What are we going to do with you?" said Judge Ralph when I saw him next, which was the Monday after Chick's funeral.

So now I'm hanging out here for a while, waiting for my probation to run. There's a sizeable restitution bill at the end of it, and a hearing before the Board of Bar Overseers in late June, at which I am professionally obligated to try and explain myself. I haven't seen Ava since the wake, and I don't think I'm likely to see her again. It's cool. There's probably a lot she'd have to get over to be able to look at me, if she even wanted to, and I'd feel bad taxing anyone like that. Unsie is putting me up because I'm required to be around a lot, checking in with various factions, and I'm learning a lot about kayaks at Asgard. How they differ from canoes, for example, and which ones you can fish in.

Jimmer's gone back to San Francisco, promising to return if needed. He's been really generous with his wealth and his time, but since he got Vishy Shetty out of the deal I feel like he should be thanking me. She went back with him, ostensibly because it was on the way to Mumbai but also because it let her check in with her considerable fan base in Silicon Valley. She apparently got the role in the Wharton pic but withdrew to be in an action movie about illegal street racing. Last I heard, Jimmer had started to look at some CAD factories in Hyderabad. He says that when the time is right, I should come out and see him. He'll hook me up.

And that is what I intend to do.

I have this theory about California, about its endless blue days and manifest destiny. Once we went out there, Kelly and me, to Santa Monica, and while she strolled around Montana Avenue and window-shopped with her rich aunt, I got a beer with her uncle, who was a talent manager and had grown up in Rhode Island. The place we were at was full of a certain kind of poor-looking rich person, jeans that cost more than my flight, and as we ate goat skewers and drank these filthy Belgian lambics, we talked in realistic masculine terms about the long-term prospects, or lack thereof, of my relationship with his niece. Would it include California? I wasn't sure—or, rather, I was, but I was playing my cards close—so I went with a bit about how weird it was for a New Englander to be in a place without seasons. How it unsettled me, and because it unsettled me it must unsettle everyone, at least subconsciously.

"I think that's why there is so much plastic surgery, so many nose jobs and fake boobs," I said. "That's why everyone gets divorced in their forties, why this house over here looks nothing like the one next to it, why there are so many nice cars on lease. A lot of these people, they're totally focused on tomorrow. There's no reckoning. Nothing to bear. Tomorrow's gonna be great. Tomorrow's their day."

Kelly's uncle looked at me with disbelief.

"Yeah," he said, eventually. "That's exactly the point."

So, right. California. Head out there, forget all this stuff. Call it amnesia and hope that it sticks.

Until then, I'm bombing around the Berkshires on a road bike leased at favorable terms from Asgard. The truck is pretty beat up, still in the shop, and I don't have money to waste getting it out, but the weather is good, though it rains for some stretch of nearly every day. People wave at me, even people who know about what happened. Sometimes they look a little wary, but it's late spring and folks seem willing to forgive. They're believers in redemption, or something. We're all in it together. I'm probably not the first one to go around the bend. So I wave back, and keep on pedaling. I'm sorry for everything. Sorry to everyone. The other day I went to St. Barney's and prayed.

Beyond that, I'm getting a lot of hill work in. Sometimes in the evening I ride up the curving road toward Richmond and stop at the overlook, stare down at Normanton Bowl, like that night in March when Chick fell asleep on the way back from the Heirloom, except that then the Bowl was frozen and now it's a blue plate in a green lawn. I count the boats. There's a lot of them, more each day. Nearby, a huge rock sticks out over the road, and years ago someone painted it to look like a shark. It's a rock shark. Nobody messes with it. The sun sinks low and sometimes I can see the moon come out over the eastern hills. Beneath me, the woods hum. I stand on the retaining wall and scan out as far as I can, past the Bowl and Fleur-de-Lys and Gable, but the hills always meet the sky no matter where I look. I went to the Midwest once, to a wedding on the edge of the plains outside of Chicago, a green summer day, the air humid and glowing. No hills on the horizon, just flatland that rolled out forever. It spooked the hell out of me.

I talk to Chickie a fair amount these days, when I'm asleep but when I'm awake too. Sometimes I don't even think he's gone. I didn't go to the funeral, being otherwise obliged, but I heard it was solid. His mom had him cremated and took his ashes back to Florida with her, which I'm sure he would have appreciated not at all. I'm sure he would have wanted to stay here. It's okay, though. It's like Jimmer was saying with graves and markers and cognitive ability or whatever. I know where to find Chick when I need him. Just last night, for example, he and I went Hill-to-Bowl, cruising down Main to Walker toward 183, he was ahead of me and the rough road was making our tires bounce and our cheeks vibrate. We turned off into the marshland by Stonover and the fireflies rose out of the night, blinking lazily in the heavy air, and the pavement got smooth and I caught up to him almost.

"Guy," I called out into the space ahead of me. "That time at the quarry. Remember? With Shaunda and them?"

He cocked his head like he was waiting for the question.

I pumped my pedals and came up behind him.

"Were you really drowning?"

It was something I'd always wondered about. There were a whole lot of things I'd always wondered about.

I couldn't see Chick's face but I feel like he grinned. A turn or two later, he started laughing. Happily, quietly.

And then I was laughing too.

Laughing as if it mattered at all. What really happened. The actual truth!

This tumbling, star-crossed parish, this lurid slab, all the great beasts that swam beneath her swells and under the feet of her citizens. Mist and shadows. The ghosts of the natives. Things you felt but didn't know. Things you didn't know you knew until after. They all rose up around me and pushed me forward, pushed me along through the dark county, the road uncoiling, the white moon high, until I was just even with my friend.

Thanks

Ben LeRoy, Ashley Myers, Tyrus Books, and F+W Media. Lauren Abramo at Dystel & Goderich Literary Management. Jim Ruland. John Leary, Pia Ehrhardt, Ron Currie Jr., and Tom O'Keefe. Roy Kesey, Pasha Malla, Pamela Erens, Marc Strange, Mark Keats, Peter FitzGerald, Matt Tannenbaum, Ben Marlowe and Eileen Donovan Kranz. Kate McKean, Mark Weinstein, Alexis Hurley, Rhonda Hayes and Clyde Taylor. Bob Schneider. Pete, Chris, Tom and Ted. Jayme, Brian, Steve, Art and Setti. Missy, Sonja, Sonia and Nichole. Matt Lenehan. Joe Malossini. Turney Duff. Dotch, Keyes, Mullen, Weave, Richard, Kev, Ian and Pete A. Sheesh and the Deacon. David, Mary, John, Frederick, Katie (always), Matthew, Bridget and Timmy. Schermerhorn Park. The Millionaires. The Zoetrope writing community. Maryjane and Jerry Fromm. Katie, Rick, Trey, and Kai Shinholster. Leo, Eliza and Jenny.

❧

The Duration was partly inspired by the legend of Columbus, a circus elephant who died while touring the Berkshires in 1851 and is supposedly buried in the woods on the south side of Lenox, Massachusetts. His remains have never been found.

• • •

Reprinted with permission from "Where Do Elephants Go to Die?" by Derek Gentile, 2004. *The Berkshire Eagle*, B1 & B4. 2004 by the *Berkshire Eagle*.

Where Do Elephants Go to Die?
Legend says pachyderm's grave in Lenox
By Derek Gentile
Berkshire Eagle Staff

Lenox—The elephant was tired. He had walked almost 15 miles on a leg that was badly injured, possibly broken. His breathing was coming in long, heaving wheezes, like a bellows.

Suddenly, despite entreaties from his handler, Columbus the elephant veered off the road, stumbled a few yards into a nearby shed, and collapsed. A week later, he was dead, and was buried a few dozen yards from where he died. Somewhere in Lenox.

That's the story. It is also the legend.

The death of Columbus occurred in October 1851 and was written about in a number of publications. This year,

Margaret Biron, a teacher at Lenox Memorial Middle School, assigned the story as an extra-credit research project for her social studies class.

"It's an interesting story," said Biron. "I'm not sure how true it is, but I thought it would be a good project for the students."

The story of how Columbus died began in Adams. According to Adams historian Eugene Michalenko, the 33-year-old male Indian elephant had been displayed in North Adams the day before he was injured.

The elephant came to America in 1818. At the time he was in the Berkshires, Columbus was apparently part of a traveling menagerie that also included a rhinoceros, a hippopotamus, lions, tigers and cougars.

Columbus, however, was one of the stars of the show, so the story goes. His handler, a man named Raymond (no one is sure if this was his first or last name, or if he was the elephant's owner, James Raymond), would attach a "salon car" to the elephant's back and allow children to ride him a short distance.

The kids loved it. It is unlikely that Raymond mentioned to anyone attending his shows that Columbus had a bit of a temper and, according to the Adams Historical Society Newsletter had, over the previous 15 years, killed four people.

The North Adams show had apparently gone well. Columbus and the rest of the menagerie were to travel to Stockbridge the next day, to set up the exhibition in a field in that town. The trip was about 24 miles, a good day's hike.

That October day, (the date is not certain) the troupe traveled down Route 8 and walked through the center of Adams. Meandering down Park Street, the elephant came to a bridge at the intersection of Park and Center streets, which spanned the south branch of the Hoosic River. The bridge is now made up steel and cement but then, said Michalenko, it was made of wood, "and probably not that sturdy."

It wasn't. Columbus, who weighed about 10,000 pounds according to the menagerie's handbill, got about a third of the way across and the bridge collapsed, dropping the elephant about 20 feet onto the rocks on the west side of the river. There was a "mighty crash," according to the Berkshire Hills Monthly, an historical magazine published at the turn of the 20th century.

Accounts differ as to the nature of the elephant's injuries. Judy Peters, an historian from Lenox, recalled that she had heard the elephant had injured one of his legs. The Berkshire Hills Monthly speculated the animal had "internal injuries." Perhaps it was a little of both.

But Raymond had a schedule to keep. He "cajoled" Columbus out of the riverbed and got him walking south again. It's unlikely that Raymond used sweet reason to get Columbus out of the riverbed. What is more probable is that he used a quirt or a whip or, more probably, a training hook—a metal or wooden rod two or more feet long with a sharp hook at the end.

Columbus rose awkwardly out of the riverbed. With his handler leading him, he headed south.

Several hours later, Columbus made it through the center of Lenox, moving slower and slower, despite the physical entreaties of his handler. Columbus continued south, along what is now Old Stockbridge Road. Route 7 would not be built for decades, and Old Stockbridge Road was the main road to Stockbridge in 1851.

But it was tough going. About two miles from the center of town, Columbus stumbled off to the side of the road. There was a shed a few yards off the road. The elephant headed for the tiny structure and once inside, he collapsed. No further entreaties by Raymond would get him up.

The elephant was in obvious pain. According to The Pittsfield Sun, a weekly newspaper, "his groans and cries could be heard from an immense distance."

But Columbus did not die right away. The curious came from miles around to see the gigantic creature. Columbus lay in the shed for about a week before finally expiring. He was dragged a short ways away from the shed and buried.

But exactly where all this happened is something of a mystery. An Eagle account of the event, written by columnist Dick Happel in 1951, suggests the shed was on the former Bishop estate. The shed was apparently located "across the road from the entrance to Elm Court."

The Bishop estate was cut up into lots for single-family homes many years ago. And any sheds or structures that might have housed a sick elephant are long gone. Understandably, none of the current residents of that portion of the road know much about it.

"I've never heard that," said Coreen Nejame, who lives at 238 Old Stockbridge Road, and whose land is not quite opposite the entrance to Elm Court. "That's an interesting story."

"That's interesting, but I don't know anything about it," said Lucille Friedson, who, with her husband, Belvin, owns property at 245 Old Stockbridge Road.

Peters, however, recalled that years ago she spoke with the late May Butler, a longtime resident. Butler's father was a superintendent at the Bishop estate and he apparently knew where Columbus was laid to rest. Peters said Butler described the elephant grave as being "near the entrance to Elm Court, across the street."

One of the people Butler's father showed the grave to was, according to Peters, the late Dick Happel. But his column about Columbus did not specify exactly where the grave was.

At one point, there was speculation that the stuffed body of Columbus was somewhere at Williams College. This was probably generated when it was discovered that the elephant's owner, a man named James Raymond of Carmel, N.Y., sold the body to the Williams College Lyceum of Natural History.

But, at five tons, Columbus was so large that there were no local taxidermists available to stuff and mount him. So the lyceum officials decided to wait a few years until the body decomposed.

They waited six years, according to this story. It wasn't enough. A group from the college dug up the body, but, to put this politely, it had not decomposed sufficiently. Columbus was reinterred, and the lyceum officials vowed to return in another few years. But the lyceum went out of existence in 1871. Columbus was never stuffed.

"I'm almost sure he never went to Williams," said Michalenko. "He's still somewhere down in Lenox."

About a week ago, a reporter drove slowly along Old Stockbridge Road, a copy of Happel's column in hand. There was the entrance to Elm Court. There was the Friedman parcel, and there, slightly to the north and across the street from Elm Court, is the Nejame parcel.

Coreen Nejame graciously allowed access to the parcel she and her husband own.

But, besides a very nice home, there's really nothing there. No shed, no huge mound of dark grass that might conceal a mighty body, no rusty training hook hidden under a bush, nothing. The next parcel is heavily wooded, with old growth. Wherever Columbus is, he may be hidden forever now.

And there is a postscript. Owner Raymond sued the town of Adams for a "defective" bridge. (Adams officials countered that the bridge was fine for people, wagons and most animals, except elephants.) Raymond sought $20,000. The case was settled out of court for about $1,500.

About the Author

Author photo by Jen Fromm

Dave Fromm is an attorney and the author of the memoir *Expatriate Games: My Season of Misadventures in Czech Semi-Pro Basketball* (Skyhorse, 2008). He lives with his wife and children in western Massachusetts. This is his first novel.

SL 5-12-16
TC 7-14-16
WH 9-19-16
OS 11-21-16
AG 1-30-17
EI 4-13-17
OM 6-15-17
PL 8-17-17

PL 8-17-17 kP